# MEMPHIS

## A GINGER SCOTT STORY

Ginger Scott

Ebook ISBN-13: 978-0-9990464-3-2

Print ISBN-13: 978-0-9990464-2-5

*For BilliJoy.*
*You are a champion to so many.*
*Fight on.*

"*Rhythm is everything in boxing. Every move you make starts with your heart, and that's in rhythm or you're in trouble.*"

– SUGAR RAY ROBINSON

# CHAPTER ONE

Liv

There are certain things you can always count on.

Like how the perfect pair of jeans is a myth. It's a simple fact of logic—no ass is alike, and it's impossible to cut denim to conform around every imaginable curve.

Roots will grow out faster than a stylist says they will. I've got a purse full of root touch-up pens in every imaginable color that prove this one true. I've been many colors, but I haven't been my own in years. No matter how hard I try, there are some traits I can't seem to dodge. Just like the Valentine last name, Archie Valentine's damn dishwater-blond hair is one of them.

There's also the rule that the best-looking men are the ones who will tear your heart apart. My mom should have warned me about this one. She knew better. She picked a man who dragged her heart across the country, to Atlantic City and back. Weeks at a time of her life were wasted—aching nights spent awake and unsure of where my dad was, who he was with, how long she'd be in some hotel room or her own bed alone. She said prayers on dirty concrete floors beneath coliseums, begging spirits to protect him or heal him after a fight. She always prayed for him to get up, to fight again, and for him to come home—no matter where he was...no matter whom he was with.

My dad counted on it.

There is one truism that should comfort me—*you can always go home again.* Only, it's those things that never change around here that make coming home the most miserable sure bet of them all. It's the way the air smells—like dirt on fire. It was sixty-eight degrees when I boarded the plane in Portland. The pilot said it was a cool one-oh-six when our wheels touched down in Phoenix.

As miserable as the heat is, that's not what sinks deep in my gut as the cab idles forward against the grain of every other vehicle heading the opposite direction.

My parents and uncle share a duplex, one of four built as a downtown Phoenix infill project when I was a kid. Time has left the place with mismatched garages, oil stains on the driveway, and chunks of broken sidewalk bits. Development plans changed to a different part of the city, forgetting this one under the scorch of the relentless sun. Trees don't grow here, just old piles of brick and barred-up windows guarding pawnshops and bail-bond joints.

V's Gym stands in the center of it all. A whitewashed stucco two-story with cracks every few feet and a thick layer of dirt from the summer dust storms and lack of rainfall. At the height of his career, my dad had enough to buy the entire block, so he did. It was going to be "the investment of the century." Like all of his grand plans, though, this one fell short too. Locals still come to train, or at least they did before I left seven years ago. The gym churns out just enough business to keep the power on. Renters in the other two duplexes and my Uncle Leo's coaching pays for the rest of their needs.

The three of them are all of the family I have left on this earth, and the last thing I ever wanted was to see them again. All it took was one good-looking man to drag my heart around Portland—dragging my name through the mud—and here I am, rolling up alongside the large mural of my father in his prime painted on the side of V's. The setting sun casts a golden hue over the chin, his light almost gone in reality, too.

The streetlight struggles to flicker to life as the cab stops. The sensors can't tell if it's day or night. The heat muddles with the computer systems just as much as it seems to with the people living here. My eyes scan over the faded words painted on the brick under the likeness of my dad's face: ARCHIBALD "THE HEAVY" VALENTINE

"Forty-six."

The cabdriver's voice startles me from the short visual trip to my past.

"Uh...yeah, right. Of course." I shift in the seat and remove the safety belt from my waist, leaning to pull my phone from my back pocket. I slide out the crumpled fold of bills from the small slot on my phone case and take a slow breath in an effort to chase away the tight squeeze of humiliation climbing up my throat.

Pulling out the two twenties and two fives I have left, I pause with the money in my hand and let my eyelids flutter with nerves for just a moment.

"I'm gonna need change," I say, handing my cash through the small window. It only takes the driver a second to realize how much I've given him.

"How much?" His reply comes out in a bark.

"Four, please," I say, clearing my throat before the words are done leaving my lips.

His fingers work quickly on his stack of folded bills, and his hand jerks back for me to take the money.

"Thanks," I say, eyes focused on the door handle and my attention on getting out of this cab as fast as I can. I drag my rolling duffle bag along the seat behind me and the cabbie takes off the moment I slam the door.

I've quit giving excuses to people. That driver would never believe me, but I need those four dollars a lot more than he does.

"You just gonna stand out there all night? Or you planning on coming inside and giving your favorite uncle a hug?" The familiar gravel of his voice fires up a few more nerves inside my chest that I thought were dead.

"You're my *only* uncle," I say as I roll my neck and look at the bald and overweight man holding the security door open leading into my parents' house. We've made this same joke so many times; it quit amusing me when I was ten. Of the three of them, Leo was my favorite. Of course, that's like picking a favorite way to get your tetanus shot. Leo would be short and sweet with a tiny needle in the arm and maybe a Hello Kitty Band-Aid at the end. My parents, they're definitely multiple rounds right in the stomach, and probably an infection from the puncture wounds.

"Come here and give me a hug."

Lips tight and eyes wide, I lean in as he wraps his heavy arms around me, wishing I felt more than a glimmer of comfort in them. I'm desperate, but I can't let that color things too much. Leo still is a selfish prick of a man. He hasn't seen me in a while, so right now I'm getting the charm. Once the newness wears off, his rust will show, and it will be nasty.

"Your mom can't wait to see you," he says, letting go and backing away from our embrace to lead me inside. "She's upstairs with your old man, giving him a bath."

I nod and drag my feet through the foyer, the edges of the linoleum peeling up more than I remember. The house smells of dirty towels, sweat, and some sort of pungent medicine.

"Let me take your bag." I feel the weight shift in my hand as my uncle takes the straps on my bag and tugs.

"I got it," I say, wrapping my fingers tighter around the handle. I don't really like people taking things from me anymore. I've lost too much.

My eyes hit his, and his lip ticks up on one side to match his shoulder shrug.

"Thing is, you're actually going to have to stay in my spare. Your mom's in the other room here. She stays up so late with her shows, and your dad just sleeps all of the time..."

My eyes drift down to his chin and I relax my grip on my bag.

"That's fine."

I guess staying with him is better than staying with my mom. It's another set of doors between us, and I'm fairly certain I'll come to appreciate those barriers. My bag looks even smaller in his possession. He holds it up and flashes a short-lived smile.

"I'll take it on over and be right back. Your mom should be down in a minute or two."

I nod and wave my hand near my leg, spinning away on the balls of my feet and hooking my thumbs in the pockets of my jeans. My mom isn't excited to see me. I guess maybe, somewhere woven into that innate motherly instinct there's a flicker of excitement in there, but mostly she's looking forward to saying *I told you so*.

I'm a Valentine all right—one big-fat disappointment to Angela Grossman, a Valentine by marriage. Just as disappointing as that man upstairs.

"You Olivia?"

My hands flee from my pockets and clutch the cotton on my chest, my heart pounding against my knuckles.

"Who the hell—" my face and arms flush and tingle with the rush of delayed adrenalin, my mouth dry three words in.

He's like a ghost the way he leans against the kitchen counter, taking big gulps from the bottle in his right hand. Black sweatpants ride low on his hips, pushed up to his calves, and the *V*-cut white T-shirt hugs his body where it's dampened with sweat. His build is vintage Archie Valentine—the build of a real boxer, a physique that almost doesn't exist anymore—but a glance up to his face shows a different kind of man. He isn't smirking, and his brown eyes aren't shifting gears to show off his charm. His face is void of ego, even after he lifts the bottom of his shirt with his free hand to run it along his face to clear it of sweat, thus revealing a sculpted row of abs that brings my gaze back down to his waist.

"Olivia, right? Leo said you were coming in..."

My eyes widen as he steps closer, wiping his palm along his right hip before reaching out for my hand. It lingers there for an awkward second before I wake myself from this frozen state and take his palm.

"Yeah, sorry... I...I didn't know anyone was down here," I stumble.

"I came in through the back. I needed to wash this out," he says, holding up his now-empty bottle, the insides gritty from some sort of green drink.

"You, uh..." I raise my hand and tap my fingertip on the edge of the bottle. "You missed a spot."

His eyes hover on mine for a beat just before his chest shakes once with a chuckle.

"Yeah, I meant before I mixed this stuff, but you're right. I should wash it out again. I'm bad at leaving stuff until later."

He turns from me and moves to the sink. I immediately recall all of the things I've left until later, until it's too late.

"I'm sorry, but...*who* are you?" My eyes roam over the muscles in his back and the curve of his thick shoulders as he rinses his bottle out at the sink. I know *what* he is. It's been a while since a body in his condition worked out around here, though. Most of the guys that come to V's are hobby-seekers. They like the workout, and telling people they box, even if it's only against other thirty-year-old wannabes in sparring gloves. This guy, though...he's different.

"I'm Memphis." His short answer is punctuated by the sound of him tapping his bottle against the sink, shaking away the beads of water.

"Unique name," I say, my nerves clearing out a little more. I remind myself that good-looking men hold no power over me.

"Thanks," he says, turning back to face me, cheeks dimpled with a proud grin. "I picked it myself."

"Ahhhh, you're a wrestler," I joke. "I have to advise you, though." I lean toward him and look both ways before cupping my mouth and whispering loudly. "Memphis doesn't really strike fear in the heart of your opponent the way, say, *Thunder* or *The Ax* does."

His grin tightens, holding in laughter.

"*The Ax?*" he repeats, one eyebrow raised.

"I couldn't think of any real wrestler names, but you have to admit...those would be good ones." I nod and fold my arms, squeezing myself at my ribs as a physical reminder to be wary.

"Those would be terrible," he says, chuckling through his words. "Pretty as you are, I can't lie."

My fingers squeeze harder and my jaw loosens as my smile drops.

"You usually lie to pretty girls?" My gut squeezes in response to my knee-jerk reaction. That wasn't fair. It's not his fault I happen to know a guy who makes his living lying to pretty girls. "Sorry, I was... I'm just tired. Long flight."

His eyes move down to the floor between us. His lashes are long enough to draw my focus to them.

"I bet. No worries." His eyes move up just then. They're a brown that's also gold. "I know what you meant."

I match his gaze, wondering if Leo told him more than my name, like why I had to come crawling back home, penniless.

"Do you really know?" My brow draws in, and his expression follows as we stare at one another. His lips part with a breath, about to speak, but in a blink his attention is behind me.

"Your hair looks like shit."

I have a feeling I could have stayed in the silent conversation with Memphis for a while had my mom not brought me right back to reality with her ever-so-warm and loving welcome.

My eyes drift closed and I turn to the side, not quite ready to fully square up with her. Angela doesn't wait, though, running her hand through my hair and twisting ends in her fingertips, pushing her glasses to the tip of her nose and studying my dark-brown split ends before glancing at the top of my head where my color is much lighter.

"I haven't been able to get to the salon," I say, falling right into my roll of justifying things that shouldn't be important or matter when the daughter she hasn't seen in seven years is standing in her kitchen.

As far from grace as my parents have fallen, my mom still gets up two hours before she has to care for my dad to make sure her hair is done and her face is covered in foundation and powder to soften the wrinkles made from a lot of hard living.

She lets my hair fall from her fingers and *tsks*, moving over to the young version of my father who bared witness to this little taste of my dysfunctional family.

"Memphis," she says, patting her palm on his chest. I catch the slight curl of her fingers and cringe. He's man-candy to her, a throwback to what my father once was.

"Good night, Mrs. V. I was just borrowing your sink when Olivia came in." His eyes flit to me as he says my name.

"Welcome here anytime, son. You've got a big fight coming. Arch is really hoping to be there for it."

Memphis nods, and nothing more is said about it. He must be close enough to the family to know that my dad hasn't left his bedroom in years, and my mom's delusions that they've had coherent conversations—let alone made plans for him to leave this house—are to be indulged and then ignored. The last time I reacted to her fantasies led to the worst impulsive decision of my life.

"Tell Leo I'll see him in the morning," Memphis says, glancing my way briefly. "Nice to meet you finally, Olivia."

"You, too," I say, forcing myself not to look at him long either. It's bad enough that I'll be seeing him again. I need to treat him like a client of the family business. I should probably treat my parents and uncle that way, too. I'm here as long as it takes for my bank account to be viable enough to survive a cheap apartment in any other zip code.

My mom barely waits for the back door to close before she starts working me with guilt.

"You should go see him before he falls asleep. I told him you'd be up, but be careful, he might not remember what you look like. It has been a while." The sarcasm oozes with her special brand of bitterness.

I gnash my teeth under tight lips and pace myself. If I start engaging with her now, I'll never make it through the week, let alone however long I have to stand it here.

"All right," I say instead of the dozens of things I'd rather respond with.

When she pulls out a stack of tabloids from the cloth bag she takes to the grocery store, I do my best to ignore her obviously calculated attack. I recognize the covers. I should—I'm on them: my head buried in a hood, a newspaper folded and shading half of my face. Enoch's lawyer ushering me toward that last luxury car I'll ever step into.

"You should go with a dark brown again," she says, flipping over one of the covers with my red locks on display.

"Maybe," I hum.

That photo was one of the first ones, right before the trial.

Life's funny. I made written promises to myself in a junk-store diary I bought for a dollar when I was twelve: I would never become my mom. But here I am...twenty-five years old, existing in the same kitchen she's in...*stuck* just like she is, in a life that didn't turn out anything like either of us thought it would.

The moment he opened his mouth at the podium in front of the packed finance lecture hall at State, Enoch Rostram breathed me in. He was this young, enigmatic spark of inspiration dressed like the men do in magazines I'd flipped through in the grocery line. He smelled of Gucci, and he wore crisp, white collared shirts that somehow didn't feel douchey with the top two buttons undone. Not on him. He was a lion, pacing in front of hundreds of wide-eyed and naïve college freshmen business students all hoping to be the next Facebook CEO or Mark Cuban.

He was promising so much too. A one-year internship with Rostram Investment Holdings that wasn't limited to only seniors. It was a chance to race to the finish line and come out ahead, and maybe land the single greatest job of my dreams.

"I got where I am not by playing by arbitrary rules like degrees and prestigious university titles," he had said, waving off the squirms of our professor in the wings who clearly disagreed. "I got here by taking risks and choosing paths that aren't expected. And today, I'd like to talk to each and every one of you."

He was completely serious. I missed my next two classes waiting patiently in a line that wound through eighteen tiered rows of seats—just to get a shot at a one-minute Hail Mary to leave the boxing world behind for good. I wasn't like the others in here. I didn't want a hundred employees or a portfolio of clients with million-dollar accounts. All I wanted was the opposite of the life I'd always known. I wanted to be someone different and do a job that I was good at, and maybe have one of those nameplates on a door to a small office one day down the road.

I rolled the dice and, during my one minute, told Enoch just that. He offered me the job on the spot. I didn't sleep with him until my internship was over—the *day* it was over, but still. He moved me into his Seattle penthouse, I dropped out of my degree program, and I got stars in my eyes at the prospect of becoming Mrs. Rostram.

He never even saw the Feds coming. Neither did I.

The final number plastered on every news site and front page from Seattle to New York was $1.4 billion. I know that number should be bigger. The money he took from me was a fraction of a fraction compared to the millions he squandered away from others in his Ponzi scheme, but when the house of cards came crumbling down, we were all left with the very same amount—*nothing*.

My bonus was getting my name attached to the biggest international fraud story to break since Madoff. There was also the little bit about me being pregnant that got leaked by one of Enoch's lawyers. My "condition," as his legal team referred to it, would buy him sympathy and reduce his sentence. They abandoned that idea two weeks later when I miscarried.

A month after that, they abandoned me.

My mom didn't call to check on me once. Until I drained my checking account and could no longer make coffee-shop pay stretch to cover rent, utilities, and well...life, I managed to survive without calling anyone in my little family. Eviction has a funny way of making dead lifelines suddenly feel viable, though.

My mom flips the tabloid closed and nudges it toward the center of the table, her fingers just following orders in her next calculated move by spinning the cover image just enough I have to look my own, terrified self in the eyes.

"I'm actually really tired, so I'll see Dad tomorrow." I turn away, a little proud that I didn't engage her and actually defied her by putting my visit with Dad off for the night.

"You start at eight, and really...the floor needs to be cleaned and the main office opened up for new registrants by then, so you should probably start at seven." She pulls the magazines together again into a neat pile as a tight, satisfied smirk begs to grow on her lips. Her eyes flutter, still heavy with the day's makeup, and eventually they open on me. "What? Did you think you were going to stay here for free and just...mooch off us?"

I press my tongue against the back of my teeth and force a small nod before rapping my knuckles against the side of the doorway.

"Wouldn't dream of it."

I can feel my eyebrows pushed up on my forehead, wrinkling my skin. She reads my surprise; I can tell by the way her pucker tightens against the push of her smile that she is dying to flash at me like a silent checkmate and I-told-you-so rolled into one. But she's not prepared for the girl who's been through hell and back with literally nothing to lose.

"In fact," I start, pausing to mimic her grin—the one she gave to me, "I'll be ready by six so we can discuss my salary."

Her eyes twitch, the right one just a little more than the left. I've fucking engaged, and it feels sickening and addictive all at once. Codependent mother-daughter relationships never really die, I guess.

"Oh..." My brow draws in. I do it for effect. I do it...to be a bitch right back to her. "Did you think I was just going to work for you for free?"

Our blue eyes duel and flicker in silence, and after a few seconds, I walk back out the way I came in and cross the yard made of stones and weeds to my uncle's place. The familiar kick of adrenaline pumps my heart faster than I'm used to, and I hate that it feels good. I don't like the person I am when I'm here. Unfortunately, this job is the only one I can get. I'm not sure what's worse—being broke and homeless, or working for my mom.

I use my toe to push open my uncle's front door, which he left cracked so I could get in. I'm relieved when the inside is dark, and I feel for the bolt lock, twisting it after I shut the door behind me. I let my head fall forward, resting it on the wood while my thumb rubs along the cool metal of the lock.

Darkness seems to be the only thing that soothes me lately. I like the idea that nobody can really see me. Maybe I just like the idea of being alone. There's no one to begin to unload exactly what they think about Enoch Rostram on me—with all of the hate and vitriol I know he deserves, but somehow becomes my burden to bear just by having been the woman who was stupid enough to love him. I did love him. He was my fortune. He was also my curse.

Rolling my head on the door, I spin slowly on the balls of my feet until I relent to the idea of sleeping in this house tonight. My fingers trace along the familiar walls, the pathway to my temporary room the exact opposite of the one I grew up in. I count the stairs on the way up, all the way to twenty-eight, and then it's only four steps until I'm able to close another door behind me and welcome the darkness in.

My bag sits at the foot of a bed I doubt has ever been slept in. The mattress is small—smaller than a typical twin bed—and it reminds me of my dorm room back in Seattle, the one I lived in during the internship. I didn't appreciate that safe independence enough when I had it. I was too busy chasing a fantasy—bitter girl swept away by millionaire Prince Charming.

I push my bag to the side to sit next to it, unzipping the top and feeling inside for the softest T-shirt I can slip into for the night. My fingers stop on what I am pretty sure is my plain white one, so I tug it out from the middle of the folded stack of clothes and stand to kick off my flip-flops and slip from my tank top, bra, and jeans.

The fresh shirt is hot from travel, warm from the Phoenix air outside and the stuffy room I'm in—my *now* home. The cotton clings to me as I move closer to the window covered by the same yellowed metal blinds that my uncle put in when he bought this pad. I twist the wand and tilt the slats open to the sky, bending the one near my sightline just enough to take in the scope of the stars. They may very well be up there, but I'll never know. It's all a muted gray, not quite black because of the light pollution put out from the city. I can *see* the heat at night, the way it swallows up anything pretty.

Breathing out a sigh of disappointment that I can't even have the pleasure of stars anymore, I twist the stick again to close the blinds. Just before the slats flatten completely, my eyes catch a glimpse of the things below my window. Specifically, the shirtless man in black sweatpants leaning against an opened RV door, one foot propped on the step. His thumbs hang from his waistband, pulling the material lower on his hips than it was when I met him minutes ago. Muscular lines that highlight clear discipline in the gym run down his stomach and curve over his sides.

"Shut the blinds, dumb-ass," I whisper to myself, somehow thinking chastising myself out loud will help me behave. My eyes don't even blink, though, and my fingertips don't twist an inch. Fifteen feet below, a man who apparently named himself *Memphis* stares up at the same dark-gray sky I found nothing in. He stares with eyes that are at peace above a mouth resting in a satisfied smile. This is what content must look like. I wonder if I've ever worn it?

His head rests cocked back against the metal siding of what seems to be his home, a tiny place on wheels with rusted trim and a broken-down vehicle cab unlikely to drive it somewhere else. He's stuck here, too. Maybe he'll never want to leave, though I can't imagine that. His right hand moves from his waist to behind his neck, adjusting his position to look up at the bleak sky a little bit longer, but a twist in position brings his eyes right to my window. I don't run, and I keep the blinds open to wait until he gives up on finding something up here.

Cradled in my darkness, I doubt he sees much, if anything at all. But the longer his gaze focuses on my window—*on me*—the more I wonder if, somehow, he sees things I no longer can. I wonder what he sees when he looks at me.

"Close the window, dumb-ass." I whisper my orders to myself again, and this time my hand obeys, twisting the blinds shut. My feet slide back to my bed, and I sit and fall back onto the blanket that smells of dust and stale air.

It's too hot to sleep under the covers, so I push the material down underneath my body until it falls to the floor, the thin sheet not doing much to shield my skin from the springs I feel in the mattress, but at least smelling less of dust.

It's only a minute or two before an RV door slams shut outside. My muscles twitch with the urge to rush to the window again now that it's safe, but I have discipline too. Mine came the hard way. And the only boxer who's going to break my heart is the one who gave me my name.

# CHAPTER TWO

Memphis

She doesn't seem as screwed up as her family says she is. I've been working out here for more than a year, and I didn't know the Valentines *had* a daughter until a few months ago when all that crap with that big-time financial guy was all over the news. When the story broke on the afternoon news, I was in the gym training with Leo and Mrs. V was working on the books in the office. We had on the small TV they used to keep tethered up in the corner. Mrs. V ripped that TV down the next morning, and nobody's brought it up since.

I watched her kick the office filing cabinet so hard she dented it, and then she began to pace in the small area behind the desk, chewing at her nails and spitting off the ends while muttering swear words. When I asked what had her so pissed off, Leo didn't want to tell me at first, but when Mrs. V went to get a trash bag and broom to sweep up the shards of glass and bits of plastic from the TV, he let it spill that the woman in the story was Archie and Angela's daughter.

The first mention referred to the woman involved as Olivia Stone, but by nightfall the media had those details sorted out and reported her real last name. Mrs. V became obsessed with the stories, and I always wondered why she never went up to Washington to help her daughter—or why there weren't phone calls. Leo wouldn't answer my questions after that first conversation. In fact, he didn't say her name to me again until two weeks ago, when he told me Oliva was coming to stay with him for a while.

I expected someone hideous. A real monster. Not the way she *looked*; I'd seen her on TV. I knew she was a pretty girl, but the kinds of shows that would blast her face on the screen never really showed what kind of person she really was. I know what she looks like running from a drugstore to a taxi, trying not to be caught by cameras or shouting reporters. And I know what she looks like when she's staring off in the distance in a courtroom wearing whatever some lawyer probably told her to wear.

She struck me as a girl who might be quiet, I guess. I didn't expect her to be funny. And I sure as hell didn't mean to watch her last night, but damn am I glad I was standing where I was, when I was. The curves of her body peeking through that thin white T-shirt would have probably caught any man's attention, but that's not why I kept looking. I'm not sure I can pinpoint exactly what it was about the way she looked up at the sky, then down at me, but the feeling made a dent in the center of my chest. Not attraction—though she is definitely attractive, in a really interesting way. It's more of a lingering side-effect type thing, like déjà vu.

I don't think she realizes exactly how much of her I saw last night, because there's not a hint of embarrassment in her today. She marched into the club this morning with a bang—literally. She was carrying this enormous box of files, and from the corner of my eye, I noticed she was balancing the box against the same office doorknob she was trying to twist open. Leo was wrapping my hands, and by the time I jumped up and rushed over to her, the files were on the floor and she was swearing.

"Nice job, hero. You got to me just in time to pick this shit up," she said, tossing the torn box on the floor with the rest of the mess.

She flung the office door open and has been sitting at the desk rubbing her temples ever since.

My inside voice keeps screaming "distraction" at me. It's also telling me to quit being nice to a girl who seems to have a chip the size of Texas on her shoulder.

"You know, you don't actually have to pick all of that up." Leo's words are slurred by the wad of chew pushed in the space between his gums and cheek.

It took me about twenty minutes to get the folders back into a pile. I can't help her with the order the pages are supposed to be in, but I can be nice.

"Nah, it's no trouble."

I wrap the pages in what's left of the cardboard and get to my feet just as Leo spits into the bucket by the office door.

"That's Liv, always telling people what to do. Hell, she didn't even have to tell you; you just went and became her bitch." He laughs out hard, the ball-busting kind I'm used to from him, but his laughter stops and his cheeks sink when he glances through the open office door where his niece is staring at him with glowering eyes.

"What? You're bossy is all," Leo says, palms out to his sides as he takes a few meandering steps away before walking over to a group of regulars who just came in.

I give my attention back to Liv, and her eyes are no longer lasers on her uncle. Instead, they look heavy, sinking into her cheeks, which are slowly sinking back into her palms.

"I guess I need to do more speed work," I say, grin twisting high on one side of my mouth. A snorty chuckle comes out. It's my nervous laugh, and I can feel it brewing to come out again while Liv simply raises her brow and moves her focus to me.

"You know, because I didn't get to you fast enough to...to..."

I step forward and set the disorganized pile of papers on the end of the desk, the side flap of the box falling open the moment I let go.

"To stop the mountain of shit that is my parents' business files from falling out of a box that's been eaten by moths every day for the last six years?"

She touches the top of the files and slides a few of the folders around with her fingertip before breathing out a short laugh and falling back into the chair. It rolls a few inches backward with the force. She looks like an angsty teenager, stiff straight legs, holes in the knees of her jeans, and some concert T-shirt tucked into the front of her pants.

"That's not moth damage. Box is just old. And yeah, sorry I was too slow to hold the paperwork mountain up." I lean into the door-frame and wait through her sigh. I'm hoping she'll look at me, but she doesn't. I don't know why I want her to. My friend Miles would say it's because I need everyone to like me—abandonment issues and all that. Maybe he's right. Whatever it is, after this attempt, I need to let it be whatever it is, because I can't be distracted by a popularity contest for approval from one single person. I don't have that kind of time. And the lineup of fighters I need to get through this year are only focused on one thing—knocking my ass out and putting me in my place.

I wait long enough for it to become awkward. Liv is lost somewhere far away. She isn't sad about it, and she isn't angry really. She's resentful as hell, but mostly I think she's just resolved to whatever place her mind is.

"Yeah, so...anyway. I'm just gonna finish my conditioning, so if you have anything else heavy, I can—"

She cuts me off.

"I'll be fine."

Her eyes move to me briefly and her mouth is tight.

"Okay," I shrug and raise my brows. I'm not going to get a smooth exit from this conversation, so I just walk back to the speed bag where a chuckling Leo is waiting for me.

"She that way with everyone?" I pull the tape around my right glove tighter, ripping with my teeth.

"Ha, you just got her nice side," he says, tightening my right glove for me. "You should see her at Thanksgiving when she's going at it with her mom. Pre-fight smack talk's got nothing on a holiday round between Liv and Angela. Been that way since she was fourteen or so."

Fourteen.

That's how old I was when I got a postcard from my real father. The postmark was from Memphis, Tennessee. The picture on the front was of Beale Street just after a rain, the purple sky behind it a perfect match for the neon lights along the roadway. Felt weird for someone I'd decided to hate to send a photo from some place so beautiful.

He signed it *Robert Delaney.* The handwriting was the same as it was on the note tucked into the blanket that swaddled me on the Fourth Precinct footsteps in Philadelphia, where he'd left me when I was just a few days old. That note explained that my mother had died while giving birth, and he had no business raising a baby. He kept his name a secret then. He didn't want to be found.

Robert Delaney made it far in fourteen years, but he still said I was better off where I was. In fact, that's all he wrote on that card—that I was better off. At fourteen, I was positive I knew better, so I ran away from the foster family I'd been living with for a year and slipped onto a bus to Memphis. I didn't have an address, but I had a street. I went to eleven hotels before someone recognized the name. Everything this man ever owned was bundled up in a box stashed behind a hotel desk, like it was waiting for me. He'd passed away days before from a stroke. I've always believed it happened the moment his fingers let the post card fall into the mailbox. The hotel was getting ready to donate his things, and I don't think they expected a kid to show up to claim them.

An army coat, a proper shaving kit, a diary of everything I'd missed—every wish and regret he had about leaving me—and boxing gloves. They were well worn, scarred from training and battle rounds in the ring. I don't wear them now, the leather's brittle and the padding thin. But I did then. I wore them at the police station while I waited for someone from Child Services. I wore them on the airplane they put me on back to Pennsylvania, and I wore them at the group home I stayed at until I was eighteen. Though, as I got older, I kept them in the duffle bag under my bed and only took them out on rare occasions.

I loved those gloves because of the words he'd written during our years apart—honesty poured from pens and pencils—the words sloppily written and often misspelled. He filled pages on my birthdays, and sometimes I could tell he was drunk. He rarely wrote about himself, but when he did, it was as if he'd planned on me finding this book one day. He wrote about his struggles with alcohol, about his abusive father that nearly beat him to death when he was fifteen, and about my mom, a seventeen-year-old he'd lived next door to and ran away with right before their high-school graduation. Their relationship was volatile, and they would lose touch but always come back together. She had her own troubles, it seemed, and during one of those times they met up again, I was created. The timing was wrong all around, neither of them in a place to parent.

For years, I imagined who he was—based on the history he'd chosen to share with me. I decided he'd gone by the name of Memphis, because that's where I'd found his ghost. I made everyone else call me by this name I'd made up, and on the day I turned eighteen, I took his last name: *Delaney*.

I couldn't tell what kind of fighter he was in real life. The only proof I have that he ever fought at all, other than the gloves, was a yellowed scorecard with Archie Valentine's name written on the back. My father was knocked out in the fifth round in some small time undercard fight in New Orleans. The way I see it, though, he went five rounds with a legend. Leo and Angela don't remember him. I'm sure he was some nobody to them. But they took me in like family when I finally got the courage to come here to train. Even if he's just a man I've built from my imagination, I'm going to honor him as if it's all true. The pretend Dad feels a lot better than the one I hated when

I was a kid. He's the truest father I've ever had, and *that's* where my focus needs to be—on training and winning.

I give everything over to the speed bag until the sweat is sliding down the center of my chest and my last clean T-shirt is clinging to me like a second layer of skin. When Leo calls it quits, I pretend to pack up and then let the door fall closed behind him before I pick back up where we'd left off—dodging and weaving, my breath timed with every punch I throw. I get lost in the rhythm. It's a vicious cadence, the perpetual thumps of my leather-bound knuckles swinging the bag with each knock until my triceps beg for mercy. I push beyond the pain, working through the fatigue until the euphoria fills my chest. It's a strange sensation to try to explain to anyone who's never challenged endurance. I feel it push my heart to extremes and flatten my lungs with desperation, but my hands...my feet...my eyes—they never stop. It's a sweet victory against my toughest challenger: *myself.*

With a final blow, I falter back until my numb legs sense the edge of the ring behind me, and I rest on the mat, my neck cradled by the taut rope, my ears pounding as my breath tries to catch up. As tough as this workout was, it's nothing compared to facing a real man just as intent on exploiting my weaknesses as I am his. I have weaknesses. I have too many.

I pull on the tape around my wrists with my teeth, ripping it away in strings, half wanting to drink four-thousand calories in protein and come right back to this bag and do it all again, and half wanting to run down to Shill's and pick up a rib-eye and slather it in butter. I decide to do neither when I hear the office door swing open. Music that sounds like it belongs in a retirement home comes streaming out quietly.

"Why Memphis?"

One hand is on her hip, and her ankles are crossed while her weight rests on the inside of the door. I tug at the tape, and only a sliver comes off, so I stand and slide my tired feet over to her, my wrists turned out. When I glance up to meet Liv's eyes, she jolts the tiniest bit, quickly looking down at my hands.

"Mind?"

She scrunches her shoulders and pushes her hands in her back pockets nervously at first, but eventually breathes out and reaches for my gloves.

"You probably did this a lot when you were a kid, huh?" Her lips twist at both my question, and the stickiness of the tape. She finally grips enough of it in her hand and begins to unravel it from my wrist.

"Not really." Her eyes flit nervously, darting from her own hands to the wide-open gym off to the side, but never up at mine. The lights are low in the gym, but the bright bulbs from the office ceiling act like a spotlight on her face.

"Your dad didn't let you watch his fights, huh?" I take over when she frees my right hand, and I begin tugging at the tape on my left.

She steps back, leaning into the doorway again, and her lip pulls up on one side as she scratches at her ear.

"I watched him train, mostly. But Leo did this kinda stuff. We didn't always live in this place, with the gym right next door. I only really saw my dad when he wasn't *on*, ya know? Like when he wasn't training for a big fight or whatever." She gives me a short glance then looks down, folding her arms over her chest and rocking on her heels.

"So...*Memphis*?" She cocks a brow, her eyes sticking to me a little longer. The light brushes her cheek, and I dip my head in response, not wanting to look so long that I notice things. There's something about Liv that reminds me of home—only I don't know what home is. I've had addresses, but until I started staying with the Valentines, I never had a place that felt like mine. There's a familiarity here. And I see it in Liv, more than anywhere. Or at least I feel it. It's like a dull pressure at the center of my chest.

It's a weakness.

"Didn't much like the name I was born with, and I like Memphis, so..." I hold out my palms, gloves and tape held in each hand, and force myself to look her in the eyes. Only a second or two passes, but I can tell she's not buying my lie. It's the only story I'm giving her, though. You share too much and people start to see all of your baggage.

"Wish I could change mine." Her eyes are serious when she speaks, and we lock gazes again. As much as I'm lying, Liv is speaking a harsh truth.

I respond with a nod eventually, then lean my weight back in the direction of my locker, falling away from her—from this conversation.

Thing is, even if she did change her name, the world already knows her face. She would never be able to disappear. All I was looking to do was belong. Liv is looking to run. It took me years to find my place, and I'm not leaving it now—no matter how hard it is to keep walking away, to not lick my lips and imagine it's Liv's tongue against my skin.

Weaknesses do not belong in the ring, and I need this one to get out of my head.

# CHAPTER THREE

Liv

It's been a week of work—the same work I did as a teenager, because helping with the family business was "expected" of me. My mother and I have always been more boss/employee than mother/daughter. When I was in high school, I think maybe I liked doing my family's books because of the praise. When I found money—discovered an overpaid bill, an underpaid invoice, an overdue account—I was suddenly just as valuable as the broken boys sweating their asses off in the gym just hoping my uncle would pick them out of the crowd and decide to groom them for a real match.

It was the only time I felt valuable. In the Valentine house, money does the talking. Somewhere along the way, though, the only words spoken were lies, and even the money couldn't compete with that.

There's no money to be found here now, anyhow. I've put more than sixty hours into these ledgers and piles of receipts, and the negative equity in this place is the only thing getting bigger. What's sad, though, is I don't even care. I'm not hungry for the praise, and I wrote off inheriting anything worthwhile from my family years ago.

The only thing driving me to the office every morning and into the evening hours is the puzzle that always accompanies messy finances.

That's a lie.

I enjoy the puzzle, but I feel absolutely no allegiance to this business or my parents or my uncle. I show up because I need the job and a place to hide until I can breathe again. The reason I come in here early and stay late...is pounding his fists against my uncle's palms, panting and grunting with every swing. Every morning I beg myself not to notice him, and by the end of the day, he's the only thing I'm paying any attention to at all.

For the last hour, I've been staring at blank spreadsheets while zoning out to the heavy whirr of the air conditioning unit just above my head. It's on its last leg, and that's an expense my mom is going to have to figure out how to eat when it goes, because she can't run a boxing club in a place that hits triple-digit temperatures without air. It doesn't cool like it used to; I think it's gotten hotter just this week. As warm as I am, though, I won't leave. I won't leave because *he* is still here.

He breaks away from my uncle just as I rest my cheek against my palm, and when he turns to grab his towel, his eyes catch mine briefly. His lips don't react, no twitch of a smile or acknowledgement that he and I now share the same space for most of our waking hours. It's been like this—cold, I guess—since I asked him about his name again a few days ago. He suddenly became closed off after that, and I became invisible, which I guess is what I really wanted.

"I hope you don't think I'm paying you for more than forty hours, just because you're working late." My mom's tone cuts right through the peacefulness. Memphis's eyes catch mine again, still emotionless, but they linger through my entire breath.

I blink slowly and open my eyes on my mom. She's dressed like a woman ready for church—her legs covered just below her knees with a long pencil skirt, a silk blouse tucked in perfectly at the waist, adorned with a strand of pearls around her neckline. She's wearing contacts today. She does that when she wants to look young. She's here for Memphis, too.

"Speaking of paying me..." I lean back in the chair and tip my chin up in preparation. It takes my mom half of one second to change the subject, and my mouth slides into a sardonic laugh.

"I'm going down to the market. My magazines came out today..."

"You mean *tabloids*," I cut in, rolling my eyes.

"That's what I said," my mom huffs.

"No," I stand, stretching my arms high and peering beyond my mom to where Memphis is still resting. My uncle has gone to close up, and he's standing in the same place he was seconds ago, his eyes down and his hands working on his tape. He's stalling—eaves-dropping.

I look back at my mom, who's lost in her own world, digging through the purse locked against her chest, searching for keys.

"You read gossip rags, and those are not the same thing as *magazines*. You shouldn't insult real journalism that way."

My voice is snarky, and I push it a little, because I'm annoyed that she's still here, after she blew right over my mention of payday. My dig at her tabloids fires her up, and she stops sifting through the junk in her purse.

"You really think you're in the position to serve as moral authority on what constitutes a legitimate career?" Her eyes narrow and my chest tightens. I stepped right into this. "If it weren't for those magazines, how would I have known my daughter was in trouble?"

"Ummm," I grab my phone and wallet from the desktop and laugh out a single, painful punch. "Maybe you call her. Maybe...*maybe* you acknowledge the fact that she's family, even when it doesn't benefit you financially."

I shake my head in disgust and glance to meet Memphis's eyes again. This time, he looks away. It's hard to ignore my mother and me when we get started, but I wish he wasn't here for this. She brings out my ugliest.

"You mean just like you rushed to the phone to tell your father and me we were going to be grandparents?"

And just like that, jagged needles punch through my insides, my chest stinging, and my heart dropping to the depths of my body. My lips part wide. I stare out the glass doorway, wishing it were closed so at least those words weren't heard by anyone other than me. I keep my back to her and her hate-laced attack meant only to remind me that she's on top. My mom wins this round in the lowest and most personal way. Without saying a word, I swallow my ever-shrinking pride and leave—my head low as I move past Memphis, my arm shoving against my uncle's shoulder as he and I pass through the doorway.

"You leaving on time tonight, Liv?"

I mouth *uh-huh,* but it's silent. His chuckle echoes behind me, and I hate him for it. I know if he had heard my mom, he wouldn't laugh. Leo isn't cruel. He's just selfish.

Without pause, I rush to my temporary room, gather the few articles of clothes I have from the places they lie on the floor, and I stuff them into a plastic bag I found in Leo's kitchen. Flipping open his cabinets one at a time, I finally find one with a coffee can tucked in a corner, and I grasp it in my hand, shaking it to make sure I'm right. I hear the change jingle, and I can feel the paper rustle with the coins. It's enough for laundry, which buys me nearly two hours of solace away from this place and the people who infect it.

Some things never change, and Suds has been open twenty-four hours a day since I was a kid. Even before we moved to the duplexes from the apartment, this is where my mom did our laundry. She liked the patio where she could smoke, or at least she did before she quit. Then she liked to come here to flirt with the men. I would cringe watching her take out her intimates one panty at a time, as if anyone really folds their underwear.

The men at Suds haven't changed, either. I walk in to leering eyes, some hazed by pot, some by pills and alcohol. Only three or four of the other people in here are actually doing laundry. A woman with thinning hair and poorly wrapped wounds on her arm is stretched out along the row of plastic chairs in the back. For her, this place is home. I would consider trading her for mine right now.

I swing my bag of laundry on top of one of the washers, a single sock falling on the floor from the overstuffed sack. Plastic bags make my belongings seem more plentiful. I smirk at the thought as I bend down to pick it up. A hand slides down the center of my ass, invasively, slapping quickly as a pair of dirty Nikes and tight black pants rush past me. I flinch and lurch into the machine, standing and turning my backside into the machine defensively.

"What the fuck!"

The man blows out a thin line of smoke, the stench of weed strong, and he coughs through his laughter as he strides to the back of the room and sits on a table next to another man, here without a good reason. They mumble to each other, and the other one starts to laugh loudly. I can tell they're talking about me, and my skin crawls.

Turning my focus to the payment slot on the washer, I breathe in deeply and hold the fullness in my chest for a few long seconds. I clutch the can between my hands and my thumb pries at the plastic lid as I waver on whether or not I'm actually going to stay. When I decide to leave, I press the lid back in place and reach to hook my plastic bag on my thumb. As I turn, though, a very dangerous reason to stay walks through the door and makes eye contact with me.

Memphis nods, politely, then carries his laundry basket to the opposite corner of the room, his back to me. My grip loosens as I watch him open a washer and drop in what looks like a dozen T-shirts and sweatpants. He pulls a wallet from his back pocket and slips out a credit card, and with his face turned to the side, holds the card between his teeth while he puts his wallet away. His eyes glance my way, and I look down quickly, pouring my pathetic wardrobe from the plastic bag into the metal bin of the washer. My heart beats fast under the notion that Memphis is watching me. I don't glance up again until I slip two dollar bills into the machine and press start.

His back is to me again, and deep down I know he didn't watch me at all, and I hate that for that moment I imagined he was. Imagining is like wishing, and wishing is like wanting. There is nothing about Memphis that I want. I don't want anyone. I want independence and a fresh start, and as far as I can tell those things don't come with fighters. At least not for me. No, that would just be more of the same old thing.

I move back until my shoulders hit the wall, and I cross my ankles, pulling my phone from my front pocket and flipping open a few news apps so I can pretend to read. The world is an ugly place, and the news spoon-feeds tiny morsels, a bite at a time, in an app that lets people actually *click* to love a story about a black boy beaten in an alleyway behind his school.

Forty-two people have clicked to heart this story, and I wonder how many of them did it because they have rotten souls. It only takes four more swipes for me to get to a story about Enoch. I skim the first few paragraphs, and I close the app when I don't see my name. My omission actually washes my stomach with a sense of relief, and I feel my shoulders physically drop an inch or two.

"Pretty ass!"

The groping jackass is trying to bait me, his mouth puckering into loud kissing sounds. I force myself to look straight ahead to the machine with my clothes. I won't engage.

"Bro, you see how she likes me? Yeah, pretty ass there likes me. She's playing all cool and shit, pretending she doesn't hear me. But you hear me, don't you, baby? Yeah, you like my hand on your pussy."

I sneer in reaction, my mouth releasing an audible hiss as I take steps closer to the door, but keep my backside against the wall. Another thing that hasn't changed about this place is the side of sexual harassment that comes with it. I hate it, and I hated it when I was a little girl and watched men say things like this to my mom. She'd giggle, and when they touched her, she laughed it off. There was some tortured part of her that fed off the negative attention. My dad wasn't living with us at the time, and she was desperate to feel like someone wanted her.

Self-hatred is such a wicked cycle. I've ridden it myself.

"Oh come on, baby girl..." The man's voice trails off, and I brace myself for his next taunt. When it doesn't come right away, I glance to the left. My eyes flash wide when I see Memphis standing in front of him, his hand wrapped around his neck, pushing the man's shoulders flush against the wall.

"Come on, we were just messing with her..."

The man's plea comes out gravely, and Memphis pushes into him a little harder, the man's face blushing and a guttural choke escaping his throat.

Memphis looks over his shoulder to me, his eyes capturing mine for a solid two seconds. He then glances back at the man he's holding. With his head falling to the side, Memphis slowly lets go of his grip and begins to step back. He raises a finger and points at the dude while he walks away, eventually returning to his laundry. This time, he sits on the counter, his eyes facing the entire room so he can stand guard. A minute later, my harassers leave.

Stragglers come and go over the next two hours. A mom with two kids takes the machines next to me, and her children begin pounding the window of the dryer whirling around my clothes. The mom is on the phone with someone; her volume is loud enough for me to hear the full conversation. It's about her custody battle. The sleeping woman has started to wake up, and she's shouting every few seconds, her body jolting violently. My head pounds with the excess sound, and my pulse races with the stimulation, my hands quaking due to jacked-up nerves.

"You're done."

"Huh?" I startle hard, surprised to see Memphis now standing in front of me. His eyes are off to the side, hands in the pockets of his gray joggers.

"Your dryer just stopped when I walked up." His eyes slide to mine briefly.

"You're watching my dryer now?" I puff out a short laugh and push forward, stepping around him to swing open the machine's door.

"I was just making sure those guys left you alone." My upper body deep in the dryer, I wrap my arms around my clothes, bringing them to my chest.

"You know that's actually how my dad won over my mom. He went nuts on some guy that was hitting on her at a bar; he beat the shit out of the guy in the parking lot. Knocked out two of the guy's teeth. My mom just melted for that shit." I swing my hip into the door to shut it and dump my clothes on the counter to begin folding, but take a moment to shift my gaze to Memphis. "I don't melt for that. *That...*" I nod over to the wall where he had the asshole pinned by his throat, "is exactly the kind of thing Archie Valentine would have done."

It's only partially true, because my father wouldn't have passed up a chance to make a bigger scene. He would have sworn loudly, and there's no way he would have walked away without throwing a punch. But the alpha-animalistic Tarzan nature of it all—definitely in the Valentine playbook.

"I don't like bullies or guys that think it's okay to harass women." I note that he didn't mention the words *help* or *rescue.*

"Noble." I hear him take a heavy breath behind me, and I make a lopsided smirk as I fold my last shirt and stack my clean clothes together so I can slip them back in the bag. "You should come here more often, because guys like that are here all day and night. You could step in and stop them from harassing the other women, too. Not just me."

I smile with tight lips as I tie the handles of the plastic bag, then walk past him. I get a few steps away, to the trash where I toss in the detergent sample wrappers, when Memphis responds.

"Jesus, you're impossible."

I chuckle to myself, planning to keep walking and leave it at that —at *impossible*—but with a few long strides, he catches up to me and soon passes me, turning around with his arms outstretched.

"I'm not impossible. I just don't need your help, Memphis." I can't even speak his name without wondering what it was before he changed it, and the fact that I spend time wondering about him frustrates me.

"Clearly!" He shakes his head, and his eyes stare into mine. I've been foolishly waiting for him to look at me all week, but now that he is, I realize exactly what kind of danger I was toying with. His lashes are dark, which makes the golden brown of his eyes a hint more powerful. He needs to shave, or rather...he *doesn't* need to shave, because fuck me is his face sexy like that. There's a small pink bruise on his right cheek—a mark left behind when Leo tagged him at workouts two days ago. I was watching him then. He was refusing to look at me. The whole cat-and-mouse situation is making me mental, and it feels...it feels like the way my dad was with my mom.

His head cocks to the side, and his mouth curves.

"I don't even get why you're mad." He chuckles through his words, and I lose it.

"I left this place for a reason. Men like you. That's the reason, Memphis. No...it's more than men like you; it's the women you turn us into when we're around you. I'm never going to become one of those women. I won't be her."

I shake my head and blink, recalling all of the times I watched my dad flirt with my mom. He'd make her feel special by standing up to some drunk at a bar or by hovering over her protectively, like a bear, everywhere they went in public. Then he'd leave her in the morning, and come home days later smelling like smoke and booze and sex clubs. The fights between the two of them were epic. She'd throw things and make holes in the walls with glasses or ashtrays. The fights never scared me, though. What scared me was watching my mom sob as she patched up the damaged wall all by herself—knowing that she'd wait for him to come back and grace her with his protective company again.

Glancing behind Memphis, I see the mom with the rowdy kids staring at us with her mouth agape. My focus darts around to the woman in the corner who just arrived, and she's staring too—though trying to pretend she isn't by pushing her pile of towels around the folding table. I swallow hard and bring my gaze back to Memphis, and those tempting eyes are waiting, slanted with confusion.

"Look, I'm tired. Working for my mom...she and I...we just..."

"I'm Memphis," he interrupts, reaching his palm toward me to shake. I bunch my brow staring at it. "I hear your name is Liv? You've been working at the club where I work out. I've seen you. Anyhow, I thought I should introduce myself."

My lip gets twitchy. It's twitchy because motherfuck, he's charming. He's actually, genuinely charming. And I'm falling for the act. I give in to the slight smile and breathe out a quiet laugh before taking his hand and gripping it tightly for a shake.

"Liv Valentine. I'm *the cleaner*."

His right eyebrow lifts.

"If you saw the books I'm working with, you'd get what that means. I've been gone for seven years, and I can tell. Leo and my dad know their way around the ring. My mom...she knows her way around a soap opera."

He laughs at that. I join him. Soon I'm walking alongside him to his laundry basket, and without even thinking, I let him take my things and put them inside it to carry my stuff for me.

"It's a good thing you're here then, I guess?" He glances at me sideways, holding the door of the laundromat open while I step out into the warm air of the Phoenix streets.

"There is nothing good about me being here. I assure you." My mouth draws into a serious line, leaving nothing for him to do but shrug at my response.

We walk the first block in silence, and I start to cringe at how upset I got over Memphis defending me at Suds. I'm leaping to conclusions that aren't even real. Memphis is kind, he is a fixture at my temporary home, and he's made an effort to be my friend. I need to quit looking at that like it's an invitation from the devil.

"I'm sorry." My teeth grip my lip the moment the short sentence passes. I'm not good at humility. That's another trait I got from my dad. We're stubborn, and we're right—even when we're wrong.

I glance to the side and catch Memphis pushing his tongue against the inside of his cheek. He twists his head a little and nods to me.

"And thank you for putting those guys in their place," I continue. "But—"

He slows his steps, and I hold up my hand.

"Those guys are just going to do it again. It's awful, but they are. Unless you follow them around everywhere they go and smack them down every time they act like assholes, it's not going to do any good. They're ruined already. You can't rehab a guy who thinks it's okay to act like that."

He's stopped, and I stand next to him as he stares at me, digesting my bleak truth. His mouth draws in tight and his head begins to nod with whatever resolution he's come to. When he begins walking again, I match his step.

"Then you're just gonna need to learn to fight."

I laugh out loud at this suggestion.

"Absolutely not," I say.

"Why? I mean, I can't believe you don't know how to already. Your dad is The Heavy." I sense the sincerity of his shock, and I hate to pop his bubble, but if we're going to be friends, then I can't let him go on thinking my dad was as good at parenting as he was at right-hook combos.

"I can count the conversations I had with my dad on two hands, and I'd have fingers left over—and half of those were either when he was punch drunk or whiskey drunk. Either way, there really wasn't much of a difference. Teaching a girl how to throw a punch wasn't a priority for that man. I mean...maybe if I was a stripper at his favorite club. But his daughter? Nah. That kinda shit was never in his skills set."

Memphis's eyes dip and his gaze falls to the basket in his arms. We make it to the main drive and the walkway that splits off to my parents' home and Leo's. I reach into the basket as he slows and take out my bag of clean clothes and hold it up in thanks.

"Appreciate the lift," I say, my smile real, but small.

I turn and reach for the unlocked front door.

"I'll teach you then," he says.

A strange rush travels from my head to my knees, like morphine. It's delicious. It's dangerous. I lean into the door with my hand on the knob, then turn to face him.

"We're the last people in that gym in the evening anyhow. I don't mean anything heavy or like hours-long lessons, just some strength training. We'll work on emergency-type situations; just enough so you can hurt some guy and get the hell out of trouble."

I take a heavy breath. I'm tempted.

"Please," his eyes rock mine with that single word. I think Memphis might actually be a decent man. "Please," he repeats, quieter, and leaning in enough that I instinctively turn the knob and step inside.

"Maybe," I relent. A weight bounces around my insides, squeezing my lungs tight and making my stomach heavy.

His smile inches up.

"Maybe," he nods and winks, and I get a tinge of regret. "Maybe she says," he hums out loud as he turns and heads down the dark path out to the parking lot where his RV is parked. Why does he live in that? Why did he name himself Memphis? Why, if he has promise, did he come *here* of all places? How did Leo suck him into this crazy place?

"Hey," I shout, stopping him before he disappears around the corner. He crooks his neck and steps back under the streetlight's glow. "If...and that's a real *if*. If I let you teach me, I want your real story."

The shift in his expression is subtle, but it's there. His jaw tightens, and his eyes haze ever so slightly. His lips fall into a near frown, masked carefully while he pretends to be thinking about my offer.

"I want to know why *Memphis*. The *real* reason."

With a blink, he looks down, his foot digging into the concrete a few times, weighing how important it is to him that I learn to fight. I won't be surprised if he lets this idea go. I won't be upset either, because the less he shares, the less I share, and that means this distance—which is already too close—will stop right here at polite.

"Memphis is the last place I know my real father was alive. We'll start tomorrow." By the time I catch my breath and let his words sink in, he's disappeared into the dark alley and rounded the corner.

The heaviness has returned to my chest, but this time it feels different. It's curious, and it's sad. It feels like it does when I want to help someone and make them feel better.

It's the sense of putting someone else before me, of a promise I made myself slowly slipping through my fingers.

"You're just like me, you know."

I don't frighten when my mom speaks. I saw her sitting on the steps of her porch in the dark. She was waiting for me to come home. Not because she cares that I get home safe; I'm her sport—her distraction from the depressing existence that waits for her upstairs.

"All right, well goodnight, Mom." I don't even turn toward her. It took me years to learn, but I've mastered the art of not completely engaging in a battle with her. Just being around her brings out my worst. Memphis saw some of that tonight.

"You still haven't gone up to visit him." She sneaks that last bit in before I can get inside. I pause at the door, lips parted and ready for response, but halted by wisdom.

I know better.

It's not like my father told her I haven't been up to see him. He doesn't talk, and there hasn't been some amazing turn in his condition. My mom seldom leaves this house, and when she's in it, she rarely leaves her room. She hears everything that happens up those stairs, and she's been watching for me to visit him. Probably, so she can pounce and fill his ears with lies about all of the ways she's trying to help me get back up on my feet. Shelter and a job—that's all she's given me. I still haven't gotten paid for the job part yet, and technically Leo is giving me shelter.

Mom hasn't given me shit.

"Tomorrow. I'm tired tonight," I say, stepping inside and closing the door with only enough time for her to shout that she'll tell him to expect me.

He was never expecting me.

I was the biggest goddamned surprise of Archie Valentine's life.

# CHAPTER FOUR

Memphis

She isn't dressed for a workout. That's the first thing I noticed when Liv walked through the gym door this morning. The next thing I noticed was Leo's black eye. The hostility brewing between the both of them is so thick, I can chew on it. I'm fairly certain both of those things are connected.

Liv's kept the office door open all day, and she's listening to classic rock, her lips moving with the words, but only half the time, like she only knows bits and pieces. A few times, Leo walked by and slammed the door shut. Without missing a beat—and without glancing his direction—Liv just got right up from her chair and opened it again.

Heatedly.

I tried talking to her when Leo disappeared for a four-hour lunch break, but I got the firm sense she wasn't in the mood. I was getting that same cold shoulder she was dishing out to her uncle, which means whatever Leo did seems to have screwed all men over in general. I ended up catching up on a few hours of sleep before my afternoon routine.

Leo's been gone for an hour now, the afternoon light fading and turning the frosted glass windows in the gym orange. The tank top from my workout is cold from hour-old sweat, and my muscles are even colder. If I tried to workout with Liv right now, I'd probably get an injury. I have work in two hours anyway.

Without saying anything, I rip the tape from my hands using my teeth and wad it into a tight ball that I toss into the metal can by the exit. I have to slide my back along the wall as I stand, my legs threatening to cramp. I was so preoccupied with Liv and her ditching our plans—and beating the shit out of her uncle—that I let my hydration slip.

Gnashing my lips at the threat of pain, I make a mental note not to slip again—no matter how distracting she is. Even in jeans and an over-sized gray T-shirt that I'm pretty sure once belonged to a man. Without looking her way again, I shove my things in my gym bag, including the training pads I planned on using with her, and toss the duffle straps over my shoulder as I head toward the door.

"He deserved that."

Her voice practically echoes as I flip the switch on the gym's main fan, killing the *hum* and leaving nothing but this glorified warehouse space and the sound of her voice. Her tone doesn't seem angry, so I stop and turn to acknowledge her. I'm surprised when she's leaning on the office doorway and looking right at me, waiting for my eyes. It's the first time she's looked at another person all day.

I shrug.

"I'm guessing you don't need those lessons after all then."

Her head cocks a little and her eyelids fall, not quite following me. I nod my head in the direction of Leo's home.

"That looked like the work of a right hook, is all. I don't think I did that kind of damage to a face until I was twenty."

Her lips smirk, just a little, and I can't help but let my lip curl too.

"Yeah, well. I'm pretty sure it was a jab. Isn't that what you call it?" She thrusts her right hand out, and her form is decent, but I think the shot she got on Leo was probably mostly fueled by luck and adrenaline. For a man in his fifties, he's still tough as fucking nails.

"Anyhow, like I said, he deserved it." She rolls her body along the frame of the door, her momentum moving away from me.

"Wanna talk about it?" I ask.

"Nope," her response comes fast, and it's accompanied by her walking away, back into the office she's been stewing in all day. I close the space between us a little, but stop at the doorway, respectful of the invisible barrier I can tell she's trying to maintain.

"You gonna hide in here all night?"

Her shoulders lift with a slight laugh.

"Was thinking more all *month*." She glances at me sideways, a pen cap held between her lips—no doubt mauled by her teeth.

I chuckle at her joke, but I don't let go of her eyes. After a few seconds, neither of us is laughing. If I could just get rid of that fortress that's standing in the way of whatever words I can tell are on the tip of her tongue, maybe I could get her to smile a little more. I could at least give her someone to talk to that didn't throw baggage back in her face. I hold her gaze through her heavy breath, and I wait while her lips fall into a melancholy line.

"I'll be ready tomorrow. I promise. I just...today—"

"Sure, yeah...we can start tomorrow," I interrupt. I can see how bad she feels for skipping out on me, and that's not what any of this was supposed to be about. It wasn't an obligation. It was...it was something else—something that I probably shouldn't let start tomorrow either, but I've already said *yes* to today.

"I'll lock up. You head out and enjoy your night," Liv says, and I can't help but read into the minor shoulder shrug that accompanies her words.

My feet start to shuffle backward, but I keep my eyes on her. She's chewing at the pen cap again and glancing from me to her work, pretending she wants me to just leave, but she doesn't. There's nothing on that paper in front of her on the desk, and I watched her put everything away already. She gives me a final smile and nods, and it's maybe the worst acting performance I've ever seen.

Liv does not want to be alone right now.

"Go with me somewhere." I lift my chin and hold my breath, hoping she'll agree.

She stares directly ahead away from me for a few more chews on the pen cap, then reaches up and pulls it from her mouth, tossing it into the trash.

"Okay."

Her answer is quick and without questions. I probably could have asked her to come help me bury a body right now and she'd be up for it, just to get out of this one-block prison she's trapped in.

I wait by the exit while she finishes locking up the office and killing the lights on our way out. I don't say anything more until we've walked around the gym to the alleyway and we're standing in front of my bike.

"I've got an extra helmet. Just give me a few minutes to change. I've got work in a bit, so I'll just drop you off here again after Miles."

Her gaze remains on my bike, and the tip of her tongue parts her lips as she smiles faintly.

"Of course you ride a bike," she says. She nods slowly and starts to laugh quietly.

I stop at the top step into the RV.

"I don't have a *bike*. I have a nineteen-seventy-two Commando," I say, leaning into the doorway of the RV and stretching my neck with pride. It's dashed quickly with Liv's snort laugh.

"Commando?" Her lips pucker as she strains to hold the rest of her laugh in.

"What?" I hold my hands out to my sides, and she lets her laughter escape completely.

"I'm sorry. You're right. It's a very pretty bike," she finally says, but her lips visibly twitching and wanting to laugh more.

"The Commando was Machine of the Year back in the late sixties. It's iconic."

"It's also what you say when you let your balls fly free," she deadpans.

I blink once, deciding that I like her here too much to tell her about the other things that make my bike special—like the fact that I know my real dad rode it across the country, and I know he wanted me to have it one day. Instead, I'll let her have a good laugh. We could both use it.

My tongue held over my front teeth, I spend a few seconds letting my grin fall in place while I consider what words will make her blush the most.

"That's the only way I ride baby," I settle on, hooking my thumbs in the waistband of my sweatpants and letting my eyes haze just a little. I'm going for smolder, whatever that is. I have compression shorts on underneath right now, but when I'm not in the ring, I like to breathe. And I kinda like that Liv is thinking about that now. I wink when I feel like she's turned the right shade of pink, then head inside to shower and pull on some fresh clothes. I catch a quick glimpse of her before I look away, and I'm satisfied by the way her eyes have widened.

I settle on my dark jeans and the white V-neck I washed at the laundromat, and I step back outside just in time to catch her swinging her right leg over my bike, her hand affectionately running up the seat, onto the chrome.

"You've done that before."

Her cheek dimples on the side closest to me with a smile.

"Leo had a bike. Not a *Commando,* but it was a nice bike. He used to take me to school on it." She glances at me, and I step forward to hand her a helmet.

"Leo around a lot when you were growing up?" I ask as I help her situate the helmet on her head.

"He was more of a dad than the one I got my DNA from," she says, planting her hands between her legs and holding herself on the back of my seat. I put my helmet on and slide in front of her, feeling her warm body conform behind me as her arms snake around my sides and flatten against my chest. I haven't had a girl on my bike in more than a year, and I don't think I've ever had someone settle in with such ease and trust as Liv just did.

I turn my head slightly to the right and she reacts by resting her cheek between my shoulder blades, somehow getting even closer to me. It's oddly intimate—almost...natural—and it halts me. My bike rumbles as I start it, but I leave my gaze to the side, catching the curled ends of her hair swirl in the breeze from under her helmet. She adjusts, and when her hand moves along my chest and grabs a fistful of my T-shirt, I breathe out heavily and let my eyes close for just a second, because it feels so good to have someone here, close like this.

"Hold on," I say, swallowing.

I give over to the road, roaring us out of the alleyway and onto the side streets I've memorized in this part of the city. There are two personalities to this section of Phoenix. The version that's busy and bright—loud, with cars and government employees on their lunch breaks wearing dressy clothes with sneakers so they can walk to some fast-food place on Van Buren, then back again. Then there's this time —the afterhours, when the streets are quiet, so quiet that the growl of cars usually means someone's racing, and the only people on the streets are the ones who live this far west of the high rises or the ones who didn't make it to the shelter before it was full.

That's how I met Miles.

His area is only a few blocks away, but too far to walk in this heat. I can feel Liv's hesitation when I slow as we get closer to the long strip of patchy grass and trees that divide one of the city's oldest roads. It's not like the movies, where bums huddle around fires burning in metal garbage cans, but it still has an edge of sketchiness to it. The smell of weed and urine is strong. When I pull to a stop right against the curb in the center of the road, her hands squeeze at my sides.

"This isn't the kind of spot you take a girl for a picnic." Her words are followed by a nervous laugh.

"I told you, we're meeting my buddy Miles." I grin at her as I slide from my bike so I can take her helmet and help her off too. She pulls the collar of her shirt up to cover her nose, and my chest squeezes with guilt. This was a bad idea...bringing her here. But if she gets it—if she sees why Miles matters—it will be a sign that she's maybe more than a distraction. Or, that I'm looking for signs anywhere I can get them, because she's also beautiful.

Liv's eyes scan the park, and she winces slightly with each ruffle of a bag that reveals a sleeping human underneath. Without thinking it through, I turn my hand outward and feel for her fingertips, grabbing her free hand at the first brush. My touch sends her gaze down to our linked palms and mine to her eyes. She lets the shelter of her shirt fall from her nose, and her neck moves with a slow swallow. My fingers pulse once, squeezing her a little tighter.

"It's safe," I say, her eyes sliding upward to meet mine again. She gives a slight nod.

I recognize Miles's plaid shirt resting against the largest tree in the center of the median, the maroon duffle bag I gave him during our last visit tucked tightly against his right thigh and a water bottle clutched in his left hand.

Smirking a little, I nod toward him and escort Liv closer. Her grip tightens with each step, so when we startle Miles upon our approach and he jumps, she squeals and jerks behind me.

"Good lordy, holy hell my man. You thinnin' out the homeless by giving us heart attacks one at a time?" I breathe out a laugh and reach my hand down toward my fallen friend. He grips my palm with his dry, cracked fingers, and I immediately notice the new bandage wrapped around two of his fingers.

"Don't worry 'bout it. Jus'a burn is all. I was too close to the exhaust pipe the other night, and I'm a wiggler in my sleep. But you know that." Miles laughs and coughs together, his breath running thin and his face reddening with his struggle to breathe. I let go of his hand and crouch down to lift him from under his arms. He's struggling more to stand than he did a few months ago.

"You talk to the man at the VA? The one I gave you the card for?" Miles scrunches his face like he's struggling to piece together what I'm talking about and I can tell he didn't. I save him the effort of lying to me. I know he doesn't like to.

"He's only going to help. You know that. But I won't force you. I get it," I say, letting our eyes lock for a few seconds. He nods and glances over my shoulder toward Liv, and I know that conversation is done for tonight.

"Look at that. Young Memphis gone and got himself a better-looking friend, I see." Miles's eyes crinkle at the corners, and his unshaven face bends with his smile. Even sixty and broken by a failed system, his Southern charm possesses a magic I envy when I hear Liv's quiet giggle behind me.

"I don't know about that," she says, stepping out from my protection and taking a hand that's lived twice as many years as hers and has survived war.

"Honey, trust me when I tell you—between the two of us," Miles pauses, pressing his lips to the top of her hand after lifting it, then winking. "You are most definitely the better-looking friend."

I glance at her and am hit with this vision—her lips puckered, trying to hold in her smile, her eyes squinting in flattery, and her cheeks high and rosy with blush.

"Well, thank you." She nods and lowers her eyes, but sweeps her gaze my direction as her hand falls back to her side. "But what I meant was this fool ain't my friend. I just felt bad for him is all. I was trying to build up his self-esteem and make him feel like he wasn't such an enormous loser."

Her smirk shines in her eyes, and I breathe out a short laugh as I tilt my head.

"I like this one, Memphis. She keeps you in your place. A champ needs to be humbled," Miles says, adjusting his weight on his legs and folding his arms over his chest.

"Yeah, she keeps me humble all right," I say, suddenly unable to turn my eyes away from Liv's.

I shake off the trance, realizing the dim light has triggered the streetlamps, which means it must be getting close to eight o'clock.

"Liv, meet Miles Dickerson, a man who has three medals of bravery for *some things that happened over in the Middle East in the early eighties.* Good luck getting him to tell you anything more than that. I've been trying to get him to talk about it for a year."

Miles starts waving his hand, dismissing my flattery, before I finish my last sentence.

"There are a whole lot of people who are worth a lot more fuss than me," he says.

"And they should take better care of them, too," I add.

Miles just rolls his eyes and moves back toward the tree and the spot he's claimed as his, at least for a while. I kneel down by his feet, nodding for him to take his right shoe off while I pull the salve and wrap from my pocket. I hear Liv take a sharp breath when she sees the dirty bandage I begin to remove. I glance up at her, pausing my hands, and nudge my head to encourage her to look away. She steps closer and kneels at my side.

"It's infected," she says, her voice almost a whisper.

"He has a hard time getting new bandages. Just getting in to see someone, so—"

I shrug.

Liv blinks slowly, her eyes grazing over my friend's dirty jeans with tears along the legs, and doubled-up socks that don't match and haven't been washed in weeks.

"We have a lot of stuff at the gym. We can bring more."

My chest kicks hearing her words, the same ones I said when I first met Miles a year ago. He'll shut her down, too, but god I love that her mind went there.

"I get by. And I'm not here long. This is temporary. My daughter lives in the Springs. I'm heading there soon."

Liv nods, just like I did the first time Miles said it to me. When his gaze hits mine, we exchange a silent agreement that I will let him continue to spin this story for now. I'll tell Liv the truth later, though, because for some reason, I don't want to have secrets between us.

Us. A beginning of us—or an accidental us, fate or coincidence... maybe luck—whatever it is, it made *us*. We are in this space together, and there was a moment. It makes breathing both hard and satisfying when she is around.

"I have to get to work," I say, standing up as Miles slides his newly wrapped foot back into his well-worn tennis shoe. "I'll stay longer next time...maybe bring some food."

"Well if I'm not here, don't worry. Just means I caught a ride to the Springs..."

"Yeah, I know the drill. Give the food to Manny, and don't let those young, druggie punks near your tree," I say.

It's the same thing I always say to him. Over the year we've spent talking to one another here in this pathetic excuse for a park, we've developed a sort of secret code. This tree is important to him. It's sheltered him from rain and brutal sun alike. And if he's gone, my job is to make sure this little plot of public land goes to someone worthy. I should feel happy that Miles has finally gotten a ride to the Springs, even though I know that his daughter died years ago, along with his wife—and that going to see her means his time has come, too.

"It was really nice to meet you, Miles." Liv's fingers sprawl and contract in a small wave, and her eyes soften as she takes in a final smile from this homeless man who insists on living in this park.

"The pleasure was one hundred percent mine," he says, fluttering his hand down his chest like a gentleman would a hat in the olden days. I can almost picture him in dress blues, cleanly shaven, with hair slicked back.

We're both quiet as we walk back to my bike, and I wait to start the engine while Liv slides in behind me and positions her helmet back on her head. Her hands quickly find the place they belong on my chest, and I struggle to keep my breathing normal. I can't show her how affected I am.

"How did you meet him?" I feel her cheek rest against the center of my back after she talks.

"He was in the ER the day I got this." I hold my palm up above my shoulder and she peels back enough to look at the top of my hand. Her right hand slides away from my body briefly until she runs her thumb along the thick line of stitches that ladder from the webbing of my thumb all the way around my wrist.

"Was this from a fight?" she asks.

I shake once with a laugh and bring my grip back down to the gears. I'm glad when her palm returns to the warm spot along the side of my chest.

"I wish I could say it was something cool like that. I was making salsa. I cut the shit out of myself with one of your mom's knives," I say.

"Ah," she responds.

We're both quiet, and as the seconds tick, I start to feel desperate to find a reason to stay right here, just like this.

"Where do you work?" She breaks the quiet.

"St. Peter's, in the community center. I run the night desk on the days they're open late. The crowd from eight until eleven is a little rough, but for some of these kids, this is the only place to go. Technically, they can't be on the streets after curfew, but most of their parents work nights too. I'm supposed to help them check out pool cues, games, or whatever—but I'm really a security guard. The girl that works there with me got beat up a few months ago, because she was working the desk alone at night. Some guys came in to give one of the teens a hard time. I guess I have one of those faces that warn people not to take a swing, so they asked if I could move from mornings to nights."

She's quiet again, and I regret talking so much.

"Can I come with you?"

I freeze when she interrupts my self-doubt, and then I smile because she can't see it.

"Sure," I answer, a small word for something that feels bigger. I glance down at her grasp, the tips of her fingers dug into the softness of my shirt.

"Hold on."

When I fire up the bike, her chin rests firmly on the center of my back, and I imagine where it puts her lips. I imagine her kissing me there, and working her way around to my mouth, then my chest, and my stomach.

"Hold on tighter," I say, knowing she's holding on tight enough. I just want her closer, and for now, that's the only way I can see it happening. She obeys, closing the fractions of space between us, her thighs squeezing around my hips. I shift the gear and kick away, my body burning up thanks to the mental torture of my own doing. This fantasy is going to need more than a twenty-minute bike ride to fade away. Probably because it seems so real.

# CHAPTER FIVE

Liv

I can see why Memphis likes it here at night. It's quiet. Four boys have come in since we arrived an hour ago, and Memphis spent most of that time playing pool with them. From the little I know about him so far, I think maybe he missed out on having brothers when he was young. He's good with them. He's good with everyone.

I never wanted a sibling. Even before I knew how twisted and awful my household was, I was aware enough to know that bringing another child into our family would be cruel. Maybe I didn't want to have to be responsible for getting someone else out of this place; I didn't want a sister or a brother to get in my way. I ended up right back here anyway.

Amy, the girl that works here, is young—too young to be working in a place like this alone late at night. She's in college. I haven't asked, but I would guess she's maybe nineteen or twenty. She's mentioned not being able to drink twice. Ah, the carefree days of college when that was what mattered.

I can tell she likes Memphis. She doesn't flirt, but her dreamy eyes are sweet. He's kind to her, without leading her on. Just one more way he isn't like Archie. My dad would have exploited affection from a college girl in a heartbeat. He probably still would if he could get his ass up out of that bed and form words.

When the group of boys move over to a video game console set up by two couches in the corner, Memphis flips his pool stick around his wrist once and turns his head toward me before walking closer.

"Come on. I wanna see how well your right hook adapts to nine-ball." He holds the stick in front of him toward me, ready to toss it, so I stretch my legs out from the chair I've been planted in and rise to my feet.

"I broke a window playing this game when I was seven," I say, holding out my open palm and catching the stick when he tosses it.

Memphis chuckles, but his mouth falls into an open awe when he realizes I am not kidding.

"With the right touch, those bumpers really act like ramps, ya know?" I shrug and move toward the table, and Memphis drags behind me.

"I'm sure your touch has gotten more delicate since then," he says.

I pick up a cube of chalk and roll it in my palm, stopping with it between my thumb and fingers so I can dust the end of my stick.

"You saw Leo's face this morning. You think there's anything delicate about that?" I twist my lips and lean my hip into the table, locking eyes with him. His head falls slightly to the side and he takes a few slow steps toward me, halting at the other end of the table. He reaches for the chalk and rubs it on the end of his cue without breaking our eye contact.

"You make a good point," he says, cutting his words short, like he has more to say.

He wants to know what happened between Leo and me, but I already told him once that I didn't want to talk about it. I don't—at least, not about that. It's not a simple story I can boil down into something relatable. It's messy and complicated, and it's woven in my family web; it won't make me look very good—not that anything else Memphis has seen of my life has been a highlight.

"You break." He racks the balls into a diamond pattern and rolls the white one toward me with a gentle push.

I stop it with my finger and line it up just slightly off center, wasting little time as I bend forward, resting my forearm on the wooden frame of the table so I can angle my shot.

"I wouldn't stand there," I say, glancing up and smirking.

Memphis takes a large stride to the right and I level my eyes back with the ball. I think Memphis thinks I'm hustling him, pretending not to be good just to toy with him, but I really am awful. Everything about the way I play pool looks good—all the way...up to...

The tip of my cue catches the side of the white ball, spinning it askew and directly into a pocket. My arms and body follow through with my motion until my chest is flat against the felt top and my stick is launched several feet behind Memphis—the crash of the wood against the tile floor *pings* and echoes. The teens gathered in the corner pause their game to stare for a few seconds.

"Wow. I don't really even know what to say about what you just did. I'm...I think maybe I'm..." Memphis pauses and furrows his brow, his eyes shifting to the faint chalk line trailed along the table's center from my massive fail to the place where my stick landed.

"Sexy, huh?" I joke, pulling my entire body up on the table and propping my chin in my palms. I warned him. My dad had to pay for that window I broke when I was seven. I wasn't even supposed to be in the bar, what being seven and all. Just one more way I inconvenienced him.

"That?" Memphis points to the cluster of balls still pooled together on the table, then gestures his thumb behind him toward my stick. He chuckles.

"Liv, there was quite literally nothing sexy about that."

He takes a few steps backward and bends down to get my stick as I push up with my palms and slide back off the table. I clap my hands together to rid them of the little bit of chalk left on them.

"Nah, I'm pretty sure that was sexy," I say, holding onto the table's edge and stretching my arms out while I lean back. My eyes meet his; I move slower, my head falling to the side to cause my hair to slide slowly across my forehead, lips, and cheeks. Memphis's mouth twitches just a little higher on one side, and mine reacts with the same, barely-there smile. A cool rush races up my chest and my pulse doubles.

Damnit, I liked that.

There are so many cheesy things he could say right now. My tingling body, combined with the way he looks holding a pool cue— his rock-solid, denim-hugged body resting his weight to the side—are the undoing of self-control. I'd be his tonight. Hell, I'd be his right here on this table, demanding he close the place early and send everyone home. All he has to do is say one word, *any word,* and I will forget the rules I made when I was a little girl about kissing boxers.

The second his smirk evens out, though, I know that the moment has passed us in a blink, and there are a few words that will erase it for good. I'm about to hear them.

"What happened with Leo?"

I roll my eyes and let my head fall forward between my arms as I groan. I kick the toe of my shoe into the ground and twist it, like I'm squashing a bug. Maybe if I wait here long enough he'll get busy and forget he asked.

The clank of the sticks being dropped on the rack happens first, and when I look up, he's resting his weight on his palms, one wrapped around the orange solid ball. His head dips and his eyes beg me to meet them. We stare at each other like this for a handful of seconds, and his mouth slowly curves up; he shrugs.

"You'll feel better if you talk about it," he says, pushing the ball forward and sending it to me. I stop it in my hand and pick it up, rolling the smooth surface around my fingertips as I breathe out a laugh.

"I've been hearing that from therapists for years," I say.

I toss the ball low in the air a couple times, then roll it toward one of the pockets on his end. It bounces off the edges and *clicks* against two other balls.

"I couldn't even win this game if I got to use my hands," I joke. Memphis leans toward my abandoned ball and rolls it back my direction, sinking it perfectly in the corner pocket. He chuckles and I roll my eyes in anticipation.

"Yeah, yeah. You're good with your hands," I say, moving back to the front desk area as Memphis follows.

"I wasn't going to say it," he says, and I shoot him a glare over my shoulder because *bullshit*. He holds up both hands, fingers stretched wide. "I swear. I was satisfied enough thinking it. It was a joke just for me."

He drags the metal folding chair so he's across from me, then flips it around and sits on it backward. It's so cliché, but I can't believe how unbelievably sexy it is. Only, he's not doing it to be suave, at least...I don't think he is. He folds his hands together and rests his forearms on the chair's back, then leans forward, waiting. Patiently waiting. For me.

This genuine attention makes me squirm a little. It's a foreign feeling. I fold my legs up underneath me in the chair and look at Amy, who's working on the computer and shuffling paper stacks on the desk next to me.

"Hey, Ames? I was trying to find those sports drinks that guy donated the other day. I thought maybe I'd put some in the refrigerator and see if the boys wanted one. You know where they're at?" Memphis keeps his eyes on me when he talks.

"Yeah, we put them all in the storage closet, by the craft supplies," she says, turning and resting her arm on the back of her chair. Memphis scrunches his face and looks at her.

"I looked there, I swear. Didn't see them." He shakes his head a little. Amy's eyes shift to me, and her mouth parts briefly then closes into a soft smile.

"I'll get them." She pushes in her chair before she leaves, her posture sunken.

"She has a crush on you, you know. And now she probably hates me, because you made her leave us alone." My heartbeat picks up when his eyes meet mine.

"I wanted you to be comfortable to talk," he says, a slight tilt of his head. Fucking charm oozes off him.

Archie.

"Ha," I huff, unfolding my legs and stretching them out in front of me, resting my palms on my thighs. "You must love how girls do whatever you say. A snap of the fingers, one look with a smile, and it's all 'sure, Memphis. I'll go get the drinks for you.'"

I snap my fingers for emphasis, and his brow draws in as his mouth twists.

"You're deflecting. And you know what? I don't think like that at all—not with anyone—but sure as shit never with you. I wouldn't dream of manipulating you."

There's a little bite to his tone, and it stings. I hold his stare for a few seconds, a part of me waiting for him to kick away from his chair and storm away from me, maybe go kiss Amy to prove a point and reprimand me. That's what Archie would have done. Enoch, too. With each passing second Memphis stares back, though, that sting— the one I earned from underestimating him—burns my gut a little more.

"Leo stole money from me." I boil it down to its simplest form, even though nothing that my family does to me is simple. I didn't want to talk about it with Memphis, because I figured he wouldn't believe me, that he'd take Leo's side. When you're under their spell and see how wonderful everything is—bright with potential and promises—it's hard to fathom the bottom feeders they actually are.

But Memphis doesn't react. He just sits there perfectly still, his face relaxed, waiting...waiting for me to tell him the rest.

"My parents didn't get married until I was seven." I shrug, but Memphis just waits. My muscles tighten, fighting against the grain. These aren't things I talk about to anyone. I never have. At least, not unless I'm paying them to listen to my problems. Even then, I pick and choose what gets said.

I draw in a full breath. If I tell him too much, he's going to look at this place—at my family—differently. It's happened before. I tell people things and the image gets shattered.

And then they leave.

"My mom got pregnant with me on purpose. My dad was married to someone else, and she was his *piece on the side.*" My stomach rolls with a wave of nausea, but Memphis is still sitting still—his face calm and assuring. I can't trust it too much, because I'll over-share, so I look away.

"Anyhow, before he left his first wife—and before you ask, no...I have no idea who she was. They all pretend that part never happened. But when he found out about me, he sent my mom money. It was really hush money, but she wanted to show how important *I* was in this mess she made, and she set up a trust that the money went into. It was totally all for show—and to make my dad feel guilty. It wasn't much, maybe five grand before he got divorced and married my mom."

I've chipped away some of the gold. I can see it reflected in Memphis's eyes. I should probably stop here, but he was right. Saying this stuff, this sludge that lives inside me and brews toxic waste that sinks everything good I try to achieve—it is freeing, if not unbeliev-able to hear come from my lips.

"Anyhow, I went to the bank to see if it was still there this morn-ing. I kinda had a feeling it probably wasn't, but then I saw Leo's signature on the records, and it just pissed me off. He's the only one who is ever on my side. Never fully on my side, but he has a shred of a moral compass, or at least I thought he did, and...I lost my shit. I came home, he had just woken up and was holding a mug in the kitchen, and I punched him in the face. I don't know what pissed him off more—the fact that he got decked by a girl or that I broke his favorite mug and forced him to spill coffee all over his dumb T-shirt."

My eyes move back to Memphis briefly, and he's let his hands fall to his sides. It's a lot to take in, and I know none of it is really surprising. My family doesn't put on a great show that hides their true selves, but they do offer this sliver of hope that maybe they're just shallow and not total assholes.

But they are. They're all assholes. Even my uncle.

"Your uncle...was he in charge of the trust?" Memphis asks.

"Yup."

I remember when Leo insisted on it. Money was tight, and my mom was talking about borrowing from it, and Leo stepped in. It's one of the few times my dad took Leo's side in a fight between the three of them. He was made trustee. She wore him down, too, though —the first withdrawal was right after I left with Enoch. Four more, each a few months apart, and it was empty.

"Funny, I found the drinks all right in the open," Amy interrupts. Memphis slides back and I twist in my chair, taking a pen from the canister on the table and pulling a blank sheet of paper out to trace my hand.

"Yeah, I must have looked right over them," Memphis says.

Amy responds, "Uh huh."

I trace my hand with the same blue pen until the paper starts to tear and I hear Memphis leave our space to join the boys and their video games. I fold the paper and turn to slip it in the trash, catching Amy's glare. She forces a tight smile, then turns back to the computer and continues typing. She's jealous. I understand. My mouth hangs open, and I almost ask her about the paper she's writing, but when her typing picks up, I decide to let it go. I don't really care, and she doesn't want to make small talk with the girl her crush brought to work for the night.

———

THE AIR IS thick and humid when we finally leave the center. A storm is threatening to pass through, and the air smells of the dirt kicked up by the wind. It's my favorite scent—the thing I missed about this place when I was gone. Oregon and Seattle smell wet, but the desert is different. There's a moment before it rains that smells like hunger. The land craves the water so much that bits and pieces literally take flight and race toward the clouds.

Memphis pulls in to the small alley space and kills the engine. When I take off my helmet, my hair sticks to my cheeks. I run my hand along the right side of my face, but stop when I feel Memphis touch the other. Our eyes lock, and he lets his hand fall away.

"Helmet head," he shrugs. He doesn't look away though.

"It's amazing how it can be this hot at midnight." I should be exhausted, but I'm not. My mind is racing, feelings of guilt for sharing too much crashing into a rush of lust and attraction. I shouldn't be feeling any of it.

I look away and kick my leg over the bike as Memphis takes our helmets toward his trailer.

He sets them on the stoop, then puts his thumbs in his pockets and ambles back toward me.

"I won't say anything, just so you know." His eyes glance up and meet mine. "I'm not into gossip or drama, and I won't let it change how I work with Leo. I don't use people's secrets. I...I just wanted you to know that. I know that was hard for you to tell me."

"Ha," I breathe out, shifting my feet and pushing my hands deep in my back pockets as I look down to my toes. "Yeah...it's not really a subject that comes up much. I think maybe I spent the last few years trying to pretend this part of my life wasn't real. But unlike you, seems I have a flair for drama."

I lift my shoulders and give him a crooked smile.

I ran away from one nightmare and moved right into the center of another storm with Enoch. They say things like this come in threes, which worries me, because I like Memphis. All of the reasons I shouldn't are there, but I like him anyway. What's worse is I think I trust him.

"Thanks for letting me hang out tonight. I think I needed to just..." I pause and look around at our surroundings. "I needed to be away from this place for a while. It was nice. I...I had a nice time."

Memphis smiles and closes his eyes for a quick nod.

"Miles will want to see you again I'm sure. You can come with me anytime," he says. His head tilts and his eyes move down my face. It leaves me feeling warm inside. It feels real, and I tremble a little, so I push my hands in deeper, forming fists.

"Maybe," I offer, the pounding beat suddenly vibrating in my chest echoing everywhere. I feel blood pumping in my balled-up fingers, throbbing in my toes, expanding and contracting in my stomach. My nerves are a mess, and this vulnerable feeling is unsettling.

"I'll see you in the morning," I say, smiling as much as my numb lips will allow and turning toward my escape. I barely make it a step before Memphis's hand brushes my wrist. I stop at the contact, and his hand wraps around my arm, pulling it from my pocket until our fingers are knotted together. The touch feels frantic and light as a feather, but we remain connected, even as I turn to look at our linked fingers, arms both stretched between us.

"I..." Memphis stops, and I look up at his parted lips, then to his long lashes shadowing desperate eyes. This is not the face of a warrior. I worry that when he steps into the ring soon he'll be killed. Archie is incapable of this vulnerability. He always was. Memphis will be easy prey.

Wriggling my fingers loose from his slowly, I take the lead. His hand remains in the air between us for a second when I let go, and his teeth hold onto his bottom lip as he smiles through it, his chest shaking with a single laugh.

"Sorry," he says, closing his palm tight and squeezing away our touch. I do the same. "I just wanted to remind you to be ready for our lesson tomorrow. No excuses."

He takes a few steps back, and I let him go, nodding before I turn and head to my corner.

"I'll be ready. I'd recommend you don't bring coffee," I say, my body feeling relief when I hear his laughter from my stupid joke.

"I'm not as stupid as Leo, don't worry. I also don't have a favorite mug for you to break," he says.

Chancing it, I spin on my heels just before I round the corner. Memphis is standing with one foot on his stoop, both helmets in his hands.

"Goodnight," I say. He lifts the helmets a little in response, then heads inside.

The door closes, and then I wait until I hear it lock. I squeeze my hand in a fist so tight that my skin turns bright pink, but no matter how many times I do it, I still feel his touch. It's burned itself in my head just a little, and I stand here because it spawned a fantasy—one where he swings open that door and runs at me, placing his palms on either side of my face and pressing his lips against mine as I lose balance and stumble backward into the wall.

I stand here until I feel foolish, and then I stand for several seconds more to remind myself of what foolish feels like. I don't like it —it leads to impulsive decisions and heartache. And like it or not, that man is going to be in a ring somewhere soon getting his face bloodied and his ribs broken.

I will not be the stupid girl waiting in the trainer's room alone while a crowd of gamblers howls on the other side of the wall, hoping his face will hit the mat.

I've seen what that woman looks like, and she's tragic. She becomes Angela Valentine.

# CHAPTER SIX

Memphis

I promised Liv I wouldn't say anything; I'd keep her words in confidence and not let them bleed over into everything else I'm doing here. But with each minute that passes that I'm throwing my fists into Leo's padded palms—his face completely exposed—the more I fantasize about finishing what Liv started.

There's more to the story, I'm sure. There's *always* more to a story, and Liv only gave me the surface. I recognize that as a fellow surface-sharer myself. This family, though—they have ugly scars, and I'm pretty sure Liv's bled all over, mentally, from their abuse.

"Ahhhhhh, just...stop. Stop there. Hell, fuck it. You know what? We're done for the day!" Leo takes a few long strides backward, unfastening the pads from his hand and tossing them to the side of the ring. I back up until my back hits the ropes and I lean my weight into them.

"We've got another hour of work to do. You not feeling good or something?" I tug at the edge of the tape around my wrist with my teeth and pull it out a few inches. I'm not done; I want to rewrap it.

"Blech!" Leo waves his hands up, like he's done with me, then slides through the middle ropes out of the ring, leaving me there alone.

"What the hell does that mean?"

Our voices are both elevated now, and the few other guys in the gym have all stopped with their workouts and are watching us. Leo's been grumpy with me before. Usually, it's when he's hungover. His eyes seem clear today, though, which makes me wonder if he had another round with Liv, or if she said something about telling me.

"It means you look like shit today. That's what it means. You're supposed to be traveling to Vegas in less than three weeks, and you're in here acting like some punk who just got outta high school and thinks he wants to fight."

Leo emphasizes his words by throwing his fists out front with weak punches that look more like slaps. My upper lip sneers, and I push off the ropes and walk to the other side so I can stare down at him.

"There ain't nothin' wrong with the way I'm fighting. You're just in a bad mood, but don't confuse the two, old man. Just because you're having a bad day and don't wanna work, don't throw that shit on me. I'm here to work. My tank isn't even close to empty yet."

I pound one fist into the opposite palm twice and rest my hands on the top rope when I'm done, staring down at the shine on Leo's bald head. Beads of sweat line the tops of his cheeks, and the few hairs he has are flat and damp. His gut sticks out like a pouch through his drenched T-shirt and his shorts hang to his knees, almost meeting the spot where his socks pull up. If it weren't for his name—or more importantly, his brother's—nobody would give two shits about Leo Valentine from his looks. All he has is history, experience that I've learned from for sure, but that's all.

Leo stares up at me, a frayed toothpick rolling out of the corner of his mouth. He's had the same one all morning, and he just pulled it out of his pocket. It's disgusting.

"I've been too easy on you," he finally says. Liv walks in behind him, and we both glance her way.

"Carry on," she says, with a wave of her hand. She's dressed for our lessons later today, a pair of black sweatpants pushed up just below her knees and a well-worn blue T-shirt hanging off one shoulder. Her eyes linger on mine for an extra second before she heads back into the office, pushing the door halfway closed. When I glance back to Leo, he's smirking at me.

"Grab your gear," Leo says, leaning to the side and spitting on the concrete floor, rubbing his saliva in with his shoe.

I pause, not sure what he means until he grabs the headgear from the equipment locker and tosses a pair of sparring gloves up to me. I squeeze them between my taped hands and narrow my eyes.

"Are you being serious right now?" I ask, holding the gloves against my chest as he grabs the tape from the edge of the ring and wraps his left hand first.

"Oh, I'm dead-fucking serious." He doesn't bother to look at me while he talks, and I breathe out a silent laugh still not sure how far he's going to go with this. He rips the tape with his teeth and then begins to work on his right hand.

"You're twice my age. Stop it," I say, shaking my head.

Leo presses on, though. Climbing into the ring and moving to the opposite side of me as he slips his headgear on and then his gloves. He shuffles his heavy feet around the mat, dragging them in these ridiculous half circles made even more absurd by the bright-white orthopedic walking shoes on his feet.

"We go until you tell me you get the point," he says, gesturing both of his gloved hands at me while he bounces like a fool.

Sighing, I look over his shoulder at the framed posters from back in the day. They're all of Archie; Leo's in the background, in a few.

"Did you ever have hair?" He doesn't laugh at my joke, so I pull my headgear on and then my gloves.

Leo ushers me to the center and holds his fists out for me to tap. Arms dangling at my sides, I chuckle lightly and stare into his eyes.

Red veins and a glassy surface punctuate deep-blue irises that can hardly focus on me. He's been punched a lot in his lifetime—and pissed off or not, I don't feel right adding to the damage.

"Leo," I sigh out his name, my mouth resting in a straight line.

He nods for me to raise my arms. I shake my head to comply, letting him pound his fists into mine as he backs away a few feet, bouncing and swaying like a kindergartener learning how to dance.

"We go until you tell me you get the point," he repeats.

I nod, then hold my hands up in my defensive position as I begin to move. My feet are quiet, just like he taught me. Every movement below my waist is smooth and a surprise. My legs feel full of energy, surged from a dose of adrenaline that comes naturally anytime I step into the ring. I need to be mindful. I can't take advantage of him and let him get hurt just to prove something to me.

We dance for nearly a minute. Leo's eyes steely and his lips parted for a light pant. I lurch forward and jab, and he blocks me just like I thought he would. I repeat this move a few times before rushing him with a combination.

I go for his body, and he blocks most of my shots but one lands at his ribs. A heavy bellow leaves his mouth and his eyes shrink from pain, but he keeps moving.

"Is this the point?" I ask, wondering if I'm supposed to watch him take all of my punches but stay on his feet.

Without warning, his left fist strikes my temple and I stumble sideways, feeling the burn.

My mouth is watering from the taste of blood where my mouthpiece cut into my flesh.

"Come on!" I center myself and pound my fists together, fueled by his cheap shot.

"Something is always coming for you." He growls the words through his mouthpiece, and I keep nodding, getting it now. This is about him blowing off some steam. Fine, if he wants a fight...

I lunge at him on the right, where I know he's weak, and my leather meets the fatty part of his rib again. He leans away with the pain, but not as much as the first time, so I slide back and regroup, looking for another opening. His eyes are like coal, pupils wide, and the blue almost black. My fists rush toward either side, my arms tight and muscles coiled to deliver a shot he'll remember—one that will make him end this stupid pissing match.

He blocks them both, then sways again, his body turned slightly to protect the place where I've hit him. I begin to move and work him off balance. One more shot there and we're done.

His fist lands against my right cheek, the pads doing little to buffer the force.

I move faster and take a shot at his other side, landing a punch. He grunts, and the sound echoes, but he comes right back at me with two more jabs to my face.

My eyes are beginning to blur, so I reach my arm up as I step away a few paces and run it over my face to clear the sweat. My cheeks are swelling, and my headgear is growing tighter.

"You get the point?" Leo's body lumbers, heavy steps moving him from one corner to the other while he stares at me with dark eyes.

I don't get the point. I know that if I stepped at him right now and went with everything I had, I could kill him. I would take his life, or leave him marred or unconscious. I have no idea what any of that would prove, but I know that the stubborn asshole in the ring with me right now isn't going to quit until I say we're done. He'd rather die first.

I shake my head, sweat drenching my hair, and close the distance between us again. Everyone in the gym is watching us now—even Liv. They're not standing close, but they've made sure to get a good view. Every now and then, someone shouts for me or Leo, enjoying the show. Liv's the only one who gets that something else is playing out here. Maybe she knows what it is. Maybe she's seen this before—this...*lesson* or whatever is happening.

"When does this end, man?" I stare him in the eyes as we circle each other, but he doesn't say a word. I'm not even sure he's really breathing.

Leo's body flinches, and I ready my hands and elbows, swerving to avoid his thrust, but he's led me early and his shot comes a fraction of a second later than I thought it would. It's a punch to the gut, and I double over briefly, still hearing the "*ooooohs*" from beyond the ring. Something is audibly missing, though.

I look to the right, where I know Liv was standing seconds ago. The space is empty, as is the office. My lips puff out, my body needing air; I shake my head to regain my alertness before I scan around me again. The gym is filled with nothing but men—men like me and men like Leo—hopefuls and has-beens.

The next slam hurts.

I stumble several feet back, my balance shot and my vision tilted. A wave of tingles rushes down my spine, quickly turning into nausea. I can't focus immediately, and for the first time since I can remember, there's a glove at my face and I'm not prepared. All I can do is think through the pain about to come and anticipate the reaction—the whip my head is about to take.

It doesn't come, though. Leo tosses his gloves at my feet, then his headgear. His face is bright red, blotched in places, puffy in others. He's favoring his left side, and his breath is ragged. But his eyes—those eyes are still black like the night.

"Two weeks ago, this wouldn't have happened. You're fighting distracted. You're in here, but you're not here," he says through hard breaths.

Leo moves next to me, his hand red from the rush of blood and tight tape. He grips the rope, pausing before he pushes it up to make room for his body, and he steps so close I smell the stale coffee on his breath and wafting stench from the remnants of his cheap cologne.

"She's family. I love that girl, but you need to stay away from that —whatever is getting in your head."

His right finger taps on my headgear several times to accentuate his point.

"Those are the rules. You've heard them before. When you're prepping for a fight, your job is to make love to the art—you live this shit...breathe it. Boxing is the only girlfriend you need. She's all you've got time for. Your eyes wander somewhere else—some place other than right here in this ring, and boxing will get jealous. She'll make you pay for it. Liv is making you weak, and if you can't shut it off for two minutes in the gym with me, you're in big trouble in Vegas."

Leo's eyes burn right through me, but I don't back down. My weight shifts, and I breathe in deep, my chest growing as I take away a few of the inches between us and stare right through him. My nostrils flare with my heavy breath. Liv's money is a topic that sits at the back of my throat. I promised her I wouldn't get involved, but she needs someone on her side. My gut is heavy, though. It's sick from the truth in Leo's words. He's right about one thing—I can't shut her out of my head, not even for two minutes.

"Yeah, I see it in there," he says, his mouth twisting in a wry smile that smells of pity. "You got the point, didn't ya?"

I huff like a child and step away as his chest begins to shake with laughter. The sound follows a second later, deep, but barely audible.

"Yeah, you got the point. If you can't quit that," he says, slipping through the ropes to the ground below, "then you may as well quit this now. I don't like wasting my time. And Angela don't like wasting her money investing in fighters who can't be faithful to this right here."

His hand slams down on the mat, and our eyes lock one last time before he turns for the door, not even bothering to quiet it when it slams shut behind him.

"Fuck," I mutter, staring at the closed door.

"He's tough for an old dude," Mr. Jello Hands says to the right of me. The guy's been working out here for a year and he still hurts his knuckles on the heavy bag.

"Fuck off," I fire back. He holds his hands up when I look at him, and he begins to walk toward the weights on the other end of the gym, laughing about something with his friend.

After dumping my gloves, I tear away the tape on my wrist with my teeth, balling the rest up and dropping it to my feet. I slip down to sit on the ring's edge and free my head from the gear before resting my folded arms along the rope, like a school child at his desk.

My face hurts, but it isn't bad. I've been hit harder. What burns deeper is the complete lack of discipline I had. More than that, I seemed incapable of it. I chose to mock the entire thing—to shrug off how serious Leo was being...to the point that I was unprepared and unable to be in the frame of mind to consider this a real fight, to consider a fifty-seven-year-old man a formidable opponent.

He isn't. Or at least, he shouldn't be.

But he was. For two minutes, in the same air that Liv breathes, he was the favored opponent.

That was his point. He isn't wrong. I just don't believe he's entirely right, either.

# CHAPTER SEVEN

Liv

Nothing makes a girl swoon quite like watching her middle-aged, potbellied uncle fight over her with his protégé who just happens to be showing up in a lot of fantasies lately. Memphis must have said something. I'm sure he didn't mean to; Leo probably provoked him with some offhand remark about me. This is always how things get settled in the Valentine house—with fists.

God forbid any of us sit down like adults and address our differences.

Leo's coming. I can smell the smoke from his cigar. He always lights up after going at it. It used to be rounds when I was a little girl, but now it's minutes that he lasts in the ring.

"You feel better now?" He stops about a dozen feet away from me leading up to the door.

"Yeah," he growls from the side of his mouth, cigar still pinched in his teeth.

I stand from the open doorway, but keep it blocked with both hands resting on the sides of the entrance. Leo doesn't move closer, instead puffing at his cigar and pulling it from his lips to admire it. I hate cigar smoke—even if it tinges of victory, thanks to the years my uncle and dad spent smoking them after big knockout wins.

"What did he say to you?" I look pointedly at him, studying his eyes as they shift down and crinkle at the corners.

"It's not what he said, sweetheart. It's what he isn't hearing."

He dropped *sweetheart* in there on purpose. He knows I hate being called names like that. It's belittling, especially the way he says it. My lips close tightly and a rush of air seeps angrily out my nose. There's a boiling sensation in my stomach, and I hate that.

"You're just like those two," I say, nodding to the house next door as I turn to head inside to Leo's. I'm trapped here. I don't want to go back to the gym where everyone watched that play out, and I don't want be in this house. I linger with my palm on the round, wooden top of the stair rail leading up to the dark room I plan to hide in.

"I hate it here so much," I pant, my voice low. My eyes sting, and I know they're red. They're angry tears forming, and the only way to dry them out is by screaming.

"I hate you all!" My voice echoes from the enclosed space, and the temporary relief in my chest lets me take a large breath just in time to ready myself for the next choking feeling.

"You ain't exactly our favorite person around here either, you know." The cavalier way my uncle speaks cuts deep, but the words themselves—from him—stab me through the heart. He couldn't be nice forever. I knew this side of him was coming.

I turn around to face him, slightly breathless, but angry enough to engage.

"What happened to *favorite niece* and all of that shit? Just an act so you could lure me here and make me watch you steal money from me?" My pulse is rattling my ribs, I'm so mad.

Leo chuckles, smoke puffing out with each laugh.

"You stole ours first, and you know you did." He tilts his head to the side; I follow his eyes, leaning mine with him.

I never asked them to invest with me, to put money into any of

Enoch's funds. My mom couldn't help herself, though. If I had something good happening, there was no way in hell she was going to let it be mine and mine alone. She was going to ride my coattails. The fact that Enoch's Ponzi scheme made fifteen grand disappear from the Valentine assets was in a way the only silver lining I got.

"Mom did that all on her own. You know it and I know it. You were here, Leo! You were here when I told her not to get involved. No...I even *demanded* it! I told her to stay out of my new life, but her greed just couldn't let it be."

I never imagined the financial ruin that was only a few years away, but I was worried about the possibility of losing her money legally. I was in love, and I didn't want the stress of having to earn for my parents to poison my relationship. The stock market is fickle, and my mom is resentful as hell. So resentful, that apparently she's willing to steal from me in a sick game of tit for tat.

His brow low, and forehead creased with a deep wrinkle, Leo kneels down slowly, smooshing the end of his cigar on the ground, adding to the collection of burn marks. His eyes flit up to me when he's done.

"Look, I was angry," he begins. This is where his guilt comes in and I get Sweet Leo. This always worked when I was a kid. I hate that it ever worked. I see through it now, with adult eyes. It's all tactics with my family, and my uncle uses several.

"I want my money, Leo," I press on.

He sighs, then stands slowly, having to push himself up with his hand on his knee. His knuckles are bloodied, and his body looks worn. He's deceptive this way—always has been. I'm sure Memphis thought he was going to hurt my uncle, but that's how Leo has always caught people off guard. While most of my dad's fights were under the lights and in the ring, Leo's were all in alleys and around broken barstools. When he was younger, Leo walked around this neighborhood like he owned it—the way Capone owned places. He's aged, but the ugly fighter still breathes inside his body.

"Liv, hon. You're gonna have to let that go. Your mom needed to pay some bills, important bills. This place is all she's got, and really... that money was dirty anyhow. You said so yourself back when you found out you had it." His eyes stick on me for a few seconds before he rounds the corner and heads into the kitchen.

Tactics.

I trail behind him, remembering how I felt when I found out that my dad tried to pay my mom to keep her mouth shut. She was a homewrecker, at least for the previous Mrs. Valentine. I was the dirty secret.

"That money was the only thing I had left, Leo," I say, my voice hoarse from shouting. I lean into the counter and stare at his back as he pulls a hunk of frozen meat from the freezer, holding it against his rib as he turns around. His skin is a deep red where he lifts his shirt, where Memphis hit him.

"That's not all you have left. You've still got two parents, too, you know. Have you even seen your father since you've been home?"

He means to scold me and inspire guilt for not visiting with my dad. He should know better than that. I step away from the counter and move in the direction of the front door, planning to leave without another word.

"Memphis left when I did. I wouldn't bother looking for a sympathetic ear over there. He's got some thinking of his own to do too." I hear the last few words from my uncle as I step out the door, and I don't pause to think about them until I'm fully outside and out of his view.

It's the same psychological bullshit my dad pulled with my mom for years. It's the reason he strung her along, warning her that the fighter life didn't have room for volatile things like love or marriage. He'd reasoned away his first wife by dismissing their relationship—promising my mom that it was more of a business partnership. But she'd seen them together—she knew he was a liar. He paraded his first wife around like she was one of those golden belts he'd won. Public displays of affection were par for the course. My mom's kisses all came in the shadows, stolen moments and when he was drunk. I learned a lot from those early brawls; eventually, my mom wore him down, and Archie won plenty of fights after they got married.

She told me once that she was a distraction of convenience. It took me a while to understand what she meant by that, but after my father lost a major title, I understood. I was old enough to know he wasn't prepared. He'd been partying hard and stepping out on us for months. He went into the fight tired—and that was on him. My mom took the heat, though. Her needs were distracting, her constant accusations—distracting.

"Loving her was goddamn distracting," he once said.

There was never any love in this house, or between those two. Never has been. There are a lot of other things—egos, codependency, anger triggers, adrenaline—fame. They got off on all of the terrible things a relationship can be built on.

When my father lost, it was easy to blame her.

It was convenient.

I, however, won't be anyone's crutch.

When I reenter the gym, I'm both surprised and not to see Memphis lying on his back in the middle of the ring. There are only two guys left from the group that gathered to watch the scene a little bit ago. They both stop their work on the heavy bag when I enter, and their eyes follow me all the way to Memphis's feet.

"Your uncle kicked my ass," he says, rolling his head to the side enough to catch a glimpse of me.

Shoulders sagging, and thumbs catching my pockets, I breathe in deeply and exhale through my nose. I dart my eyes to the right and get a peek at our audience. They aren't even pretending not to eavesdrop. I forgot how much being a Valentine fascinates others. Living here, where gym members look up to everyone in this family as if they're special, is a lot like reality TV—only there's no roses or opportunities at the end—just gossip, and a clientele that will *always* take the side of the men in the family.

I sway my hips with my thumbs still hooked to my jeans and

swing my elbows back and forth, brushing into his right foot. He lifts his head in response, propping it up on a fist behind his neck.

Shrugging my shoulders, I hold his gaze.

"I don't suppose I had anything to do with the ass-kicking you got?" I hold my breath and suck in my bottom lip to prevent me from saying anything more.

His mouth curves and he breathes out a short chuckle, shaking his head slightly and closing his eyes. He opens them slowly, back on me, and we stare at each other in silence under spying eyes from assholes waiting for more show.

"Come here," he says quietly, nudging his head to the space to his left.

I look down at my feet and let myself feel the tightness in my chest. I promised myself that I would listen to the warnings my body gives me from now on. My heart throbs heavy beats and my insides squeeze. I've strayed out of my lines, and this is where I'm supposed to force myself to get back on track.

My hands fall from my pockets and I reach forward, latching my fingertips on the rope above Memphis's feet. He's pulled the tape from his hands, but it's still tangled in a pile by his side, his gloves and headgear on the floor next to me.

"Why do you even want to be here?" My eyes flit up, catching his waiting for me. I roll my gaze from side to side and lift my brow. "You know this place is just a name, right? Valentine—V's. My dad was a big personality, and yeah...he won a few fights, too. But look around, Memphis. Look at the walls crumbling, the people who show up before the sun who haven't gained an inch of muscle in a year."

I scan to my right and briefly look at our audience. The two men start to move toward their cubbies when I glance at them—either finally feeling awkward or insulted by how I categorized them. I was being honest, though. V's hasn't produced much of anything in years, and my uncle isn't the man he used to be when he trained my dad.

Memphis draws his legs up, bending them at the knees, and lifts his torso to rest his weight on his elbows. I follow his movement with my eyes and stop when our gazes meet again. The thumping in my chest has grown stronger, but its sound is muted in my ears. I shouldn't have come back here in the first place, and now that I have, I should leave before I get too close. I can feel this line—this...decision that's impending in the air we're both breathing. I allowed myself to have a friend, but I was never strong enough to cage my feelings completely.

Memphis curls the left side of his mouth and leans his head to his left, glancing next to him once more and silently inviting me to join him again. I hold his stare until I hear the door close behind the last two people who were in here with us. My hands fall from the rope until my palms are flat on the mat. I dip my head, but keep my eyes on Memphis's as I crawl under the only line that was physically dividing us, missing just enough to clip the top of my head and rip out a few strands of hair. I roll my eyes at my own clumsiness. When I'm positioned even with him, I rest my cheek against my palm to hold my head up as I lay on my side. He turns to face me, doing the same.

"Why do *you* even want to be here?" His question stops my breath. I wasn't expecting it, and my mind doesn't know how to understand it.

Shaking my head, I draw my brow in tightly, the line between my eyes deep and painful. His words somehow hurt me to hear.

"I don't," I say, shaking my head.

Memphis doesn't add to his question, instead studying my face with a softness that leaves me slightly numb. His lashes flit as his focus moves from my eyes to my cheek, down to my chin, his gaze tracing the strands of hair that have clung to my arm while I lay here. He lifts himself slightly, reaching forward with his right hand and uncurling a few strands of my hair from my skin. His touch tickles, and my nerves begin to fire away. I'm sure he can see me tremble, so I adjust my weight to mask it. His eyes flit back to mine when I do.

"I didn't say a word to Leo about the money. I wouldn't do that to you unless you wanted me to help," he says, his fingers trailing down my arm to my elbow. He leaves a fraction of an inch between us when he rests his hand back on the mat.

I nod and flash a short-lived smile on one side of my mouth.

"Thanks...I guess."

Memphis chuckles and rolls from his side to his back again, taking his hand with him. He folds his fingers together and rests them on his chest, and I take the opportunity to look at his bruises.

"You need to put something on that cut. It's not deep enough for stitches, but it's not good," I say.

His head rolls sideways and he starts to laugh. I pull in the corners of my mouth at first, a little pissed that he's dismissing me, when I realize what he's doing—he's showing me the other side of his face, where the cut is *much* deeper.

"Yeah...that one? You might want to have Leo sew you up," I say.

"You do it." His response is fast, and it leaves several seconds of quiet between us again.

"Okay," I say, pushing myself into a sitting position and sliding my way back to the edge of the mat.

Just like last night, though, Memphis stops me with a touch on my wrist. My reaction is the same—I'm frozen. I glance at him over my shoulder and our eyes lock again.

"I want to know you," he says, and I stop my breath. He doesn't really. The more you know of me, the uglier it gets—the baggage is endless.

"What's to know?" I respond.

He scoots forward so he's sitting next to me, but his hand stays on mine, our fingers not totally threaded, as if we're both pretending that this touch is completely accidental and not impulsive. That would be a lie on both of our parts.

"About your family, and the problems you all have—at least as it relates to you—have I seen it all? Or...is there something I should know?" His mouth has grown serious. His eyes have lost the spark that's usually there. I think maybe he's scared.

"Memphis, I don't need you to rescue me," I say. His hand reacts, finally gripping me with a slight force.

"That's not it at all," he answers, squeezing his eyes closed and running his other palm over his face. "God, I don't even know what I'm doing, but I just—"

"I get it," I say, turning my hand under his until we're grasping each other. I look down at where we connect, and imagine what a life like that would be. "Yes, I've told you everything. My mom got pregnant on purpose to trick my dad into marrying her. They're both selfish assholes, and my uncle isn't any better. They're terrible business people, all three of them, and they've lost every dollar they've ever invested. You probably saw my last few years on the news. I'm just like them, it turns out, and they blame me for every financial hardship they've ever had. That's everything—my existence in one breath. I know you can't focus with *all of this*," I say, holding my other palm up and gesturing it across the room, a symbolic move to represent my messy family and life.

I laugh lightly and pull my hand away from his finally, resting both of mine in my lap as I bite the tip of my tongue and smile as it finally hits me. I turn to look Memphis in the eyes.

"I can't be your convenient distraction," I say, forcing a tight-lipped smile when I'm done.

"So don't be, whatever that means," he says. I reach for his face and rest my palm along his unshaven and bruised cheek, blood from the few gashes drying already.

"You don't really know me. And all I know about you is you're ambitious, and you work really hard in here every day. You have to have something to show for all of that, and if I sit here for another minute, we'll both regret it. You'll regret it more—they always do." My hand skims along his cheek lightly until it completely falls away. I slide myself under the rope to my feet, turning to face him once the rope barrier is back in its place—between us.

"I'll get the kit and stitch you up, then tomorrow I'll shut the office door and we'll both just do our jobs," I say, smiling through my words. I wait for a beat, then spin toward the training room, my mouth falling with every step I take until I'm wearing my real feelings.

I flip the switch for the training closet light and step inside, my hands finding the kit; a flash of my past races through my body at the touch. I stitched my dad up a few times—he taught me how. Leo wasn't gentle enough, but I had "the touch of an angel."

Glimmers of good dot my memory, and I wish those things never happened. I wish there wasn't one percent of it that was good—it's easier if it's all rotten.

When you feel one of the good things it makes you hate all of the bad shit even more, and the good parts just feel like tricks to make you stick around.

The closet door closes just before I turn. I grip the plastic case for the medical kit tight against my chest. This space is small, and Memphis takes up most of it. My eyes naturally dart to either side. Sensing my panic, he leans back on the door to give me space.

"Don't, Memphis," I say.

"Don't what?" His arms rest heavily at his sides, his chest moves in and out slowly, and his eyes are red from taking abuse.

"You are beaten and defeated, and right now I look like a life raft," I say, hugging the box against me tighter.

His focus moves to the spot where my hands are folded over the red cross on the box, and it stays there for several seconds. My legs begin to feel weak, so I shift my weight, and my slight movement startles him out of a trance. His eyes instantly move to mine.

"I grew up in a group home," he says, his eyes unflinching in their hold on mine. "I spent fourteen years wondering who my parents were and how I got there. Then one day, this postcard shows up from Tennessee."

"Memphis," I whisper.

He leans his weight into the door behind him, sliding down enough that his feet stretch out a few more inches.

"I ran away to find him, but by the time I got there, the only thing that was left was a diary, a few of his things, a pair of boxing gloves, and a score card with your dad's name on it."

His gaze settles just below mine.

"That's why I'm here, Liv. I spent a lot of time training on my own, in other places, but really...the only thing that mattered was chasing a fucking ghost." His chin lifts and his eyes meet mine. A second passes before he shrugs one shoulder. "I'm not under some delusion about this place. Ha, I mean...Liv...I have eyes! Your mom has always been good to me. I've learned about Leo's past, and your dad is a legend—but this place is a shithole, Liv. Your family is certi-fied—I see that!"

I swallow during his pause. His words are hard to hear, even if they're everything I think.

"Do you even want to be a fighter?" My voice croaks the words, and I allow the absurd idea that his dream is something else run through my mind. I've seen him move, though. He was born to do this —just like my dad.

Memphis draws in a deep breath through his nose, standing straighter as his chest fills. He readjusts his feet as he moves toward me slowly, his jaw set and his lips pursed in thought. He glances down to the floor between us. My palms begin to sweat, and I flinch when the medical kit slides from my grip just a little. I catch it, but not without Memphis helping me—his hand covering both of mine.

"A fighter is the only thing I know how to be," he says, letting one hand fall away from me while the other opens the doorway behind him. "I'm not here because I think the mojo will rub off on me and make me a better fighter. I'm here hoping the spirit of Robert Delaney, who passed away in a cheap motel in Memphis, will find his long-lost son and guide him...just a little."

His eyes leave mine as he turns to exit the tiny space, but before he can leave the room, I let the medical kit fall from my hands and I grab onto his cold, damp shirt. He turns to me quickly, but before he can speak, I grasp another handful of his shirt in my other hand and lift myself up with my toes, pressing my lips lightly against his. I catch his lips partially opened, and the slight breath from his surprise tickles my mouth. My right hand lets go of his shirt and finds the hard line of his jaw, tense and warm under a single stroke of my thumb. I'm not sure which one of us is trembling, but a vibration is there where my hand rests uneasily along his face. His lips move subtly as I begin to slip away, and just before our touch breaks, his mouth reaches out for mine with one desperate pass of his lower lip against my upper.

His hands cradle my elbows as I leave the tips of my toes and fall back to earth. We both stand under the arch of the doorway, medical supplies spilled on the ground at one side and the glow of outside streaming through the open gym door—where my mother stands motionless. My heart stops; I know she is going to ruin this. It will never be anything more than a stolen moment I leapt at in a storage-room closet.

I was foolish anyhow, to think that I could compete with a ghost. Memphis Delaney was born to fight. I am an inconvenient distraction.

# CHAPTER EIGHT

Memphis

My head is all fucked up. Liv left it that way. Her lips were like sugar, and I'm a boy who has been forbidden sugar for *so* long. I wish I could figure out why it's so different with her—why I'm so invested.

Obsessed.

I wasn't sure what I was going to get from her when I stepped into that tiny space. I was prepared to get decked. I wouldn't put up a defense; I'd leave my hands at my sides and take the full brunt of it.

And then she kissed me.

She didn't bother to stay to experience her mom's reaction. I'm sure if she had, it would have been different than the one I got. She played coy. I've never actually seen someone pretend to blush, but Angela did. She giggled and said seeing stolen kisses reminded her of when she was younger and visiting Archie. She was quick to dismiss what she'd seen as anything serious. That much she was very direct about.

"I know you won't let this little infatuation she has with you get in the way, but if you need me to talk to her, please just let me know. Somethings are easier coming from your mother."

I smiled and nodded, knowing full well that was the last way Liv wanted any communication delivered. The longer I'm here, in their family web, the uglier the threads that hold them all together seem.

Angela offered to sew me up when Liv ran off, but I've seen the scars on Archie's face. I'm doomed to get a cold or flu in this emergency room, though. I might have been better off with horror-movie stitches from Angela.

The man next to me is wrapped in a blanket that smells of urine. I've moved seats four times in the last hour, and every single time someone takes the seat right next to me even though there are dozens of open seats in this waiting room.

"Memphis Delaney?"

Thank you, sweet Jesus! I leap to my feet, wasting no time rushing toward the doorway held open by a woman in pink scrubs.

"Rough waiting room today," I say, chuckling a little.

She glances at me sideways and smiles on one side.

"It's hot out. We get a lot of homeless this time of year—it's usually dehydration." She starts flipping through pages, stopping on the chart of basic questions I already answered for the triage nurse.

"Stitches, huh? Let me see what we've got," she says, setting the clipboard to the side and scooting her stool close to me so our knees are almost interlocked. Her eyes catch mine; I must react because she smirks and tells me to relax.

"That's a nasty one. Let me guess...I should see the other guy?" She winks and scoots her chair back, moving toward a cabinet filled with basic supplies that all look like the ones Liv spilled on the floor back at the gym.

"I'm pretty sure I got the worst of it actually," I say, wishing I had Liv's phone number now or a way to check on her. I'm not sure who would be worse to call—Leo or Angela?

"Well, he must be a pretty tough guy...unless...a girl kicked your ass?" She unwraps a few things and tilts my chin before she begins cleaning the area near my deepest cut.

I laugh, but am careful not to move my face as she inspects me closer.

"Everyone's kicking my ass lately, it seems."

I look at her from the side of my eyes, but she's focused on my cut. I notice the reflection from the diamond on her finger, and I feel a strange relief—I don't have to walk the fine line between polite and flirting like I do with Amy at work. I'm also relieved because, for some reason, I feel like flirting wouldn't be fair to Liv.

Leo was right about her invading all corners of my mind. I can't even handle a visit to the ER without considering her.

"This is gonna sting at first, but...it will pass..." She tilts her chin down and bites her tongue, pushing the needle through with one hand while her other holds my skin together tightly. It hurts, but I have a high tolerance, so I barely wince. Pain is relative in my world.

"Not my first rodeo with stitches," I say through the side of my mouth.

"Ah, a professional ass-kickee, huh?" She pushes through again, and I feel it even less.

I chuckle silently, careful not to move my face.

"That's one way to put it. I would rather people call me *champ*, though," I say.

Her face crinkles.

"I box. I've got a big fight coming up at the end of the month, actually. This was sort of the result of some tough love," I say, glancing to her just as she ties off the third and final stitch.

"My older brother used to fight. Amateur stuff, down at that club on Central. Sometimes at the college. You local? Maybe you've heard of him...Tommy Vargas?"

I shrug and shake my head.

"I don't know a lot of people, though. I've only been here a little more than a year, and I spend most of my time in a dark gym with a jump rope and a speed bag," I say.

"Well, like I said, he wasn't really serious about it," she says, moving her attention back to the paperwork. I stand while she signs off on a prescription.

"I hope the guy you're supposed to fight in Vegas isn't as tough as the guy who did this," she says, handing me the script. I breathe out a sharp laugh and take it from her.

"Yeah, me too," I say, keeping to myself the fact that Leo's in his fifties and a bit of an alcoholic.

She swings the curtain open and I catch her name on her tag —*Laura*. I'm about to thank her when I hear a recognizable hacking cough a few curtains down.

"Miles?" My brow pinches as I step forward and scan to the right.

"That you, young prince?" I grimace at the familiar response and follow the sound.

"Which one's you?" I look for signs, or his bag on the ground. I find him three beds down sitting up with an IV in his arm. I glance back at Laura.

"He's a friend," I say. She nods and follows me into Miles's space.

He shadowboxes me when I step closer, and I do it back. His face is pale, and his unshaven cheeks look like they're sinking in a little more than normal. His hair is combed back, and its damp, which makes me wonder if he finally spent a night in the shelter.

When I first met Miles, I begged him to stay with me. It took me weeks to convince him to just try one night, and he was gone by the time I woke up the next morning. I found him back under his favorite tree.

"You go for a swim or something?" I gesture to his hair and he puts his hand flat on his head and looks up, laughing when he feels it.

"You might say so," he says, pausing to cough again. "They say I passed out in one of those fountains by the school board building. I must have gotten too hot."

I look to Laura for confirmation as she reads through Miles's chart, and she absentmindedly nods to herself as she takes in the report.

"You know, I can get you some water you can keep. I can bring more when I visit, or—"

"Bah, you know those vultures will just take it. I'm fine; I'm fine. I'm not the one who looks like he got his ass kicked," he spits back through a raspy cough.

Laura laughs with him this time.

"Yeah, yeah. I've still got three weeks. I'll be ready; you wait," I say, taking in the state of my friend's shoes. I tried to give him a new pair last month, but he refused those too. I guess when you've experienced loss like he has, a lot of things don't seem so important anymore —even survival.

Another nurse pops into our space and urges Laura to step outside to assist her with something. Miles breathes slowly and falls back into the bed with his eyes closed, his head sinking deep into the cool pillow, a smile touching the corners of his mouth.

"Hey, man. You do what these doctors and nurses say, okay? I'll watch your tree for you. You just get better," I say, stepping back so I can keep an eye on Laura before she leaves completely.

Miles waves me off, like I knew he would, and I follow Laura just before she continues on to another patient.

"Hey, I'm sorry...but...how long do you guys keep people here in his situation?" She slows her walk away to let me catch up, and when my eyes reach hers, I can tell she hears a lot of sympathy stories and has become hardened to them.

"Mr. Delaney, look—"

"Memphis," I cut in. She sighs.

We both pause right by the check-in desk. It appears she's stopped me here on purpose, to show me the waiting room filled with people just like Miles. I mash my lips and breathe out my nose slowly.

"He's different," I say, feeling the twist in my gut, because I don't *know* that. That room could be filled with people as warm and generous and...and as familiar as this man my heart pretends is my dad, even though he's not.

"If you want to help him, Memphis, you really should connect him with the human services organizations we have here in the city. They can get him started in the right direction."

I close my eyes, because I've tried that. He isn't interested. He's broken from loss. He's scarred from being forgotten, and he's genuinely selfless. Miles isn't a drain on the system; he isn't asking for anything. But it doesn't mean he doesn't need help.

"Check his foot," I say, turning to square my shoulders with Laura.

She cocks a brow, glancing over my shoulder at the full house waiting for beds to open up and for triage to rank them as important. The only reason I jumped up in the line was because I was bleeding slightly. Every single person here is needier than me.

"He's here for dehydration, and he hasn't presented anything..."

I hold up an open palm.

"I know, it's just...he's a veteran. He's lost his entire family. The man lives in a park littered with trash. People...they just drive by and throw half-filled Styrofoam cups and old chewing gum there, and it's where he *lives*."

She looks behind us, back down the hallway, where my first real friend will be sent back out into the streets in minutes.

"His foot is infected, and he can barely walk. He won't get help for it, but it puts him in danger. How can he get away if someone tries to assault him? He's defenseless. The man went to war, and he can't defend himself. Please...just..."

"I'll look at his foot," she stops me mid-plea. "I can't promise you anything, but if it's bad enough, maybe we can treat him and give him a safe place for the night."

A thousand pounds roll down my shoulders. The last time I looked at his foot, I was worried. He's lost weight. It's so hot out during the day, I know he's suffering.

"Thank you, Laura." I nod, unable to hide my growing smile.

"I'm not promising," she repeats.

"I know." I close my eyes lightly and nod, then hold up my

discharge paper. "If you ever need to kick someone's ass, I owe you one."

She flashes a crooked smile as she walks backward.

"Awe, that wouldn't be a fair fight."

I wait an extra second or two as she heads down the hallway, just to make sure she really stops at Miles's bed. When she slides behind his curtain and draws it closed, I exhale, still not completely rid of the squeezing in my chest that comes along with caring for someone.

I can't lose Miles.

———

PAIN PILLS AREN'T an option for me. I can't afford not to know every single thing going into my body, especially this close to the fight. Alcohol is off the table too. I stop at the market near V's, and instead, buy a steak. The sun is down now, so it's cool enough to grill.

With my small bag of groceries tucked into my backpack, I straddle-walk my bike into the alleyway, parking it close to the trailer. My eyes go right to Liv's window. It's dark, which means she's either gone, hiding, or asleep.

My face doesn't sting as much as the bones hurt underneath. I haven't really examined the damage yet, so once I get through the door, I drop my grocery bag on the foldout table and slide into the bathroom stall.

"Shit," I mutter.

I'm sure the glow of the fluorescent bulb isn't helping, but my face looks like hell. My bottom lip is busted, the dried blood having stained a perfectly straight line dividing it in half. My left eye is slightly swollen, and the deep bruising has become purple. It's going to take the full three weeks for me to look like I belong in the ring in Vegas.

I've been beaten up worse, and the dull ache I feel everywhere doesn't compare to my first few fights, or the climb up the ranks I had to endure after my eighteenth birthday, when I made the commitment to become a professional. Guys that have paid their dues aren't real keen on welcoming in the new kid. When you flatten a few badasses in your first sparring rounds, though, you earn a certain respect.

I let that go to my head. *That's* what Leo's point was. I'm still a nobody on the Vegas stage—no matter how many fights I've won off the Strip. *Fast hands* and *endurance* are buzzwords that won't mean shit if I lose focus.

Leaning in close, I tuck my chin and turn my head slightly to inspect Laura's work. Now that I see it all tucked together, I feel stupid having even gone. I probably could have just glued it. It feels vain to care when I take punches for a living.

After I flip out the harsh lights, I grab my steak in one hand, the propane tank in the other and step back out into the alleyway. A good kick of my foot on the side of the small camping grill knocks off the gristle from the last time I used it. I nudge it to a flat piece of ground a few feet away from my RV before squatting and hooking up the gas tank.

It's body temperature outside. It's strange how cool that can feel when you're used to one-eleven inside a humid brick building. The small flame flickers to life, and I unwrap my freshly cut meat and place it on the center of the grill before standing and stretching my sore arms into the air.

My eyes just go there—to Liv's window. What was black on my way in is now dimly lit. I stare at it for almost a minute straight, my mind tricking me several times that I see her moving in the shadows. For a few seconds, I feel like we're looking at each other and I start to smile like a fool.

Eventually, I look away and move back inside to grab a fork to flip the meat. I check her window again when I come back out, even glancing up a few times as I kneel down and push the steak around the grill. I like the way it sizzles and pops.

"This is stupid," I whisper to myself, then chuckle.

I flip the meat and rest the fork on the grill handle before standing and patting my hands on my shorts. I'm still a mess from the gym. I haven't cleaned myself from earlier, and I look like I was found on the side of the road after being tossed from a truck. She kissed me, and I looked just like this.

She kissed me.

It takes me seconds to jog to the front of Leo's place. I knock lightly at first, uncertainty controlling my hand. I wait for several seconds before I lean to the left to look inside through the kitchen blinds. They're tilted up, but not completely. I can see a few fast shadows pass, so I grow confident and knock a little louder.

When a few more seconds pass, I rest my hand on the door and lean in to listen. There's the faint sound of Leo's television, and nothing else. I rush around the side of the house to the back door that leads into the kitchen. I rap on it a few times, then test the handle. It opens easily. The news is playing from the living room, and the sound is louder inside. A plate with a half-eaten piece of chicken sits on the counter.

"Liv?" I call out in a loud whisper first and my regular voice a second time.

"Liv, you here?"

I get to the bottom of the stairs and take two up when I hear a short cry, like someone stepped on something sharp, and my legs climb even more in the next breath.

"Liv, are you..."

It isn't Liv. Nobody stepped on anything. They haven't heard me. I am invisible and unnoticed.

The moment my eyes register what they're seeing, my mind works defensively in a flash. Leo's lying on Angela, his bedroom door wide open, his shirt on the floor, and his pants pulled down just enough to get his dick out. Angela is half dressed, her skirt pushed up around her waist and her blouse open over a black bra. It's a sight I will never be able to erase, and I can't even understand so much of it.

I'm in control enough to keep my mouth closed and my breath in check—as I glide my feet gently, but quickly, back down the stairs.

I'm too rushed with adrenaline to be able to tell if I'm sick with panic or with what I've seen. I'm sure Angela gets lonely. I've never really thought about her life other than the time she spends taking care of Archie. Leo is with me most of the time, and when he's not, he's drunk—at least, I *thought* he was spending his time at a bar or here alone with a bottle.

Maybe this is the first time they've done this. I don't think it is.

Angela is married to Archie, but he's not really able to be a companion. He's alive though—he's very much alive. Can she leave him? And Leo...she chose *Leo*.

I mentally race through questions on repeat until I make it back to the door I came through and I run into Liv. My body vibrates with the new dose that fills my spine. Whatever her situation is with her family, she can't add this on top of it. Not after today. She doesn't need to process this tonight.

"Uh, I was..." I stop and suck in my lips, moving enough to the side to hide the half-eaten meal on the counter. It's a clue that begs questions and Liv isn't stupid. "Do you like steak?"

It's the reason I came here to begin with—to ask her to join me. All I want is more time with her.

She reaches for the door to open it wide enough to step inside with me. I step outside instead, brushing her shoulder, coaxing her to turn her back on everything inside. I leave my fingertips on her bicep and I wonder if she can feel the volts pulsing through them. She glances at my hand briefly, and her eyes widen just a little.

"I guess. I mean, I like a lot of foods if you're taking a survey, but...do you need something? I'm not sure if we have steak, but I know Leo bought chicken..."

"No, no..." I interrupt quickly, praying there aren't any sounds that trail from upstairs to her ears right now. "I meant...would you like to share steak? With me? I...I'm grilling, and I got a big cut, and we both had a day, and..."

I stop rambling and let my mouth relax into a soft smile. I'm nervous, and it isn't just because of what I'm trying to hide from her.

It's mostly that, but it's also the simple fact Liv makes me nervous as hell.

"Eat with me." I shrug and take a step back, gambling that she won't go inside—that she'll pick me. My nervous hands find the band in my shorts, and I hook my thumbs and smile crookedly, like a schoolboy.

Her eyes hang on mine while she takes a deep breath through her nose, her lips puckered just enough to curl the corners. So goddamned kissable right now. Her throat flexes with her swallow, and her head falls a little to the side.

"I could eat," she says.

I nod toward the alley, my eyes lingering on the place where her hand still holds the door. My stomach thumps with nerves until she grabs the knob and pulls it closed behind her.

I lead the way toward the scent now smoking near my trailer. A tangled mess of thoughts—what I just saw and what I need to do to protect Liv and my own desire just to have her here—swirl in my head so loudly that I don't hear her speak at first.

"Your stitches?"

I bend down to take the fork and flip the meat one more time.

"Oh, ummm...I'm sorry?" I can suddenly feel the wound more than I have all day.

"I was asking who did them for you." I glance up into sad eyes. I bet she thinks Angela took over.

"I went to the ER. It was just easier," I say, unfolding one of the chairs I leave propped against the back wall. "I'll stand."

Liv looks at me for a second before taking the seat. When she settles in, I duck inside for two plates and some silverware. Everything I own is mismatched and donated, so I find the best pieces I have clean and bring them out, handing her the nicest one. I cut into the meat to test it, then glance up at her, her cheeks warmed by the flame. I instantly wish we were camping somewhere far away from everything else.

"Rare good with you?" I ask.

"Bloody," she smirks and I shake my head with a laugh.

"Well, I'm afraid it's not still moving, but it's pretty rare," I respond.

I cut the beef in half and give her the best part.

"Thank you," she hums, sliding the plate to balance perfectly on her knees before she begins sawing with her knife.

I'm drawn to every movement—the way her fingers hold the fork, the way her arm flexes with the knife, the slight part of her lips as she blows just a little before taking a bite. Her eyes flit up to me just as she hums, and I'm too late to look away.

"Sorry, I wanted to make sure you liked it." What I mean, but don't say, is I can't stop being awed by her.

She smiles through her swallow, nodding and holding up a thumb.

"It's really good. I was hungrier than I thought I was." She doesn't hesitate, cutting right in for another bite, talking with her mouth still full from the first. I watch it all. I can't stop.

"Are you gonna eat?" she finally asks, her dimples deep from the attention.

"I am," I say, smiling back and watching just a few seconds longer.

When our eyes meet, every single time they meet, there is this tumbling sensation that happens in my chest. It isn't scary, and I worry a little that it's going to go away, but it hasn't. It's there now. I don't look away until the flutter stops. I don't want to waste it.

I take three bites for every one she takes, and I'm done with my meal in minutes, my belly rumbling for more. I'll make a protein shake later. I have time left before I have to make weight, but I've always started worrying about it before I need to. I work my body to exhaustion, then cut off its supply without warning. It turns me into a beast. I guess that's the point.

"I guess I wasn't very hungry," she says, looking down at her lap with a plate still covered in steak. "You want mine? Or...maybe we can take it to Miles."

"Shit!" I stumble in place for a few seconds, unsure of what needs to get done first. I forgot about his tree. That pact was serious; I can't break my promise. I freeze for a beat and draw in a deep breath to center myself. When I look down at Liv, her brow is high and her eyes are wide with confusion.

"Miles is in the hospital, and I told him I'd check on his spot."

I reach for her plate, taking it along with mine inside. I fumble around looking for something to wrap the steak in to save it for later, settling on the plastic bag from the grocery store. I move to my mini fridge, but Liv beats me to it, her hand holding the door closed.

"What do you mean Miles is in the hospital? Oh my god, is he okay?" There's actual worry in her eyes. The look on her face hits my chest and weaves itself inside for me to remember later—for me never to forget.

"He's okay," I calm her. "He was dehydrated and someone brought him in. I saw him there when I got the stitches, and I convinced the nurse to look at his foot. It was my ploy to make him stay inside for just one night, but I knew he'd worry about his tree."

"Why is that tree important to him?" She takes the steak from me as she talks.

"It's his home." Her eyes rest on mine, and they dim while she considers what I said. "There's no way to really explain it, other than when your life is shit, sometimes you fill it with the first place that feels like home. It's hard to give that up. It's like a sense of comfort, I guess."

Liv looks at the steak in her hand then glances to the side, her eyes roaming around my small sink piled high with a mix of dirty dishes. She takes in the space behind me, used as a closet and storage for my gear, then the fold-up table to my left and the bench piled with my dirty laundry. My bed is bunked high above her, a warm space over the cab of the truck that hasn't run once since I parked here a year ago.

Words aren't necessary. It's an increasingly common thing between us. Her eyes come back to mine after surveying my mark on this world—everything I owned shoved into a ten-by-seven space. It's barely functional, and most would argue it *isn't*. But in here, I am home. I am comfortable. I can imagine. Liv understands it all; I can tell just from one look.

"You go to the tree. I'll bring him some steak." The bag crinkles as she holds the meat up between us.

"No, I can do both. I don't want you walking or being anywhere alone." She touches my hand, lightly at first, and somehow her fingers find the right fit when our eyes meet again.

"I finally got paid; if you can believe it," she says through a crooked smile. "I'll take a cab."

Every piece of me wants to kiss her again right now, to kiss her for real—like she deserves. Instead, I settle for grasping for more of her hand and squeezing it a little tighter when I find it.

I'll think of this tonight while my back rests against my friend's favorite tree. I think of it now, in the moment. I may never stop thinking about Olivia Valentine and how unbelievably different she is from the people who made her.

# CHAPTER NINE

Liv

The last time I was in a hospital, I lost a baby. It's amazing how little I've thought about that moment until right now—faced with a long walkway, flanked by buzzing lights attracting bugs, ambulance bays to the right, and an automatic sliding door in front of me ushering people in and out.

I'm sweating, and not just from the heat.

With my eyes closed, I tug my purse close to my body and grip the steak I'm sneaking in to Miles in my other hand. I take tiny steps, and I don't open my eyes until I'm six or seven paces in. Sheer will is the only thing that moves me through the doors, and by the time I get inside, my eyes are tearing and I'm a little out of breath.

It's busy here tonight, and I'm grateful that nobody has idle time to pay attention to me. I don't need it. I don't *want* it.

There was a nurse that took care of me months ago. She forced me to attend one counselling session. It's the only reason I went, and the only thing I remember—said by the woman who led the group— was that I would have to mourn, eventually.

That day isn't this one. I stop at a bulletin board littered with pamphlets and brochures about heart disease, bloodborne pathogens, and addiction; it distracts me for just long enough to get my breathing back into check. My eyes dry, I turn my attention to the information desk.

"I'm here to visit a patient." I slip the wrapped steak into my purse, where I've also hidden a plate, and plastic utensils.

"Name?" The woman looks at me above the rim of her glasses as she pushes back the mouthpiece on her phone headset. I glance down and see the nearly dozen lines flashing on hold.

"Miles," I say, suddenly realizing that's all I know. Her face bunches, but before she can ask me for a last name, I wing it and hope I can spin a good lie. "He's homeless, but he's also a veteran. He talked to my little brother about the war yesterday while we were touring the state capital. Anyhow, he seemed really nice and we knew he was probably just there for the shade, and well...my brother wanted to get him a meal, so we filled a bag at the gas station and then tried to find him, and just as we finally spotted him—*bam!*"

I smack my hands together for emphasis, so invested in my manic adventure to do good with a baby brother I don't have.

"I don't think we have any hit-and-run victims." Her eyes are on her computer screen, and I can see the lines of text scroll by in the reflection of her glasses.

"Oh...no, it wasn't a hit-and-run. Not that kind of *bam*. He fell over from dehydration..."

The woman stares at me with narrowed eyes.

"That was the sound of him falling. Like...*bam!*" I do it again, just like before, and my heart is racing because I'm losing my way in my lie. I'm going to get caught.

"Uh huh," she murmurs, not even parting her lips.

I grow desperate and my mind races for a way to keep her invested, to make her want to help, when her finger stops rolling the top of her computer mouse and she glances up at me again.

"Curtain four. He's moving to a room soon, though, so you better head down there before...*bam!* I lose him." She smirks at her joke, and I chuckle, because I can't call her a bitch.

"Thank you," I say, my hand squeezing the top of my purse closed tightly as I move down the hallway she gestures toward.

I count the curtains carefully, not wanting to startle a stranger, and I'm relieved to see Miles is sitting up, glasses pushed to the tip of his nose while he flips through an old magazine.

"You know there's a lady up front who wears those same exact glasses." He jumps a little, but lights up when our eyes meet.

"My princess, look at you. Memphis told you I was here, didn't he?" He pulls the glasses from his face and rests them in his lap before reaching out his hand for me to take.

"He was going to come visit, but he's keeping an eye on your tree." I can actually see the relief paint his face as if he suddenly switches from black and white to color.

"I brought you something," I say, peeking around the curtain to make sure we're hidden enough. I pull the curtain just a little more to be safe, then work quickly, pulling out the plate and steak together.

"Good lord, you're a magician. I don't suppose you can pull brandy out of that bag of yours? A Guinness perhaps?" He chuckles as his eyes linger on me, then begins to cough as he makes short work of the wrapping around the meat.

He cuts a bite quickly and pops it in his mouth, a slow grin pushing up his cheeks with each movement of his jaw. His eyes slide up to meet mine.

"It's still warm."

It pleases me to see him love this simple indulgence.

"I hear the food in this joint ain't so good," I whisper, leaning into him. I make a gagging gesture with my finger in my mouth, and Miles shakes with a short laugh.

"The food here is pretty okay with me," he says.

I guess it would be. I wonder when the last time was that Miles ate like this? I know Memphis brings him things, but it must be a far cry from sitting at a kitchen table and letting flavors linger on your tongue.

"You should stay with Memphis until you get better. I saw that foot of yours, and it's not going to heal itself, you know." He doesn't react to my words at all, just like Memphis said. He cuts bite after bite, eating as if it were a race until his plate has no evidence that food was ever on it.

"Memphis said you were in the service?" I ask the question as he hands me the empty plate, and it gets no response, so I tuck the plate and utensils in the spare plastic bag I brought and sit down in the chair at his bedside.

"You see him fight yet? Our boy?" I look up with a lopsided grin and decide to let him change the subject. I have things I don't like to talk about either. Usually, boxing is one of them.

"Only sparring, maybe a little in workouts." I don't even need to close my eyes to draw in the image of Memphis's movements. He's so smooth on his feet, his entire body dipping and swaying. He becomes an impossible target to predict.

"I've only seen the videos he shows me on his phone. He's something I've never seen before." He leans back, resting his head and folding his hands over his chest, looking up at the ceiling.

"You ever try it? Boxing?" I know that a lot of servicemen fight, some for sport and some to keep their sanity.

Miles laughs, a raspy cackle from deep in his chest. He sounds like he has pneumonia.

"I got my ass kicked a few times, but what he does? Where you *actually* have a fighting chance not to get your teeth knocked out? Ha, nah. I was more of a runner."

I smile and nod, piecing that together with a man who has three medals for bravery. The pictures don't match.

Our eyes meet for a few seconds in the silence, and I can see the familiar shadow in them. His mask is better than mine—the way he tucks certain things in a corner and doesn't let people see the truth. I'm fairly certain he's more of a fighter than he's letting on.

"I don't know much about his upcoming fight," I shrug, a tinge of guilt stabbing at me. It's in Vegas, and my mom is excited about it, which means the purse is probably decent. She doesn't usually get excited unless there are five digits on the table.

"He's going to win." I start to chuckle to myself, but when my gaze hits his, I stop, letting my lips fall into a closed smile. I nod and agree, because something about Miles's confidence is infectious. It's comforting, and it feels like truth.

"How'd you two meet?" My lips pucker at his next question, and I blush a little when he wiggles his eyebrow.

"We're just friends," I say, the stab of guilt reminding me it's there with a dull ache this time.

"Okay, and I'm a twenty-year-old figure skater. Now that we've both made shit up, tell me a little bit about how you and the Champ became *friends*."

He winks.

I shake my head in small movements and pull my purse between my feet on the floor to make room for my now-bobbing knee.

"My Uncle Leo trains him. It's my family's gym," I shrug and instantly avoid eye contact.

My hand glides to my thigh and I try to temper the shaking in my leg. When I look at Miles, I catch his focus on my hand, his mouth drawn in a serious line. He glances up and I swallow in reaction.

"My wife..." He stops abruptly, his lips parted in a painful smile over gritted teeth.

"It's okay," I say, recognizing the expression of a man forcing himself to talk about something painful. "I don't talk about my family much...if I can help it."

I move my hand to his, the touch bringing his gaze down as his chin tucks into his chest.

"I can give you a shave sometime...if you want," I say, and the left side of my mouth slightly curls.

The long pause grows longer, and I start to feel trapped, afraid to pull my hand away because his focus is so intense on it. I'm growing anxious, and I can feel my hand tremble slightly and I know my palm is going to begin to sweat.

"Anna owned a resale shop. She was incredibly handy," he chuckles.

I'm frozen.

His dimples deepen as he blinks a few times.

"She's the one the Army really could have used." The smile fades quickly, and his eyes flit to mine. "We had a daughter, Felicity," he says, flashing a brief smile that breaks my heart.

I shake my head just a little, part of me wanting him to stop sharing. I wonder if Memphis knows any of this?

"They were on the way to the airport to greet me after my last deployment. I was done. I was coming home and then that was it...it was all over." There's a strange calmness in the way he's looking at me, the way he just spoke those words. He might not speak about his past often, but he's made peace with it.

"Is that why you live in that park?"

His eyes glaze slightly and his tight lips echo sweet sadness as his head bobs slowly in confirmation.

"How do you go home after something like that?" he whispers, unable to force his voice any louder.

I squeeze more where I'm holding his hand, and he pulls his bottom hand out from our pile and places it on top of mine, like a sandwich. His eyes move down to his foot, treated finally the way it deserves. His other foot is in a clean sock, probably donated from the hospital. He stretches that foot forward, pointing the toes and groans lightly from the movement.

"You thank Memphis for me, will you? For watching my spot?"

Standing, I let our touch slip away and pull my purse up on my shoulder as I nod.

"Will do."

It's getting late, but it's never quiet in a place like this. It doesn't seem to bother Miles much. I think distractions are welcome to his ears, and maybe that's why he lives on the streets.

I look back one last time before I leave, and he's already put his glasses on. The metal rims look a little bent, so I make myself a mental note to steal a pair of Leo's readers from home and bring them to him the next time I see him.

Managing to catch the route just in time, I take the bus home. The cab ride to the hospital nearly gave me a panic attack, because I couldn't remember for sure what the cab driver I stiffed a few weeks ago looked like. I don't think it was him, but the jerky driving that had my seatbelt working overtime gave me pause.

The bus is easy. People don't talk, and as long as you take a seat near the front, but not right by the driver, you can count on being left alone. I've always preferred the bus, and not because I'm cheap. I like the idle time it gives me. When I was a teenager, this route was my savior. It got me to the west part of town for the mall, and the east side for clubs I was too young for and college boys I could never have, but whose attention I still craved.

The ride was always my favorite part, though. No screaming echoing in the hallways. No parents threatening each other to walk out or weeks on end of living in an abandoned neighborhood all alone. Nobody to remind me of my big fat mouth and how I ruined the family fortune by telling the truth.

It was quiet. It's quiet now. Even as I step through the door and land at the dusty curb, the world is quiet.

Silence disappears when the bus rumbles into gear behind me, the sifting noise of the door closing startling me enough to step forward a few quick paces. I glance to the left and watch my chariot fade, bathing in the exhaust. The nearby intersection light flashes green, and my quiet is overruled by drag-racing twenty-somethings, business people leaving work late, and people passing through or cruising the streets for trouble.

Home.

I might understand the tree even more now.

My chest fills with air once the smog dissipates, and I breathe out heavily through my nose as my attention turns to the walkway and dark porch in front of me. I haven't been inside since I left for the gym this morning, and I really didn't put in a full day of work there, either. My mother will take it out of my pay, and I won't argue, even though I've put in plenty of *extra* hours sorting through bank statements trying to make books match reality. She walked in at the absolute worst time—and the fact that I haven't had a lecture from her yet about how I ruin everything, and how I'll ruin Memphis too, is worth losing half a day's pay.

I can't seem to get myself inside now either, though. I'm still wearing the sweatpants and T-shirt I tossed on this morning, and it's comfortable enough to wear to bed. I don't want to *be* in my bed, though. I want to be under a tree, standing guard because of a promise. I want to watch the sunrise out there with a guy I made a pledge to my younger self would never be my type.

Instead, I settle on waiting for him, abandoning the walkway that leads to the dark room I've been living in and replacing it with an orange-lit alleyway. The back of my uncle's house still smells of smoldering burnt cuts of meat. I toss my purse in the chair Memphis put out for me, and I shut the propane tank off, killing the small flame threatening to melt the tiny grill. I busy myself for the next thirty minutes cleaning up the area outside, making things look as neat as spare bike parts, old boots, and a broken lawn chair can. I kick larger rocks off to the side and out of his bike's path, then give into the temptation to see if Memphis's door is unlocked.

I twist the knob slowly, waiting for it to catch, but it falls open easily. One step inside and I'm swallowed up by everything I know about him. My hand dusts along the fringe of an old quilt hanging off the edge of a loft bed behind me, while my eyes rake over the other side of this space. It's a cave, in many ways, but it doesn't feel dark inside despite the long-set sun outside. The buzz of a fan clipped to the top of a cabinet hums a passing breeze through my hair, and when I draw in through my nose, the scent is familiar. My hand automatically moves to my mouth, fingertips trying to find that same feeling of Memphis's lips against mine.

The cab of the RV doesn't look drivable. Laundry is stacked in the driver's seat, although it's folded, which is impressive. Everything inside seems to have a place, even if it's not what the space was intended for. A small collection of tools—screwdriver, wrench, and some ratchet-looking-thingy—live in the center console cup holder, and a few books and magazines are tucked inside the flap behind the passenger seat. It all feels so permanent for a home meant to be on the road.

A few books are sandwiched between two protein tins on the small counter space near the single-burner stove. I slide one out and smile when I read the spine—TOM SAWYER. I wonder if it's his favorite book, or if it belonged to his dad. I slide it back in and run my thumb along the next few books, stopping at the other end against the metal ridges of a spiral notebook. I slide it out and flip a few of the first pages, clippings from small town newspapers taped to the centers of pages.

He's skinny in the first picture I flip to. The muscles on his arms are these tiny bumps, and his eyes are swollen shut from the beating he took, but the referee is holding his arm in the air. There's an intensity to his face, even at eighteen. It's a look he was born with, that much I know. I watched people come in and out of our gym, rise and fall against my dad. There were only a handful that had that look in their eyes. My dad had it, and it's in every picture I flip to that shows his face.

Weigh-ins.

Press conferences.

I chuckle when I see one where he's standing next to his opponent, fists formed on each of them—the typical comparison and a big show for the media. His opponent, Joseph Gomez, is smiling. Memphis is already there, in the ring, winning—I can see it in his eyes.

Curious, I flip through the pages from beginning to end, counting twice. There are twenty-three wins in here. Fighters keep all of their fights—even the losses. They use them as reminders of sore moments, weaknesses to erase. There are no losses in Memphis's book.

He's good. He's *more* than good. And this fight that's coming up is bigger than anyone is saying out loud.

I close the book and slide it in just as I found it, my chest growing heavier with each breath. Memphis is the real thing. I know the ride his life is about to take, and it's...filled with temptation. It's more than shortcuts and women and parties and celebrity—it's a sense of feeling like a god, above the rules we live by to make sure we don't hurt one another. It's easy to forget those things when you're invincible.

My eyes fall to the floor, my black running shoes disappearing into the darkness. I can't see where I end and Memphis's home begins, and the parallel that draws makes my heart flutter dangerously.

I move back to the doorway, pushing it open to let the glow from the streetlights flood inside, and I turn around to look at everything he owns one last time. His space is warm and sad, somehow kind of perfect, yet lonely. I pull my phone from my pocket to check the time, surprised to see it's well after midnight.

Frozen to the top step leading to his place, I glance up at my window, picturing his view of me. I fantasize a little about what he sees—what I *let* him see. When a smile touches my lips, I step down and sit on the top step. With the door pushed shut behind me, I lean against the gritty metal siding and pull my knees up to my chest, hugging them.

I waste more than two hours in my own thoughts, reliving in my own head the nightmares I've survived. My eyes can barely stay open, and my sleepy mind is starting to make me panic about being doomed to repeat my mistakes. The memory of his touch, his lips against mine, is starting to fade more quickly, and I'm beginning to think I remembered something that wasn't real at all.

Standing in an effort to force myself back to Leo's house, I wish for the butterflies to die inside me. I decide to face things with a clear head after a few hours of sleep—and the aid of sunshine and obscene amounts of caffeine. The quiet streets make his approaching bike stand out even more, though, and I stop with my back against his door, hairs rising on the back of my neck, some things still refusing to give up the fight inside my chest.

When his headlight shines on me, I breathe in deeply, knowing this bit of air will need to last. Memphis walks his bike forward another foot or two, finally coming to a stop and killing the engine. He doesn't get up right away, instead sitting where he stopped and keeping me in the spotlight.

I lose a little more of the air I've been trying to save, and my throat closes with nerves. Memphis still doesn't move. While I was here, staring up at my temporary window and this dirty strip of land that divides my old life from everything else—thinking about all of the reasons I should never have kissed this man—Memphis was somewhere staring and thinking, too.

Fear starts to trickle into my bloodstream, down my spine, and spread through my nerve endings. My fingers grow numb, and I squeeze my hands into fists just to feel them. I'm afraid—afraid that Memphis was thinking of all of the ways I don't fit in with the plan he's clearly following, based on the spiral notebook filled with win after win. I'm afraid he doesn't care that I'm a distraction, instead listening to momentary lust and greed. I'm afraid of what would happen after, if he had me and threw me away.

I'm terrified about tomorrow, about facing my mother and feeling either shame or regret, because just like her, I am falling for a fighter. Neither is good, and Memphis has the potential to drive me right through both, but I still can't move from this spot. Because as terrified as I am of the next five minutes, something is keeping him there on his bike, staring at me—just as unsure.

"Miles liked the steak." I had to say something.

Memphis kills the light, and I'm finally able to see his form as he kicks his leg over his bike and pulls his helmet from his head. He holds it in both hands, in front of his chest, and a small part of me is hoping he'll just put it back on and speed away.

"It looked like they had him on some antibiotics, or some sort of IV. Maybe just hydration, or...I don't really know how hospital stuff works." I shrug, my knees shaking.

Memphis looks down, and as my eyes adjust, I can make out the faint smile curling the edge of his lips. His head angles and our eyes meet. Ten, maybe fifteen, feet of dirt and gravel between us, but this barrier seems to hold steady.

"He was glad you went to check on his tree." A small, airy laugh falls from my lips, and Memphis's smile curves a hint more just before he nods.

I move my fingers slightly within my closed fists, my palms moist from nerves. The more I speak, the more content I seem to be with this—living just on the edge of possibility. There's a certain rush from him being there, me being here—space between us to go along with a growing desire that fills the air from both of our staggered breaths.

It must be three in the morning. The sky is as pitch black as it comes, and the thin amount of dust in the air colors the lights so everything feels like one of those old-time photographs. His bruises have darkened, and the swelling has settled a little. He's one hell of a man to look at normally, but standing there—like this—still wearing the same sweats and white shirt he wore in the ring earlier, blood stains dried on his collar...well...only my mother would understand why this is so beautiful.

And now it seems I do, too.

"I don't why I'm here." I shake my head and let my eyes blink to the ground as I fold my arms over my chest and squeeze at my sides, undoing my fists. I can't mask the hard swallow, and when I glance back up to Memphis, I know he saw it.

His jaw flexes, and under his scrutiny I start to feel embarrassed, like I missed some nonverbal cue to leave. I never should have been here.

"Why am I the only one talking?" My teeth catch my lip, and a quiet chuckle pushed out by my boiling nerves escapes. My right foot leaves the step, but I pause at the sound of Memphis's feet shifting along the rough ground.

"I...I don't know what to say?"

His mouth falls to a straight line, and I nod a laugh before letting my arms unfold so I can push the butts of my hands into my tired eyes.

"Right," I say. I nod again, then look up at the dust particles dancing under the streetlamp. "I...uh..." My chin tucks back toward my chest and my eyes meet his again. "I'm just gonna go."

I make it two steps this time before Memphis stops me.

"Wait," he says. I don't look at him at first, instead my eyes on the other option—on leaving. It would take seconds for me to walk around the edge of Leo's house and through the back door into my lonely, but safe, existence. I know Memphis wouldn't follow me, because he's a gentleman. He'd respect my need to be gone—away from this moment right here.

"I can't be that girl, Memphis." I let my words linger for a breath before I dare to look at him. He was waiting for me, his fingers drumming on his helmet's surface and his feet planted firmly where they stand. "This world...the things you are going to go through..."

Flashes from my past run through my mind. All of the times my dad went home with someone else after a fight, the shouting matches I tried to drown out when he was making weight—his never-fully-won battle with opioids, a chronic craving from so many broken bones. And then there was the stroke—all of the signs leading up to it. You can only burn bright in this world for so long, if you ever burn bright at all.

"I promised myself I would leave this place, that I would leave the people here in it."

"I'm not them," he interrupts. His chest rises with a slow-drawn breath and he looks down where his hands grip his helmet.

"You don't see it like I do," I say. His eyes snap to mine, and I pause. He's undefeated. He's on the verge of what fighters like him dream about when they first slide their hands into a pair of gloves they only hope will fit them one day. He is what my dad had been searching for—*a champion*.

"I know how good you are." There's a flash to his eyes, almost like the thought of someone praising him is a curse. He's going to need to get used to hearing it. I can sense it coming—he is all this world will be talking about.

"You can't grow up in this family and not recognize it. There have been very few." I glance up at the wall painted with my dad's likeness and chew at the inside of my cheek.

"My bike was in some pawnshop in Ashland, Wisconsin."

I draw my brow in, but keep my eyes on the brick wall and let him continue, even though I can hear his feet moving along the ground.

"It was my dad's," he says, something I think I maybe knew deep down. It hits me with a punch, even still.

"There was this picture of him on it, and he had this smile on his face like he'd finally made it, you know? Like...all he had to do in this world was get enough money to buy this bike, and he would be a satisfied man."

He laughs at the memory, the sound from his chest soft and warm. I run my hand over my opposite arm to stir away the tingles, and to embrace myself at the same time. I turn my head just enough to see him still taking slow, sauntering steps toward me, his helmet now down to his side.

"He left me this box of...old...shit," he smirks as he says it, his eyes flitting to mine then back to the few paces left between us. "Some unlucky lottery ticket with a girl's number on it...which I called to see if she knew him. She had no idea who he was, and I'm pretty sure she was a prostitute."

We share a short chuckle, though it isn't really funny.

Memphis glances to the side, tossing his helmet to the ground next to his trailer, then takes a few more steps toward me, stopping where I'm just out of reach.

"There were a few unsent birthday cards he probably didn't even know where to send, and a bunch of pictures of him with this group of guys at this bar. I fantasized for a while that maybe he owned it or something, but I killed that idea with a few phone calls."

He lifts his head, mouth crooked, the smile of a spiritually defeated man. I recognize that, too. His gaze rests on mine, and I wait to see where this goes, despite every experience in my life screaming at me from the pit of my chest. I can't help but wait—I can't help but fall into his eyes. I can't help it because this man is rare—dangerous as he may be to my heart, he is rare.

"Was Ashland, Wisconsin in the box, too," I say, with a slight waggle of my head.

Memphis laughs loudly, the sound penetrating deeper into my head, scratching at something familiar. I think it's him—I've gotten so used to him, to the sounds he makes that I love, that when I hear them my body feels whole. His dimples sink and lips part. His smile is just a little crooked when it's genuine.

"No, Liv. That's not what was in the box." I like the way he says my name, like we have a regular banter between us, a part each of us play. He's gotten used to me, too.

I blink quickly and shrug, my hand now wrenched around my arm, holding tighter with each slight movement he makes closing our gap.

"There was an old registration copy in there, and I called around until I got someone dumb enough to tell me things they shouldn't about a bike that wasn't mine. I had four thousand dollars saved up, and a car that barely made it a hundred miles at a time without stalling out. I drove it for thirteen hours straight from Philly to Wisconsin, willing it back to life from gas station to gas station. My dad's bike was parked in front of this old barn filled with tractor parts and backhoes. Someone got in some trouble, and it ended up there somehow after they stole it from whomever bought it from my dad. I offered the man five hundred bucks, and for a thousand, he threw in the camper."

I turn so our feet are squared and glance at his home that I think he probably knows I went through while he was gone. Somehow, the money he paid for it seems not enough and too much all at once. My gaze shifts back to his, and he steps forward until the toe of his left shoe rests against the right of mine.

"That's a nice story, Memphis. I'm glad you found the bike, but I'm not sure what that has to do with me," I say, my breath catching as his fingertips trace along my jaw, his touch so faint I find myself leaning my head to encourage his palm to rest along my cheek more boldly.

He brings his other hand up with more confidence, and I'm caught. The other option I had, to walk away, is gone. I never really wanted it, though.

Memphis dips his chin, hunching slightly to bring his eyes in line with mine. We're so close that I can feel the tickle of his breath along my lips, and they tingle at the familiar. Each experience with him weaves itself into my heart in this way that terrifies me. This is how people lose themselves.

But I let it in—each breath, each sound, the smells and words. His story. I am surviving on the very being of him, and I think I have been for a while now.

"I was eighteen when I tracked down that bike. I knew it was mine..."

"I don't belong to you, Memphis," I cut in, my heart pounding.

His mouth forms a crooked smile. He holds my eyes hostage in silence for few long seconds.

"Maybe it works the other way," he says, his eyes moving over my face with a softness that feels intimate and vulnerable. His forehead falls forward until it rests gently on my own, and I let go of the grip I have on myself, exchanging it for fistfuls of his T-shirt. My knuckles run along his chest as I gather the material and close my eyes, his muscles hard from discipline.

"I can't watch you get hurt. I can't..."

His hand moves to my chin, and he lifts it until our eyes meet. Suddenly, breathing just got a lot harder to do.

"I won't lose, Liv. I work too hard, and I study too much. I will never be in a ring I'm not supposed to be in," he says, and I breathe out what sounds like a laugh, but feels like hurt.

"My fifty-year-old uncle kicked your ass in some display of alpha-male, teacher-student bullshit. I couldn't watch that...how am I supposed to watch you step in with some guy who really wants to kill you? How am I supposed to kiss you knowing that your lips might never be the same after a fight? How—"

Memphis's mouth takes mine before I can protest anymore, nothing like our stolen moment from earlier. His hands cup my face and his mouth moves possessively over my bottom lip, sucking it in and letting it slide loose through a graze of his teeth. He turns my head with a gentle nudge and kisses me deeper, and his hands fall from my face in long, possessive drags down my shoulders to my waist, stopping with his thumbs just above my hips and his fingers splayed out around my sides.

My hands roam up his chest and neck until my thumbs run along the roughness of his chin, and my touch seems to somehow make him hungrier.

"My god." He breathes the words against my lips, restraint giving way as his hands slide around my ass and lift me to him. My legs wrap around his waist and my hands move into his hair. I hold on with the short strands threaded through my fingers, and our lips part as his head tilts forward, resting on mine.

He's walking, and the brief break from his kiss gives me a few precious seconds to think. Thoughts are muddled, though. My body is fighting rigid rules I made a long time ago, and with every step Memphis takes, my pulse radiates heavier until my back hits the door to his trailer. I think my heart may tear its way out through my ribs.

"Promise me," I say, the words coming out more pleading than I want, but the tone is necessary. This decision right now is everything to me—this is either a leap of faith or the recklessness of a foolish heart.

Memphis loosens his grip on my legs until I slide from him and stand on my own, his arms caging me as his eyes work from one of mine to the other.

"I will win for you, Liv. I promise you. And I will never lie."

His words squeeze at me, and my lips tremble because I'm afraid.

"You need to promise me that you won't break me," I say.

I breathe in deeply to center myself, and Memphis lets his hands slide down the doorway until they're resting at his sides. His chest rises quickly with deep, but rapid, breaths as his eyes seem to ache, a heaviness drawing down his face.

It's as if my words were familiar, like some spell he's been waiting to hear, and now that I've spoken them, somehow everything has changed. I start to panic internally, wondering if I've messed up—if my pride, my failures, my parents' terrible character has ruined me and doomed me never to feel anything good again.

Before I can speak, though, Memphis steps into me, his hand gentle against one cheek as his lips press a tender kiss to the other. I tremble as he lingers there in this small, intimate space. I grip at his shirt once more in desperation. His other hand covers both of mine, and he squeezes them, halting me. I would feel like one of those desperate groupies I used to see cling to my dad if it weren't for the tender way Memphis's lips were now brushing along my ear.

"I have been waiting to kiss you like that since I saw you looking down at me from that window up there, and goddamn, Liv, was it ever worth the wait."

He breathes out and his shoulders relax, but his grip on my hands remains steadfast. My eyes flutter closed, and I nestle my face into the crook of his neck, somehow feeling safe by this small little inch I've removed between us.

"I'm sorry," I say.

"Don't be." His answer comes fast, and I feel a slight shake to his head that matches his words. Here, in his arms, sheltered between his body and his patched-together home, I feel strangely at peace. It's the first time since I answered a Seattle apartment door to a throng of vicious and invasive gossip reporters that I've been able to fill my lungs completely.

"This...whatever it is we are doing or becoming," he says, pausing as his chin lifts and his hands finally free mine so they can both caress my face. He presses a kiss to my forehead, then holds my gaze to his. "This is too important for doubt. I want you, Liv. I want you because when I touch you I feel it in every square inch of my body. I remember where you were, how you smelled, every small sound you made. I have dreamt about the time I simply touched this hand."

He reaches down and threads our fingers together, then brings my knuckles to his lips, holding them there while his chest fills once more.

"And I will remember tonight," he says, stopping as his mouth curves on one side and his shoulders lift just a little. "I will remember the almost, and I will wait for the what ifs. Because this is too important, and you don't get into the ring with someone unless you know who they are and how they can hurt you. I will wait for you to really know who I am, Liv. I'm confident in the man I am. I'm not those men upstairs who disappointed you, but I understand your guard. And I will wait until you believe I won't break that promise. Breaking you, Liv, would be one of the biggest regrets of my life. And I just don't do regrets."

I feel weak, maybe even dizzy. My head and heart work together to process what Memphis said with what he's doing as he steps back down to the ground and tugs me toward him where our hands are still attached. He kisses my head again then steps around me, letting our hands drop apart.

"It's late, and we both have full days tomorrow. And you have now missed two lessons."

My lips pucker into a timid smile, my cheeks burning from embarrassment. I feel like a tease, but he's right—this mountain I've made between me and a man like him is built on a lot of shit from my past. I want him, too. I want him in a way that's not temporary, and if that ever has a chance, then I need to start forgiving some really old wounds, and letting go of a whole lot of hate.

"Goodnight, Olivia," he says, his brow raised flirtatiously. I shake my head and roll my eyes at my formal name. I start to slide my feet toward the corner of the building and Leo's back door, but then it hits me—I still don't know.

"What were you...before Memphis?" If I'm going to know him, I need to know every bit. Even the parts he doesn't like to share.

He smirks and looks down at his feet, kicking the back of his heel against the metal first step to his place. When he glances up at me, a few strands of hair fall along his forehead. This is how I want to dream of him later.

"Michael Parrish. They named me at the Catholic church that helped place abandoned babies at the precinct. It was on Parrish Street." He shrugs, and the ease of it all lets me exhale.

The corner of my mouth curves as I fall back toward the edge of the building.

"I like Memphis better," I say, satisfied with the way his eyes settle on mine.

I turn around and walk back into one of the suffocating homes that made me how I am, but I feel the remnants of electricity everywhere. His mouth—his skin and hair and chin. His breath and eyes. It's invaded me. But that part he let me see inside—his character—that's what inspires me most.

Memphis Delaney is rare. He also might be worth it.

# CHAPTER TEN

Memphis

There's this not-so-secret secret in the boxing world about sexual frustration helping a fighter in the ring. Maybe it's a myth. Whatever the fuck it is, it's done something to me today. My fists are bombs. Fast and wicked, though—not sluggish and heavy. They land with precision, they land with speed, and they sting and punish. It's like I can see things before they happen, my body working one heartbeat in the future.

It isn't that I held out. It's not that at all because that... *that*...knocked me on my ass for the entire night. Liv put on a show, taking her time undressing just out of reach from my gawking, pathetic eyes. The smirk on her lips when she stepped in to close her blinds crawled down my chest and stomach and there was no stopping it. There are fantasies, and then there are the things I imagined last night.

Morning greeted a new man, however; one with an edge on everybody else. It's like suddenly I have something that I'm fighting for—something real, that I can touch and hold and feel next to me one night. I've always fought for myself and for the Delaney name that I want to earn, even though there isn't a living soul who cares about that legacy. I know, because I've looked. My dad was it, a man with no living parents and no siblings, no aunts or uncles. He cruised the world with friends just like him. Their names are mysteries. They all may as well have been made up.

"How's that eye healing?" Leo spits, taking a potshot at me as an excuse to back up and pull the pads from his hands. I'm hurting him today, which pleases him, because he thinks he knocked me into shape just in time. The irony of how very opposite it is only makes my lungs feel stronger, like tired isn't a thing.

"Three stitches, old man." I pull off my gloves and slide through the ropes to grab my water. I would give anything for a beer right now. Hydration has been my weakness before, though. This time I started weeks before the big match.

"Memphis, I've got a few things to show you...minute?"

Angela likes to announce her entrances. She always has, and I used to think it was just a personality flaw—a need to draw the room's attention to her and whatever it is she's wearing. Last night clarified a lot of things, though. Angela and Leo play into each other's worst parts, all to put on little shows for each other. You'd never know from the outside, and I'm nearly positive Liv has no idea.

It's so clear now, though. The reason she dresses up the way she does, when the only person she really sees outside of that house is Leo. His blatant sexual harassment is practically expected, and a week ago, I wondered why Angela had put up with it so long. They're performing. That's what this is. She's showing off for him, reminding him she's here, of what he can have but can't tell, and he's putting on a show to make everyone believe something like this could never be possible.

Liv could have just as easily caught them yesterday, though. They're getting careless, and that makes me wonder if they want to be caught—if they want Liv to be the one to do it.

It's all so sick.

"You see that outfit in one of those red-carpet movie star photos in one of your magazines, Ange?" Leo whistles then purrs like a tiger, and when I glance to Angela, she rolls her eyes.

"He's such a fucking pig. He's good at his job. It's why I keep him," she says to me as we move to the table and chairs tucked in a corner. She takes a seat, then gestures for me to join her; so I do.

"That's not the only reason you keep him around," Liv says behind me.

I'm a little surprised to hear the words myself. They were in my head, but they came out in Liv's voice. When I turn, Angela is better at her reaction—she's perfected the performance. I'm still new at this.

"Oh, I suppose you're right, him being family and all," Angela says, laughing it off and waving a hand at her daughter, who is still paused at the vending machine a few steps away from us.

"I kinda meant that he owns half of everything," Liv says, a tiny smirk inching up her lip. I wonder if only I notice it.

"We both know you don't give a shit about family." Liv mutters that second part as she walks away, but it makes it to Angela's ears. Pretending she doesn't hear isn't something she's practiced, and Liv's words make a direct hit at her pride.

I kinda wish Liv didn't do that, though. She gets so easily sucked into their game. This is her baggage, and words like that don't help her free herself from the burden she carries around at all. They just make it heavier.

"We have some sponsorship opportunities. You thought the purse was big for Vegas? Wait until you see some of these deals I've been able to nail down. First, you are going to be getting some wardrobe items."

I must look confused, because Angela pauses when her eyes meet my face and she begins to laugh.

"Suits, maybe a few nice shirts and ties, pants. Good lord, you would have thought I signed you up for Miss America by that look on your face," she says, sliding over a packet of material that I flip through and pretend to care about until I get to that last page—the one full of numbers.

"Hey, Liv?" I call out for her, and Angela noticeably shifts in her chair.

I fold the top pages underneath while I run my thumb down the grid of dollar signs and decimals, doing my best to figure out how the percentages add up. I've been diligent with every deal I've ever made, and it's because of the system I grew up in. Good guys are always balanced out by the bad, and products of the state foster system see a mix of both. It makes me question everyone when it comes to money.

"Yeah?" she says.

I feel her next to me before I hear her. She purposely stood close enough to allow her hip to brush into my elbow. I want to let my hand fall free to the side so I can run it up the leg of her blue leggings that contour around every muscle and curve decorating her. It would make her uncomfortable, though, and that's why I don't. It's the only reason.

"I've never really had someone around to ask about these things. You think this looks like a good deal?" I turn the pages slightly so she can see them better, and Liv glances from me to her mom. A few breathless seconds pass before she finally looks down at the contract.

"I don't really deal with things outside of the operations. You should maybe have a lawyer—"

"If I win this fight, I'll get a lawyer," I cut in. "For right now, I can afford asking a favor of..." I let the end of that sentence trail off, letting her imagination insert the word. I could have said *friend*, I could have said *woman I'm seeing*; it could have been *girlfriend* or *colleague*. The way her lips purse, but bend, signals that she knows she gets to fill in that word.

Whatever smile was there, fades when she looks back at her mom, and I glance over just in time to catch the hard stare she's giving her daughter. This isn't about questioning what Angela does for me as a manager; it's about letting her daughter lend advice on something that she's territorial about.

It's stupid. And it's a big part of the problem.

Liv clears her throat and slides into the open chair to my right, her eyes flitting to me a few times before she gives all of her focus over to the numbers. She holds a finger by one line of digits for a few seconds, closing her eyes and moving her lips silently like a human calculator. It takes her seconds to do what I spend a long night and three Red Bulls doing on legal pads and phone apps.

"The payout is more if you win, of course, but the upfront is really good. It's in line with what you're worth, especially based on your r-record."

She stumbles a little at that word. If she hadn't, I might not have fully noticed what she said. She knows my record, which means she's done her research on me. I keep my grin in check, but I feel it pushing from the inside.

"You should see eight thousand, maybe eight five, upon signature. If you win, that number doubles. Even if you lose—"

"I won't lose." Liv glances my way. The way she trembles and blushes, pretending that her smile is just there because I'm amusing, is goddamn adorable.

"God I love your arrogance, Memphis," Angela cuts in. I lean back and fold my hands behind my head to look her in the eye. "Archie was the same way. That confidence is going to take you a long way. You out-talk before you out-walk. That's what he used to say."

"Hell, he did," Leo interrupts. The table has gotten crowded, and I can feel Liv's leg bouncing in the space next to me, so I adjust my position and scoot my chair in close, sitting up and moving my hands under the table and out of Leo and Angela's sight. My right palm finds her knee, and the moment I squeeze lightly, she freezes.

"Oh, I suppose you're going to take credit for Archie's sayings too, huh?" Angela rests one arm on the back of her chair, turning enough to cross her legs—a movement Leo leers at.

"He only repeated things," Leo says, finally looking Angela in the eyes. He taps two fingers at his temple and starts to back away. "Brains of the operation, baby. I'm all the brains."

Angela laughs loudly and Leo winks. I chuckle out of courtesy, but Liv...she stays absolutely silent. God, how did she survive this messed up life?

"So I sign here?" I bring our attention back to business, and Angela clicks a pen. She's invested in this. I'm not the contract genius Liv is, but I know that Angela walks away with at least one and a half, maybe two grand.

We spend the next thirty minutes reviewing two more deals—one a quick commercial spot for a local car dealer that will only run in the Valley for a weekend in September. The pay is all right, but I sign because it's really only an hour's worth of work. Everything gets balanced against the scale with time. My time is valuable.

My dad taught me that. It's the first thing that I accepted when I got his diary. It's a running theme from him, maybe because his was so short.

The last deal is a little trickier. It's for a major sponsorship. It's for Fuel Factory Athletics, one of the biggest gear suppliers in Boxing on the West Coast. This deal wasn't supposed to come this soon—my first title-fight not yet on the books.

"This feels a little...presumptive, I guess?" I squirm in my seat and draw the contract in close, resting my forearms on either side of the pages. I had to study like this in high school, to block out the noise and keep my head focused on the work. I was never meant for college, not that I wasn't smart. My heart was always pulling me on a different path, though—*this* one.

My head falls forward until my thumbs catch my temples and my fingers rub my forehead.

"I thought you were going to win?" Liv nudges me with her knee when she speaks, and my hand falls under the table to touch her instinctively as I chuckle. It's the most simple thing that shouldn't mean anything to anyone, but I feel her grow stiff under my fingers. I pop my head up to Angela.

She's making note of these little intimate details.

I'm not sure what to do here—do I pull away and create space, try to erase what she saw to keep the peace in Liv's life, or do I stand my ground and force Angela to get used to her daughter being happy for once?

If only Angela knew what *I* saw.

"I don't know..." I lean back, but keep my hand right where it is.

Angela's eyes are practically boring into her daughter, but Liv is deliberately looking away.

"That's a lot of money you're leaving on the table there, Memphis. There's nothing superstitious about good business decisions," Angela says.

I can see Leo hovering over her shoulder. He gets a cut of her cut, too. They all get a cut. They call fighters on the rise *alphas*.

*Alpha.*

I'm the leader of a starving pack all right.

"Let me think about it," I finally say, pushing the contract back in Angela's direction.

She reaches for it hesitantly, pausing with her palm over it for a second before letting it fall flat on the papers. Her fingers drum on it a few times, long, golden nails with black tips pattering against the table.

"Have dinner with Paul. He's the CEO, and he was worried you would be concerned," she says.

I cock my head and lift a brow suspiciously.

"You are not the first boxer they've sponsored, Memphis. He understands the fabric of superstition that runs through this sport." She laughs lightly and pulls the contract back into the folder with the rest of them.

I look down at the empty table where I just let several grand float in limbo, and I swallow hard. Superstition is a part of it—absolutely. But it's not just how it plays into fighting. It's about my life, and a promise I made to myself never to take the easy way. I earn everything I get. The small and the grand—they all have a story of work behind them. Long days in a shipping yard in Pittsburgh earned me enough money to get across the country to the bike and my RV. Handiwork bought things at yard sales along the way. Roofing jobs kept me in the good graces of small-time gyms that helped me get fights and train. Nothing was easy, but that's what made it feel so good.

There is power in the word *earned*.

"It's dinner, Memphis. I'll go with you, if it helps."

Angela's words strike me fast, and I throw back an alternative.

"I'll take Liv." I lift my chin and meet Angela's eyes.

She knows.

I'm daring her to mess this up for her daughter by putting the one thing she cares about most on the line—money.

"There might be questions she can't answer...about the business or the fight." Angela is grasping. Liv is still frozen, but her gaze has moved, from the open sliding doors that lead out to the parking lot, to me.

"I can answer most of it, and Liv knows numbers. But I mean really..." I smirk. "It's just dinner, Angela."

Her expression shifts the tiniest bit into a sinister one, but she nods lightly. Her eyes move to her daughter in a blink.

"You can borrow a dress." The chair scrapes across the concrete floor as she slides it angrily backward.

"I'll get her a dress," I say. My pulse is kicking with an anger similar to the one I feel in the ring. I'm grateful for the deals, and I know that Angela and Leo are the ones I have to thank for being in this position. But I also have come to realize that they aren't very good people.

Angela glances to Liv then back to me, and in that time Liv's hand quivers as it slides gently over the top of mine, which hasn't left its place on her knee. I turn my palm open just enough for her fingers to curl into me, and I grip her hard, squeezing to let her know she is safe. She squeezes back with the same force.

We both wait, our eyes now a team, staring at our opponent.

Angela licks her bottom lip, then pulls her papers and messenger bag together, tucking the strap over her shoulder and the bag against her hip.

"I'll make the call."

She nods and leaves with a swagger in her walk that I know is meant as some sort of *FU* warning to her daughter. Leo announces he's taking a break seconds after the door closes, and he follows her.

"Can you talk to mice and make birds sew ball gowns?" I ask.

Liv turns to meet my eyes and her lip curls on one side with an airy laugh.

"I really am Cinderella, aren't I?" she says, laughing a little harder.

I move my hand finally, bringing them both up to either side of her face and my lips to her forehead.

"Ready to rule the kingdom?" I ask, smiling against her skin. I rest my forehead on hers, and we both breathe in deep. We're in this, and I'm a little scared. I've always been in this alone—in everything alone, really. I made a promise that I won't break her, but I'm so afraid I will. I don't know how to walk through life with someone else.

"Are you ready to arm me for battle?" She leans away from me then stands, eventually nodding her head toward the ring where I promised her a lesson. I wonder if her words have a double meaning for her, too? I think they do.

"Don't punch me in the face," I say, pressing my palms flat on the table and standing to meet her eyes.

Her smile mocks me.

"Don't count on it."

# CHAPTER ELEVEN

Liv

It feels good to hit things.

No.

It feels good to hit people.

A terrible thought to have, but it's all that keeps running through my mind as I take swing after swing at giant pads Memphis is holding in place along both sides of his body. It's only been a few minutes, but already I feel a strange empowerment. It's addictive.

"Ahh," I grunt out, making one final swing with my right arm, landing a punch directly in the center of his left-side pad. It bends a little from the force and I'm thrown two steps back in reaction.

I giggle from joy as I run my arm over my suddenly drenched forehead.

"It's harder than it looks, isn't it?" Memphis lets the pads fall, and I jokingly lunge at him. All he does is cock his head to the side and squint his eyes.

"I don't know," I pant, shaking the gloves from my hands and letting them fall at my feet. I move over to my water and suck down a few gulps. "I'm a little winded, sure, but I was hitting you. That last one was hard, right?"

Memphis chuckles and moves closer to me, resting his back against the corner.

"It was pretty hard...yeah."

My eyes lower in suspicion.

"Yeah..." I hum, twisting my lips and waiting.

"Yeah," he says, nodding while a tight-lipped smile spreads across his face that says the exact opposite of *yeah*.

"I mean, come on!" I shove him in the arm and he leans with my push, laughing harder this time. "I know I'm not a pro or whatever, but those were some damn good punches. They felt amazing. You just don't want to give me credit because I'm a beginner. Mood spoiler. You're...you're a big, giant mood spoiler!"

Now his face is red from holding in laughter. The corners of his mouth are sinking in more with each passing fraction of a second until the burst explodes from his chest and he bends over with the force of laughter.

"I'm sorry. I'm sorry..." He holds up a palm, but keeps his head down and his other palm on his knees.

My brow drawn in, I fold my arms and jut my hip until he looks at me and feels bad. He sucks in his bottom lip and rolls his shoulders, shaking his arms a little as if he's dusting off everything left that might make him laugh.

"I'm sorry," his words are followed by that same face he wore the very first time we met: eyes so sincere, dark lashes and slowly blinking lids. His beard is thickening a little because of the stitches. He didn't shave this morning, and I wonder what it will be by the night.

"Come here," he says, calling me with a finger.

I wait a second before giving in, letting my arms fall to my sides as I take the few steps from where I am to where he is. His hands wrap around my biceps as soon as I'm near enough and I breathe in fast, just once. His eyes widen a little.

"You're stronger than you look," he smirks.

My gaze is held by his when he speaks. He holds it hostage and when I start to look away, his hands slide down to my wrists and he shakes them lightly until I look at him again. His head tilts, and he waits until I get it.

*I'm stronger than I look.*

"Thank you," I say, pulling my lip in tight, so afraid I'm not. I'm stubborn for certain. I'm hardened and jaded. I'm not sure if any of that makes me strong.

My muscles bend to Memphis's will as he threads his fingers through my right ones and lifts my arm, his other hand holding my elbow into my side. He lets go of my fingers and wraps his palm over my knuckles forming a fist and then moves my entire arm forward slowly, stopping when my body lunges with it.

"Here. You lose everything...right here," he says, stopping my fist where it is, then placing the tips of his fingers on my hips.

Memphis's eyes are intent on where his hand rests at my waist, and he pauses to take a breath, his tongue pinched by his teeth, his lips twitching up at the corners, his eyes blinking fast—all in a second.

I think about kissing him again right now.

"Your weight is already spent, and you haven't even made impact with something yet. Think about it," he says, eyes flitting up to mine.

I shake my head a little from the brief gaze and silence we share.

"Okay," I say, following his lead as he brings my arm back and steps behind me.

"You hit me hard, but that was without everything you have behind it. Imagine," he begins, adjusting his hold on me, his right hand sliding down my arm and covering my hand, feet straddling one of mine from behind, his chest against my back, his breath at my neck and a thousand beads of nerves dotting my skin.

"You're here," he says, his voice low and right at my ear.

My eyes flutter when his left hand runs down the side of my body to my hip, and my breath hitches when he grips it more forcefully.

"Your opponent is standing right there. Do you see him?"

I nod.

"Yes," I say, my voice barely audible.

"He's cocking," he says, and I giggle at the word while his nose moves closer to my skin, tickling against my ear. "You're such a child."

I clear my throat and wriggle my hips and roll my shoulders, all under his touch.

"You're right, I'm sorry," I say, still smiling.

A short breath escapes him in laughter.

"He's about to swing, okay?" he says, coaxing me to focus.

"Trust me." His voice falls to a whisper, and my eyes close.

Memphis drives my body—the space between us gone so much that I am lying against him while standing. His hand brings mine up, tucking it close to our bodies. His fingers splay on my thigh, and my leg feels strong. He leans with me, our bodies in sync as we twist to the left, our right shoulders stretching backward, necks rolling until we're nearly back where we started.

"His balance is off," he says at my neck. There are no areas of my body that aren't affected by the vibration of his voice. "You have him. He's yours. You have balance. His is gone. This is where you win."

His hand holds my left side still, and his right hand brings me back to swing with a tighter form than I had before. He takes me through the motion once slowly, almost like we're just part of some intimate ballet performance, then he brings my fist back in and tucks his chin into the side of my neck.

"Again," he says, this time leading me through the motion faster as his hand slides from its hold on my hip to my diaphragm.

"Breathe out," he says, and I do slowly at first, but with each swing we repeat, the motion is faster.

My air escapes with my thrust, my body something mechanical now, parts working in unison until I'm able to do it all on my own.

"Keep going," Memphis says as he steps away. My eyes flit open, and I imagine everything that has ever hurt me. I see their faces—my parents, Enoch, the angry crowds at trials, reporters.

Memphis picks up one of the pads and steps closer as I swing, bending down to lift one of my abandoned gloves, eventually holding his palm out for me to pause.

"Put it on, and I want you to hit me now...not like before. Hit me with what you know. Hit me with what you feel, but always, there is balance. You can't give that away. It's not theirs to have."

My eyes lock on his as he slides the glove over my knuckles and I form a raw fist with my other hand. He takes two small steps back and readies himself before nodding.

I clear my lungs and consider his words and everything he just led my body through. I was so strong. I'm stronger than I think I am.

My feet shift to find the perfect fit against the mat, and I bring my hands in, fists raised and ready.

"He's going to swing now," Memphis says, and I react just as he taught me.

I dodge. The motion so swift and natural I barely remember doing it before my legs steady themselves, my middle twists and my arm swings forward, fist landing in the same spot as it did before—only this time, my body doesn't stumble. Memphis does. Inches, but there is reaction to my action.

"Ha," I breathe out in disbelief. My eyes lift from the fist-shaped dent in the pad to Memphis, and my lips part in awe.

"Yeah," he says, glancing around to the front of the pad. "You did that by yourself."

Giddiness takes over my face, my mouth stretching wide with parted lips. Memphis lets the pad fall again, and the physical proof from my force disappears as the padding evens out. It was there, though. I fought back, and left a mark. More than seeing it, I felt it. I still feel it.

"I want to do that again," I say, blinking as my vision slides from the pad to Memphis's proud smile.

"Baby steps, Champ. Let me show you a few drills, and then maybe you can punch me one more time before we're done," he says, chuckling.

"I wasn't hitting you," I say, handing him the glove.

He holds it in both of his hands before bending down to pick up the other glove, pairing them together. His gaze hits mine.

"I know who you were hitting." Silence settles in for a long second. I don't have to respond; Memphis doesn't expect it.

He gestures with his head to the bags in the corner, so I follow him through the ropes for my next lesson. Every bit of him is solid. I can't imagine anything ever being able to take his balance away. I can't imagine how he could ever lose. But there is always someone better. There is always someone who has trained just a little harder. What happens when he meets his match? Who does he become?

Memphis leads me through four or five bag drills until my body is spent, and his phone is ringing from his locker. I wait while he rushes to it, patting the butts of my hands against the bag a few times, wondering how I had so much energy an hour ago.

"Shit, I didn't realize the time!"

I glance to the clock when he says that and note the hour hand between the seven and eight. He has work soon, and I'm sure he wanted to check on Miles.

"I can visit the hospital. I'll see if they discharged him," I say as he gathers his things into his gym bag.

"They said they'd call me when they did, but you never know," he says, slamming the metal door of his locker shut and flinging his bag over his shoulder before jogging back to me.

"Wait for me," he says.

His fingers feather out toward mine, one of them catching one of mine and shaking it a few times. The nervous, awkward flirtation between us is a rush. This is always my favorite part, though. Enoch flirted, in his own way. He was nothing like Memphis, though. Nothing is quite like Memphis. He's full of the little things, all of those little things that come in between big gestures. The stuff you wish someone had a year down the road, when you're over the newness and struggling to hold on.

"We'll check on Miles together, if you're up," he says, eyes moving from our hands to my face.

"I'll be up," I promise. I will literally put toothpicks in my lids like a cartoon to stay awake for him.

He leans forward and my mouth tingles with hope, but he kisses my cheek. He's still waiting. He's making me stronger. I won't be broken.

"I'll call you when I'm on my way," he says, holding his phone out for me to type in my number.

I smirk and type it in, then add a text to myself that reads: LIV OWNS THIS BITCH. I hit send and hand the phone back to him.

"Funny," he muses, winking at me and sliding his phone in his pocket. "Of course, you sent it to your phone, so..."

"Don't worry. I'll send it back just to be sure." I strike a cocky smile and wiggle my head a little, making him laugh.

"All right then. I'll be sure Amy sees my phone," he says.

"You do that." I answer fast, not that I'm jealous of Amy. I'm not really, but I'm also a little possessive suddenly. Memphis is nice to her, and she flirts in her own way. But he's waiting for me.

I'm stronger than I think I am.


IT'S the time when I'm alone that's always been the hardest. I've always had so much time alone. This is when my mountains feel impossible. I'm standing at the foot of one now, a literal fork in the road with one path leading into Leo's house and one to my parents'.

I have been home for almost a month now, and I have yet to breach my father's door. My mom has quit asking me to, and I'm sure she's not expecting me after today's meeting with Memphis. It's exactly what makes now the perfect time. I know that seeing him is the first of many steps I need to take. It's also the hardest.

Without giving myself a chance to change my mind, I veer to the left and take long strides through the rocks and dirt that were never quite a lawn, pushing open my parents' door. It's dark inside, and Leo's sipping a brown liquor from a clear glass at the kitchen table.

"You here to inspect the place?" he says, laughing at his own stupid joke.

I sigh.

"Mom upstairs?"

Leo's brow pulls in, and I know it's because he's surprised I would ask for her. I'm not. I'd prefer her to be gone is all.

"She ran to the store. I wanted chops tonight, and eating alone sucks. We didn't expect you to be around, otherwise I would have had her get three," he says.

My eyes slit.

"Uh huh," I say.

That was all bullshit. I've been around, alone, pretty much every night. I have a loaf of bread at his house, and some strips of turkey and cheese. I'm almost out of the mustard.

"You want me to tell her you were looking for her?" I ignore his question at first, instead pushing on to the stairs, my hand gripping the bar and my chin tilting up.

"Nope," I say, taking the first step, followed by the next.

Each time I climb higher, I think about stopping and turning back. I might have if I didn't hear Leo move from his chair so he could watch me. I won't look back at him, but I sense he's there. I won't retreat from this in front of him, because he'd like that. There's a certain satisfaction they all get from the fact that I can't bring myself to look at my dad. It's this dare they hold over me, like when I was a kid and they all used to tease me by shutting out all of the lights and forcing me to feel for a switch.

I reach his room and slide my fingers against the grain of the door. Mom's TV is off, so I know she's definitely gone.

The door sticks a little, but the man on the other side won't jump. Even before the stroke, very little scared him. I honestly think the only thing that really ever frightened him at all was the idea of being a father. It scared him so much, the reality never took hold.

The light is dim in his room. The walls are lined with his things, like a museum. Bronzed gloves, headlines framed, and belts hung—

his room is filled with everything that ever mattered to him and my mom. There's a television in the corner, the cabinet doors half opened. I doubt he watches anything. That's how it was before I left —Mom wanted to watch shows together or inspire him with young fighters that he could judge. He'd always look away.

The chair near his bed looks comfortable, and well worn. I wonder who sits here more, my mom or Leo?

I can tell he's heard someone come in. His movements are small. The doctors told my mom that it wasn't that it hurt, but that his brain just couldn't give his muscles enough direction. When his brain said to point, the message his finger got was to twitch. He can't feed himself because of it, and he hasn't spoken a word since the ambulance took him away.

"It's me," I say from the comfort of the doorway.

His body twitches. He recognizes me.

My eyes scan the room, one side heavy with the things that are distinctly my father, the other side clinical—like a hospital. The clutter of equipment that is supposed to help my dad gain his strength and practice his balance isn't set up to be used. Blankets hang from bars, and a walker holds old sweatshirts and jeans. Archie could be doing more than existing in this room. He's able to walk. That's the one thing that seems to be unaffected, the strength in his legs. Maybe my mom exaggerates it because she doesn't want him living down in the sitting room where he would be the first thing anyone would see. I don't really think she has suddenly taken on visitors, though. The truth is probably closer to her not wanting to see him when she walks into her home.

"I'm sure Mom's told you, but I've been here for a while." I continue to look around while I drag closer to the bedside chair. She's added to the collection of things for him to look at. They told her it was good for him to be surrounded by familiar things, but I think she thought it meant that he would suddenly be cured and snap out of his new normal.

Strokes don't work that way.

I fall into the seat and sink into its softness, leaning back and stretching my hands out along the armrests. Archie's eyes hit mine, and a jolt hits my chest. My eyes have found their mates.

"Hi, Dad."

It's only ever taken a subtle movement or two for my dad to express himself through his eyes. He could always get his way with just a glance—one that said he'd love you forever or another that warned someone to back off. He's frightened of me. His eyes are telling me he's afraid.

"I didn't tell her. I know that's what you're afraid of. But I didn't." I roll my eyes and shift in the chair, leaning to one side and resting my chin on my elbow. "She wouldn't believe me anyhow. She believes what she wants to believe."

His breathing never picked up, but his eyes dim a little and his body sinks deeper into the bed, his head rolling in the pillow. I'd tuck it up higher to prop his neck so he could see me better, but I don't really want him looking at me. He doesn't really care to look. Those things I said were all that mattered to him. The rest of this visit is just for me.

"I think I need to tell you how everything unraveled from my point of view, though," I begin, my eyes moving from him to a small thread at the end of the chair's arm. I touch it with my finger, then start to pick at it to pull it free.

"You never really cared about what that lie meant, about what it drove her to do in retaliation. You just knew that you couldn't let her know you were ever weak and felt something for someone. Not Archie Valentine."

His breath stutters a little. I've learned that's his laugh. His eyes fall shut and the little control he has of his facial muscles tugs at the cheek closest to me, drawing it up in disgust.

It doesn't take me long to mentally drift back to being twelve. I've told the story to therapists over the years, and it always falls from my lips in crystal clearness, as if it just happened a day or two before. I close my eyes and relive it, every single time.

When things started to dry up on the development side my dad had invested in, he and my mom turned to management through the gym as a way to dig themselves out of the financial hole they were falling into deeper by the bill. They owned the land, but the buildings were another story. They leveraged a lot to get work done, sometimes stiffing contractors. There were threats, too. I heard my dad bully people into jobs. By the time the gym was done, nobody was looking to build here, and the foot traffic he counted on for high-end clientele he could dazzle with his stories wasn't around to pay for memberships.

Fighters like Dad aren't common, though. This business is hard, and when you make money, it usually goes right back into training for the next step. There were a lot of decent mid-level guys that worked with my dad and Leo. They took a lot to Vegas, too, and sometimes they won.

Once you get greed in your veins, though...it doesn't ever leave.

"I sat there on those steps just outside this room, Dad, and I listened to you pour your heart out to a man who I know you loved. I listened to you beg him to stay, even though you and Mom had stolen everything from him. And you know what?"

My father's eyes flicker under their lids. If he rolls over to avoid me, I'll drag this chair to the other side of the bed.

"I was so proud of you. It might have been the first time that I was proud of you. I was proud of you for fighting for a person, not just yourself. I was proud to hear you admit to him everything terrible you had done. And I know it hurt that he left. I know it hurt like hell—it hurt you as a fighter who lost someone he believed in, and it hurt you as a human who loved another human."

That man's name was Charles. He had a decent future in fighting, and my dad was in love with him. My mom shaved money off every deal they made for him, though. My dad let it happen, because he was afraid. And when finances started to get tough again, she shaved a little too much. Charles noticed, and my dad, for once in his goddamned life, couldn't lie. He told him everything.

He sure found a way when my mom asked who told him, though.

"'Liv's always looking at the books,' you said. Do you remember that? I was playing office, imagining running something like this one day. I liked the numbers. Hell, I just fucking liked math. I didn't know what was really going on in those books. You could have said anything. You could have told her that he must have figured it out on his own. She wasn't exactly a surgeon at theft, Dad!"

His eyes slowly open on the ceiling, and I'm tempted to stand up to get a better view, but I don't need the confirmation. He isn't bothered by any of this in the least. He loved someone other than himself for a brief moment in time; other than that, he hasn't loved anyone since. I am simply just a casualty for careless behavior in his mind.

"Mom took the money Leo put in the bank for me, but she probably told you that. Technically, she had Leo take the money, but it's all the same. I'm sure you agree that she deserves it. Just like how she took away my college money when you told her I was the one who ran off your best client. That was my punishment for hurting the family business. State school, instead of fulfilling my dream. I could have gone to Stanford, or Duke or *any* school!"

Any school other than the one I went to that led me to Enoch. I ponder that last part, not wanting to say his name out loud.

I'm breathing hard now, thinking about the dominoes of my life and how they all fell one by one. My dad's mom was a decent woman, and she had set up a college fund for me. She was alive when they stole it, but too old and mentally fragile to do anything about it.

My dad was dazzled by Enoch, and my mom loved the way he talked about money. I begged them not to invest, because I didn't want them poisoning what was mine.

Irony is such a bitch, I guess. Enoch walked away with all they had and turned it into nothing. I looked at those contracts quickly today, and I fought every urge to grab them in my hands and run. The numbers I saw looked right, though. And I've been through the books, and I've fixed a lot of messes. Unless my mom or Leo has magically gotten better at covering up fraud, they haven't stolen from Memphis.

Maybe it's just that they haven't stolen from Memphis yet, though.

"I'm not coming up here to see you again," I say, standing and peering over my father's pale body, a fraction of the mountain it once was. His skin is spotted from sun abuse, and his hair is thin. My mom cuts it too short.

"Memphis is a great fighter, Dad. He's better than you."

I smirk and make sure he sees it. Once that jealousy and anger colors his irises, I'm satisfied.

"Everyone is going to love him, and he didn't have to screw a single person over to get where he is," I say.

There is no temptation to hold his hand, and no desire to embrace him and wish he'd suddenly be able to form his mouth into shaping words. There's just a shell of a man who screwed my mom and got her pregnant with me. And the little girl who used to dream that she'd have some magical relationship with him died right there in that room when he threw her under the bus to save his own ass.

The toughest champ alive is, in fact, a coward. He's afraid of the truth.

I step away from his bedside and move to the door, closing it behind me before I leave down the stairs. My uncle has returned to sitting at the kitchen table alone, and he toasts me with his newly refilled glass as I walk by. I don't even bother to comment. I've said everything I needed to tonight.

Now I'm going to wait for a better man to come home and visit a homeless veteran with me. I can't wait for it, in fact. I wear the smile all the way to my room at Leo's house, and then I wait by the window and pull out my phone to send Memphis a text.

*Liv owns this bitch.*

I type back the exact words I sent to myself from him, then I wait for him to respond.

*Liv owns a lot of bitches.*

I laugh loud, cupping my mouth and glancing out into the hall. Leo will be gone for a while. I stare at his words and think of the perfect thing to say. I type a few things that I delete, including letting him know that I visited my dad. Eventually I settle on simple.

*Liv owns just one.*

His response is almost instant.

*Guess I'm your bitch then.*

It's such an unromantic way to tell someone they're yours. It's utterly perfect, and lacks all traces of fairy tales. It's not how this awkward early flirting usually goes.

It's different.

Memphis is rare.

# CHAPTER TWELVE

Memphis

I could get used to pulling up to my home to find Liv waiting for me. She has something in her lap this time, and I swear to god if it's baked, or involves more than a single ingredient, I will marry her on the spot.

She stands as I shut off my bike, so I wait here for her. There's something about the way she walks. For a girl who's been knocked down so often, she doesn't show it in her body. Her steps toward me are bold and comfortable, and I'm grinning like an idiot by the time she reaches my bike.

"Why do I feel like you're making fun of me in your head?" She scrunches one eye, and I shake my head.

"I was just admiring the view," I say. The cheesy line earns me an eye-roll, but I'm still glad I said it. It's true. I was.

"What's in the bag?" I nod down to the small wrapped bundle in her hands. It's too small to be bread or cookies.

"Oh, I uh..." Her lips purse and she bunches her face in thought, holding the flat package in her palms in front of her and staring at it. She takes a deep breath.

"I went up to see my dad."

I let a second or two pass for her to feel the moment. I know how hard that was for her. It's been a roadblock.

"I'm proud of you," I say.

She chuckles a little.

"I'm not so sure you should be. I wasn't very nice."

Her eyes fall back down to the package in her palms, and my hand instinctively moves to her chin. I lift her gaze back up to mine, and I hate the shame cast in her eyes.

"Sometimes, we have to just say the shit that's on our minds, otherwise it poisons us. And I'm sure it wasn't as mean as it could have been, and maybe, it was a little nicer than he deserved," I say.

I run my thumb along the edge of her jaw and dip my head to smile at her softly. Wide eyes blink open on mine, shame still there, no matter what I say this time it seems.

"You didn't wear a helmet," she says, a change in subject I let her have.

"It was nice outside. I wanted to feel it." I shrug, knowing she'll be right about every response she's bound to have. It's reckless, and I know it is. So is this sport, though.

"Leo almost died on his bike when I was a kid. Some asshole on the freeway cut him off and he slid three lanes over and stopped when his tires tangled with the wire divider in the median. No helmet. You can still see the gravel scars around his right ear."

Shit. That's not the response I expected, but it sells her point well.

"Helmet from now on," I say, slicking my hair back from my forehead while stepping over the bike and closing the tiny space between us. My fingertips graze her bare elbows, still bent as she holds the mystery package. She's showered and changed since our workout, the ends of her hair still wet and thick in waves. She put on a black T-shirt and these white shorts that hang low on her hips and look like they belong on a beach just like she does.

"That have something to do with your visit to your dad?" I gesture toward her hands.

She offers a lopsided smile and then hands the thin bundle to me. It's wrapped in a folded page from a spiral notebook and a rubber band. I begin to slide it off as she explains.

"You're facing Omar Morales soon. My dad always saved his scorecards, and I got to thinking...Leo probably saves things too. My dad had a theory that a man fights the way the man behind him taught him to."

I start to flip through the stack of cards, none of them Omar's fights. I'm not sure I understand. Omar never trained here.

"I snagged one of the boxes up in his room on my way out, but I found most of these in Leo's files in the office."

My brow pulls in, still confused.

"Here, look." Her hands tangle with mine and I'm no longer really looking at the cards, just her—her hands, her arms, her body moving into position next to me. She's close, arm brushing against mine as she flips through cards. I should look at what she's doing; I should pay attention. She put effort into this because she felt it was important, but my God her hair is falling in her face and twists are sliding down her bare shoulder until it masks my view from everything.

I breathe.

She sweeps her hair over her neck opposite of me and tilts her head, her eyes meeting mine. There's the quiet laugh. And then the smile.

"Sorry, my hair is not cooperating today," she says.

"I like it, I mean..." I lick my bottom lip and bite the end of my tongue, laughing at myself. "I mean it looks nice."

A pink blush hits her cheeks, but just for a flash.

"Thanks," she whispers.

After a long quiet second or two, I clear my throat and look down at the cards again.

"Right, like I was saying. It's the same guys working with Omar. We've seen these guys a lot. Between my dad and Leo and the guys that have come and gone through this place, we probably have the mother-load of data at our fingertips. Unfortunately, we don't have a single technical soul in a ten-mile radius to do anything with the data, so I guess you'll just have to see what you see in these things. But I thought...well... these are the guys prepping Omar, and here's their history. Might help you better understand the man you're stepping in the ring with."

Her gesture puts a pause in my heartbeat, like a skip. Maybe it beat, but I didn't feel it because of feeling so much else right now here with this amazingly thoughtful woman.

"Is this dumb? Maybe it's dumb, but I don't know. My dad said he learned more by seeing where a guy liked to rack up his points than he did from anything. He'd look at these and then close his eyes and recreate the entire damn fight from numbers and rounds, and—"

"It isn't dumb," I cut in.

Her lips are parted and a little desperate for approval. She eyes me, suspiciously. She thinks I'm placating her, but I'm not. I'm awed by her for other reasons entirely.

"Really, I promise," I say, taking the cards into my hands completely and folding them together to bundle again with the rubber band. "I like it. I mean...I think it's a good idea. It was..."

I stumble because I don't want to belittle what she did, and calling it sweet feels like it does just that.

"Kind of you," I say, instantly knowing that wasn't the right set of words either, and maybe even worse than sweet.

"I mean, sweet. Or helpful...thoughtful. Fuck." I run my hand up my face and through my hair, leaving my palm on top of my head, fingers gripping at strands while my face heats up.

Liv's lips close and form a tiny smile that turns into a kiss on the corner of my mouth. She smells so damn good that I want to sweep her up in my arms and set her on my bike and throw the cards all over the parking lot, but I made a promise that I would wait for her to say when, and more importantly, for her demons to be put to bed, if at least not put on warning.

"Let me put these inside real quick, then we can check on Miles." I linger on her face for a beat, sliding steps backward gradually while I gnaw at the inside of my mouth looking for her flaw. I don't think there is one.

I drop them inside and grab both helmets, handing her one to wear and doing as I promised, I put mine on, too. It's a cool night, August slipping into September. The bite from the harsh summer heat isn't as smothering as it usually is, so the wind that hits us on our ride is exhilarating rather than painful.

Liv's hands hold at my hips, so when we pull up to a red light, I reach down and thread my fingers in between hers and slide her grip forward, to my stomach. Her head rests in the center of my back, her fit so natural. It's like my dad knew one day I'd find this bike and the girl that went with it.

I glance enough to the side to see her knee hugging my thigh, and I smile.

"Hold on," I say, punching it when her fingers grip at my T-shirt.

The streets are empty around this part of town this late at night. It's the reason so many homeless find their way to this park; fewer people to hassle them. I throttle down as we round onto the one-way street that's closest to where Miles normally is, and I roll to the curb so we can look closely.

"I can't tell if he's here," I say, after taking my helmet off and scanning the dark park for nearly a minute.

Liv's hands run along my shoulders, and her weight shifts until she's slid from my bike to the ground. She pulls her helmet off too and hands it to me. I won't let her walk through that park alone, so I kill the engine, rest the helmets on the seat, and pull the keys, gripping them in my right hand and taking her hand in my other.

"Something's wrong," she says, noticing just as I do. Miles is back where he usually is, but his chest is bare, and so are his feet. The closer we get, the clearer it becomes that he's been jumped, probably defending this stupid tree.

Miles told me once that people have to act a little crazy out here, even when they're not, to make people question the worth of messing with them. The problem with that is it's hard to sort out who is really having delusions and who isn't. The act just goes on and on, too, because getting mental health care out here is damned near impossible.

"I'm fine, Champ. Don't worry, it was just a setback and I've got some new things on the way." It's clear when Miles talks that his lip is swollen, and he's sitting enough in the light that I can see the red bruising on his eyebrow.

"You just wanted to look like me, I know how you are," I snigger, kneeling down as I joke. He's embarrassed, and doesn't want me to think in any way that he can't stick up for himself. It's the war hero in him.

"Hell, I ain't as ugly as you are, fool." His laugh is a welcome sound, even if it's eventually drowned out by his persistent cough.

"Yeah, yeah." I say, relieved to at least see the fresh bandages on his foot are still there. "I tell you what, how about until I need them, you hang on to these for me."

I fall to my ass and lift my foot up to pull my shoes off. Miles reaches for my hand to stop me, but I brush his attempt off. He doesn't have anything new on the way. He's going to *deal* with it; that's what that means. I can deal with riding home shirtless in my socks a lot more than he can survive out here like that for a night. I toss the first shoe at him and start unlacing the second one. My size is a little bigger than his, maybe by a half, so I make a mental note that the next time I come I need to bring another pair or two of socks.

"I'm leaving them here, so if you don't put them on, one of those punk-ass druggies you're always talking about is going to pick them up and I know you don't want that to happen to my Jordan-Eights," I say, standing.

Miles sneers at me, but after a few seconds, he starts slipping his injured foot into the shoe. It goes in easier than normal because of the size difference. While he starts the next one, I reach behind my neck and pull my shirt up over my head, tossing that in his lap next.

"Boy, you stop this. I don't need your damn shirt," he says, tossing it to the dirt next to him.

I shrug and push my hands in my pockets. I glance to Liv at my side and she gives me a crooked smile, her eyes scanning down to my feet. I move my toes up and down a few times, and she giggles silently before shaking her head.

"All right then, you give them my shirt if you want to. That one's just a Hanes, so no big. I'll see you tomorrow," I say, walking away without giving him any more time to argue.

Liv rushes up to my side quickly, fitting her hand back in mine, and I glance down at how natural and easy that was for her to do.

"You can't drive a motorcycle like that," she says, and I grin away from her. I thought the very same thing, only I'd already gotten Miles to take one of my shoes by the time the thought hit me, so I came up with plan B.

"I know," I say, my pace unchanged.

"Okay, so..." I know she's thinking what I'm thinking, but there's no way in hell she'll utter it out loud. She figures if she doesn't say it, it won't happen.

We get to my bike and I hand her my helmet. Her head tilts and her eyes narrow.

"Absolutely not," she says.

I shrug and start to walk back toward Miles. I get a few steps before I turn to face her, but keep walking backward.

"I'm not going to get my shoes back, just so you know. I figured if we're staying here, might as well be by the best damn tree in the world," I say, pointing over my shoulder.

I slow my steps when she huffs, and when she holds her hand out to take my helmet, I begin to drift back toward her.

"You'll do fine. It's just like riding a bike." I snort-laugh, and she punches my arm.

"Ow," I chastise.

"Well someone shouldn't have told me about balance and all that shit. Just show me what I've gotta do." She gets on the bike without pause and puts her hands on the grips, feeling around at the gear and leaning from side to side looking for something more to do.

"It's really that simple," I say, slipping the other helmet on and sliding down the shield on hers. If she's in front, I don't want her having anything interrupt her eyes on the road.

"Your gears are here," I tab next to her left foot. "When I tell you, you're going to squeeze right here and lift here with your foot," I take her hand underneath mine and we feel the grip of the clutch together. I show her where to shift, the best place for her to put her hands for the gas and brakes, and the ignition. Then I move to her feet, showing her how to hit the gears, something we can probably get away with only doing three times if we can hit the lights just right. It's a pretty simple bike, really. It looks like there would be more to it, but the rumble this baby makes is more bark than it is bite.

"That's a lot to remember," she says, turning to face me, her eyes lit up by the streetlamp. I lean forward and nudge my helmet against hers, so we're staring closely.

"It's two things. Maybe three. Now stop being a baby and drive our asses home." She glowers a little, but her lips hint at a smile, too.

I slide in behind her, my legs balancing the bike for us while I move my hands to hers one more time as a refresher.

"I will be right here. If you get nervous, ease up here, and we'll stop. Take an hour to go two miles if you have to." Her helmet-covered head nods, and I let her go through things again on her own as she mutters my directions back.

"You'll be fine," I say, closing the space between us. Her shirt has slid off her left shoulder, and her bronzed skin shines under the light. I'd kiss it if my damned helmet wasn't in the way.

I slow my breathing and let my chest rise and fall so she can feel it; eventually she mimics it in her own body. She turns the key and the bike rumbles to a start. She gives it just a touch of the gas to kick in.

"Good," I say, liking how it feels to hold her here, like this. She's so small against me right now, and all of those instinctual caveman things are filling my chest with this overwhelming need to hold her tighter. This is too dangerous to make her do, and she's too exposed. I should call us a cab, just leave the bike. Or call someone, Amy maybe, to come pick her up first. Hell, even Leo.

Without much warning, Liv squeezes the clutch and pops the gear and we're rolling.

"Shit, Memphis! Shit, shit, shit." Her body grows tense with her panic.

"You're fine; this is fine. Watch the road, and give it gas. We're gonna go up another gear," I shout over the motor's roar.

We cruise around the park, taking the corners at a crawl until we have nothing but green lights and a straight shot ahead of us.

"Shift and go," I say, but she doesn't go at first, and the bike feels a little wobbly under us.

"I can't, Memphis. I need to stop. How do I stop?" She's yelling, and her hands are feeling around frantically, so I lean forward and hold her arms, doing my best to steady with my weight.

"You're fine, Liv. Trust me, just give it some gas and find your balance," I say, waiting out the next five or six seconds while she looks for courage. The green lights ahead are stale, so I know she's got to hit the next gear now and punch it for us to get through this without starting all over.

"I've got you," I say, focusing on the feel of my chest filling with air, my body against her warm back, the small movements she makes that affect me.

"Okay. Hold on," she says, squeezing and moving up another gear, giving it a burst of gas that jets us forward a little faster than she wants. "Oh my God!"

"Just one more. Right now; do it now," I yell.

She does it without hesitation because at this point I think it's easier than stopping, and we sail through the first of four intersections. She's in a zone. All I do is hold her steady with my hands at her waist. My eyes are on the road as I peer just over her shoulder, and the white dashes of the lane striping are beginning to blur into solid as we pick up speed.

One more intersection down. The walk sign ahead is starting to flash, so I lean my chin over her shoulder, lifting myself a bit on the back pegs.

"You better gun it," I say, and she starts to turn her head to look at me, but flashes right back to the road.

I'm not sure if it's the vibration of the bike or her nerves shaking her hands, but it doesn't stop her. She starts to squeeze the clutch, so I sit down and focus. Her shift is smoother this time, and we don't jump forward or hiccup like we did the first time. The bike gains speed quickly, which means steering and balance are more important now. We fly through the final two intersections. I guide her through gearing down and braking, the bike slowing quickly until it's at a comfortable crawl that lets me help her guide it up the curb and into the back alley, close enough to my RV to leave it for the night.

She makes quick work of killing the engine, and she doesn't wait to pull the keys out before she crawls off the bike and pulls her helmet from her head, her hair matted with sweat and her knuckles white from squeezing so hard.

I pull my helmet off and grab the keys, kicking my leg over and taking her helmet, which she's desperate to give back to me.

"I am much better at riding on the back," she says.

"Oh, come on, you love the thrill," I chuckle. I walk to my steps and unlock the door, tossing the helmets inside on the floor before sitting on the top stoop and resting my hands on my knees. My socks are jacked, but it was worth it seeing her do something like that, something she probably never thought she could.

"I'm over thrills, Memphis. I'm all about sedans and seatbelts," she says, shaking out her arms and flexing her fingers to bring feeling back to them.

I laugh because she's cute when she's free. I lean back, my elbows resting on the floor inside my place, and I spend a few seconds admiring her until she starts to realize what I'm doing and guards her motions and words a little more.

"What are you looking at?" Her brow is pinched in the middle.

"I wish you could see what I see right now," I say, my eyes roaming down to her feet then back up to her bit lip. "There she is."

"Who?" she asks, twisted lips in a cockeyed smile.

I don't answer because there aren't really words for this moment right here. I don't want to ruin it with my small description. She doesn't need to hear it anyhow. She knows. It's the reason she's glowing, the reason her lips are cherry red and effortless in their smile. It's why her eyes are bright and wide, and her arms aren't folded around her chest, closing off the world.

Instead, I watch and wonder, letting my eyes focus on all of her little, nervous habits, and the small things that make Liv who she is. Nails that are bitten down to nothing, beads and string for bracelets, and a small tattoo on the inside of her wrist. Her hair has nearly dried, the twists tangled and a little wilder from being ripped in the wind under her helmet while we rode the bike. Her socks are short, barely there at all, and her legs are long and muscular and smooth, like she maybe thought about having them touched.

My lips settle into a comfortable smile when my eyes make their way back to hers. Her head tilted in suspicion, she's still blushing from the attention. I think she's worried I'm going to throw her back on the bike or some other thing she's never done just to watch her experience a first time.

She's right in a way. I am.

"Stay here with me. Tonight."

She blinks, but doesn't flinch, and her expression stays just as it was, her mouth pulled in on one side and one eye closed more than the other.

"I will be the perfect Boy Scout, and you can say *no* if you want, but if you do, I'm just going to sit here all night and look up there, waiting for a glimpse of you," I say, nodding up toward her window.

Her eyes stretch to the corners and she lifts her chin enough to glance at her darkened window.

I get to my feet and step up into the open doorway and reach out my hand.

"I'm getting up to run at four in the morning. If you want to, you can go back to your room then. Or..." My lips tighten into a more defined smile. "Or fuck them all, and you can just stay here...with me."

Her chin dips down as she sways side to side with indecision, her eyes at her shoes rather than on me. I'm practically ready for bed now, having given away my shoes and shirt, so I move back a little into the doorway and undo the button on my jeans. Her eyes lift at the sound of my zipper, and I chuckle knowing what she thought.

Commando.

"It's a rare boxer night," I say with a wink, showing off the top of my favorite pair showing from under my jeans.

She laughs without sound, then looks at me sideways, her spirit leaning forward, but her fear of judgment nailing her to the ground. Most of those headlines are months old. New gossip has taken over the rest of the world, but in this house, it's still her story that leads.

"Maybe tomorrow then," I say, hoping still, even as I lean against the small table behind me and prepare myself to say goodnight.

Her eyes flit down at the steps then come back to me, and her lips grow tight, a hint of her nerves in the dimpled corners. I count all seven paces it takes for her to climb up my steps and take my hand. Then I count the single second it takes for me to push the door closed behind her.

"Boy Scout," she says, blinking and waiting for my pledge. I hold up two fingers, not really sure if that's how it's done, but it makes my point.

I pull out the small wooden ladder that slides in the corner and hook it on the edge of the loft, then I take Liv's hand and help her get to the first rung so she can climb up on her own. Once she's cleared the ladder, I kick away my jeans and climb the bottom three rungs before lifting myself the rest of the way with my arms.

Liv's eyes are at my waist, slowly sweeping a line up the center of my chest. I can talk trash and fill my ego against tatted-up dudes that want to bust my head open, but one slow glance from her makes me feel vulnerable as hell. I'm not prepared for this.

Maybe I'm not as ready for this woman as I thought. She wasn't part of the plan. And I have absolutely zero control.

"Do you want one of my shirts? I have some up here," I say, reaching into the corner where I left the shirt I wore last night. I drag it toward me and smell, debating whether or not to get up and grab her a clean one, when she takes it from my hand and pulls it into her chest, breathing it in and closing her eyes.

My breath stops for just a few seconds, a tightness forming in my chest at seeing her mouth curve from something as simple as the feel and scent of my shirt. She's sitting with her legs folded, her head almost touching the roof of the camper.

"I'll look the other way," I say, turning on my hip until I feel her hand at my arm, stopping me.

My gaze flashes back to hers, surprised.

"It's okay," she says in a faint voice that I worry is coming from the wrong kind of nerves until she lifts the bottom of her black shirt up over a lacey bra. Her hair falls from above when she pulls her shirt away, landing over the curve of her breasts. My gaze drags, caught by her curves, but intrigued by her hands as they move behind her to unclasp her bra.

My eyes blink slowly and I tilt my head as her straps slide down her shoulders and her hands move to cover herself.

I should turn around. This isn't part of the promise, and I should turn around.

"Liv…"

"Shh," she hushes, in a long drag of her lips. They suddenly seem so full, and fuck, are they seductive as hell.

Her arms cross, opposite thumbs hooking under satin straps on her arms, dragging them down until the only thing that is left is her bare body in front of mine.

"Hold me," she says, in a voice so frail the breath runs out of it. "Like this. Just for a little while."

I nod and lower myself flat along the mattress that covers this entire space. The curtains were worn off long ago, but I doubt anyone can see through the dirty windows. The orange glow of the light is muted by them, and it somehow makes this beautiful creature look like she's touched by fire.

"Come here," I say once my body is stretched out diagonally, the quilt I've slept with at the group home bunched at my feet. Liv tucks herself against my bare chest, her arms folded into her body, and I wrap both of my arms around her, bringing her in tight. I feel like the gladiator protecting the maiden from a storm.

"I like it here," she says quietly, lips stopping when they're parted, to press a kiss to the center of my chest. I feel it dead center of my heart, cold like ice yet the burn of lightning.

My fingers slowly trace the curve of her spine, beginning at the small of her back and gently tickling their way up to her neck then back down. I soak in the smoothness of her skin, and my lips fall to the top of her head, kissing her as my touch drums both of us into a trance.

"Thank you for the cards," I whisper.

"Mmmm," she purrs.

I swallow carefully, not wanting to disturb this small little slice of heaven where I can feel her breathe against me, her heartbeat where our chests touch, skin scorching and forbidden tempting me. I could talk her into anything right now, but that's not how I want her. I don't want to talk her into anything, I just want it to be.

I strum her body for minutes in silence, moving to her hair, where my fingers drown in the softness, then feather it out against her skin before sliding it away. There's so much of her to touch that I'm content, though I'm gonna throw some hella hard punches tomorrow.

"My dad was a really good fighter, Memphis," she says, my hand maintaining its rhythm along her neck, then shoulder, then down her back again.

"He was one of the greats," I say, smiling lightly where she can't see me. I'm struck by her words—they're the first kind ones she's said about this man.

"I'm not quite ready to close myself off from the things that make me proud of him just yet. I think I'll hold onto those things for a little while longer," she says, and I stop my hand long enough to pull her in tighter.

My lips kiss the top of her head again before I cradle her under my chin.

"I think maybe you get to keep those things forever. The bad, too, if you want. But the good...that's what makes you happy," I say.

She nestles against me without words, but she hums lightly in what I think is agreement. Her breathing slows, and eventually my own breath chases hers. My eyes heavy, I give over to the late hour and the warmth of the girl in my arms, and I sleep so well that I never feel her leave.

But she does. Sometime before my phone alarm chirps urging my body to get up and run. There's an emptiness that settles in with her absence, and it hurts until I notice my shirt is gone, and her things— they're here.

# CHAPTER THIRTEEN

Liv

The next day, Memphis asked me to visit Miles with him after his training and before his work. I didn't leave his side until he was asleep. After four or five days of the same, he quit asking. I just came along.

He didn't always have work, and on the days he didn't, I'd watch him pull off miracles. At least, they seemed miraculous to me. He's jumped on top of boxes that I could rest my chin on, and he sprinted the basketball court down on Central about a dozen times in a row with seconds in-between to catch his breath. Then he'd walk a lap and drink water to do it all again.

Sometimes he pushes himself so hard he vomits. And sometimes he gets mad when he doesn't see a physical toll, like he's not pushing himself hard enough. I remember when my dad would train. I didn't get to watch much, but I got to see him work with Leo when I had no other place to go. Leo made my father vomit a lot.

His exhaustion means when he hits the pillow, he's out. Last night, I laid on him and watched his body move with every breath.

He dreams often, and his body twitches a little, but last night his muscles were still. I can see the effects of this final hard push. His muscle tone is like a suit of armor, and his speed—both in his feet and his hands—feels like it's doubled.

Every night, we both strip down almost completely, and I crawl under his heavy quilt that I've learned has been with him since he was ten or eleven years old. He never pushes for more, though I know he would take the invitation in a beat. He lets me dictate every step of whatever this is we are in. Somehow, because of that, I've been able to separate my two worlds—the brightness I live in with Memphis and the burden I clock in with in the morning.

Today, though, I can't seem to stay focused on paying the electric bill, filing quarterly taxes, or closing out August's books. He's dressed for his fight today, and Leo's brought in help. Seeing him with his name on his waist, his game face on...it scratches at a part deep inside of me, and no matter how hard I try, there is no tuning this out. Eventually, I give in and close the laptop and file of receipts and move out to the lockers where there's a carpeted bench made for this purpose—to stare in awe at people who can do things others can't.

I used to sit here and watch Archie.

"He's going to try to burn you out early, so don't take his bait," Leo says, circling behind the opponent he's brought in to play the part of Omar Morales.

When they go right, Memphis circles left, his feet weaving in easy steps, gliding like a hockey player on ice until one of them disrupts the pattern, faking and flinching. Sometimes, Memphis reacts, but most of the time, he remains smooth on his feet. He could go on like this for days, and that's the point.

"He might hit you. If he gets in a good shot, then that's on him, but you trust your defense. Don't fall in just because he says it's time; you tell him when. You get to say when it's time for you to fight, and when it's right, you hit him with those fucking bombs right there."

I smirk at my uncle's words. He's always had this passion for this part of the fight. He can make even the weakest boxer twice as strong simply by shouting a few things at him in the ring. His words stick, and they show up when a fighter needs them. A reminder to hold back, a lean to the right, a weak side—it calls up weeks of muscle memory behind the words in a blink.

"Come on, punk," Memphis's sparring partner says. "Whatchu got? Come on."

He jabs at him, and Memphis simply changes up his rhythm. Eyes of a hungry tiger circle the ring, his lids heavy, blocking out everything but the form in front of him. He sees his feet. He sees his fists. It's his torso, though, that gives away all of his secrets. If a fighter can conquer speed there, be faster at changing direction than an opponent, then he's got them.

They dance, trading light jabs to keep it interesting, and Memphis never falls for the trick. He gets hit once in the side, curving away from it to lighten the blow. He won't be hit hard now anyhow. It's too close to the real thing. His body needs to be peak.

While the fighters continue to circle each other, Leo steps in and says something in the other fighter's ear. He motions with his fist, pulling it in tight, unable to help himself from acting out his directions. Memphis doesn't waiver, though—his eyes stay narrow, distractions don't exist, in his mind, he's already in the moment.

"That your pussy over there?"

And in one breath, both Memphis's and my centers of strength start to crumble. Fake Omar pushes the one weak button Memphis seems to have—me. In doing so, he sends me right back to the beginning, where fighters live in one world and those of us who have living, beating hearts must survive somewhere else. We can't possibly live together because when we do, focus isn't perfect, champions slip up, and fragile feelings get swallowed by regret.

Memphis flinches just enough, his narrowed eyes suddenly open, and Fake Omar moves in on him, stopping before it becomes real.

My eyes flutter closed. I wish myself small, too numb to slink back into the office and close the door.

"That's what I was talking about, Memphis. You let *that* happen in Vegas and the next thing you see will be the side of the ref's shoes and a tilted world that might never come back in focus. Distractions...goddamnit I told you about the fucking distractions. You couldn't help yourself, though, could you?"

My eyes begin to sting with the welling tears. I feel dirty sitting here, the subject of this lesson, and I'm angry that Memphis isn't saying anything, even though most of me doesn't really want him to because Leo's partly right. I'm a distraction.

The heat beginning to turn my face red, I get up without offering as much as a glance toward the ring. I shut my office with my palm, careful not to slam it behind me. I tap the music app on my phone and turn the volume up as loud as I can without the sound becoming tinny. Then I open the computer and stare at the last line I completed before I took a break. I let my worlds bleed together, and now it fucking hurts.

There's no working after that, and if I did, I'd make errors I'd only have to reconcile tomorrow. Instead, I pretend to click around, then pause to make a dot in the margin of my receipt list. I perform, and eventually, the panic felt in my heart strikes away the need to cry. I hate this world, and I hate how easy it was for me to get sucked in.

A crashing sound echoes beyond the glass door of my office, and I only let myself sense it with my periphery. Leo's thrown the metal stool a bunch of times in my life. It may have been a few years since I've heard it, but I recognize it.

It's only a few more seconds before the office door flies open, crashing into a wire bookcase and tilting it enough to spill dozens of files on the floor. I could let this all hurt, or I could fight. I could box it out and let it be noise, because really, that's all it's ever been.

My eyes blink as I stare at a week of work tossed carelessly thanks to a grown man's temper tantrum.

"I just got those perfect, you fuck," I say, a little fire lit by my boldness.

"This isn't a game, Liv. You didn't need to come back here and mend your little, broken, fucking heart. You needed a job, good. We gave you one. You needed a bed. Fine, I gave you one. Don't fuck with business, though, Liv. This fight matters; it matters a whole lot more than your goddamned spilled files and your batting eyelashes that for some goddamned reason my fighter can't fucking ignore."

The only reason I look up at the end of his words is because he's pointing at me fiercely with his finger. My lips sneer automatically because it's so rude. And if a little smack talk can get in Memphis's head in here, then maybe Leo should be focusing on his fighter instead of me.

"One, I'm pretty sure you're over using the *F*-word, and two...those fucking files are keeping you from being audited, and I'm fairly certain you and I both know how much that's worth. So yeah, they're pretty fucking important."

My eyes level his. I take in the drunken tint of red in his whites, stains from tobacco on his teeth as he licks at the back of his mouth and twists his dry and wrinkled lips enough to silently growl at me.

*I'm stronger than I think, Leo.*

He doesn't bother to shut the door behind him, but he's never been one to leave without making a scene. He walks to the center of the gym and picks up the discarded stool and chucks it out the open garage door into the parking lot, one of the legs coming off and ricocheting into someone's hubcap.

"I need a break! You!" He spins on his heels and points at Memphis as he walks backward, feeling in his pocket for a lighter as he moves toward the parking lot behind him. "This isn't a day we can just quit and pick up tomorrow. We're out of time, so get your shit together in your head and we're going to dance until your feet fall off when I get back."

The handful of people in the gym watch Leo leave, but quickly go back to their workouts, not stunned by his outburst either, it seems. Fake Omar stands a few paces away from Memphis, staring at him with his gloved-hand held out. Memphis finally pounds his own glove on top.

"I'm sorry, man. He said to try rattling you with that, and I don't know. I didn't know it was something personal," the guy says.

"It is personal," Memphis interjects. "And it's fine. Whatever, I've got it under control."

The man purses his lips and stares at Memphis for a few long seconds before his eyes shift over to me. We both know that Memphis is lying. The guy leaves the ring, though, mentioning something in a softer voice about heading out to grab lunch. Memphis waves him off then slides down with his back against the corner, one knee up and the other leg straight out in front of him. His teeth move to his tape, and eventually he flings his glove off with enough force to bounce it out of the ring.

His chin lifts and his heavy eyes settle on me behind a desk, a dozen yards away. His tired eyes widen upon seeing me, and his chest lifts with breath, but never seems to fully exhale.

"Do you want me to leave?" My voice carries, and a few guys working at the heavy bag nearest to my office stop to watch. We're like a regular show, it seems. Stay tuned, boys—this soap is getting good.

My heart is squeezing with mixed emotions. I'm angry that Leo made me an example. I'm pissed he was right and that it worked. I'm mad that Memphis isn't able to shut me out, and I'm terrified that I'm not going to get to watch him fall asleep again tonight.

"No," he says, voice gravely and without much life.

His eyes blink slowly, and his head never moves from the fixed position it's in resting against the corner post.

"I'll shut the door...when Leo comes back. I won't watch," I say.

"I want you to watch." His response is fast, like he had it ready.

I turn in my chair and fold my arms over my chest, leaning back by pushing with my foot on an open drawer down low. I bounce a little by bobbing my leg, and I consider his request.

"You're making me a part of your training, like I'm a hurdle you have to overcome," I say.

"You are." The speed of his answers stings a little, and I wince.

"This doesn't work for me, Memphis. Not like this, and you know it." I stand up and move to the door, but by the time I get to it, Memphis leaps to his feet and swings his legs over the ropes, rushing to the door just in time to stop it with his foot, holding it open for me to have to listen.

"I'm not Archie, Liv. You have to have faith to know it. I think you know me enough to trust it. I've shown you who I am," he says, his head falling against the door, sweat-dampened hair falling over one eye.

"I'm not a hurdle." I inhale through my nose, keeping my mouth closed tight after I speak.

His jaw flexes as his throat moves in a slow swallow, his eyes dipping below mine briefly before coming back to challenge me.

"You are in here. In that ring back there, with your crazy uncle and his head games, yeah, Liv...you're a hurdle. Doesn't mean I want to get rid of you or block you out or choose fighting over you. Just means I need to know I can do my job—that I can win—with you in the room." He shrugs and shakes his head lightly.

"I don't have to watch. I wasn't planning on it, really. Watching you in the ring in Vegas would be like watching him—or like my mom watching him. The person it would turn me into..."

"You have to come. And you are not her just like I am not him, and you know that too." Memphis brings his left hand up to his chest, patting it on his heart twice then curling his fingers into a fist and squeezing. "I'm no champion at all if you're not there to see it."

I breathe out a short burst of a laugh, but grow silent when I meet his gaze and see how very serious he is.

Well damn.

My hand eases its grip on the door, and Memphis pushes it open, stepping into me in one smooth motion, just like he moves in the ring. His right hand slides up my neck and into my hair, his left hand claws at my jaw. His mouth covers mine without stopping to breathe, and he kisses me until I think I might float away. This kiss is aggressive. It's possessive in its very existence. My weight in his hands, he arches my back and bites at my lower lip, letting it slide from his grip slowly as his mouth morphs into a smile against my lips. His nose grazes along mine in a tickle, and his body exhales a low grunt, as though I've been conquered—my worries and apprehensions slain like a dragon.

"Oh," I manage to squeak out, sucking in my top lip to taste what is left of him. "Just so you know, my uncle is going to be pissed."

"Fuck your uncle."

His eyes burn into mine, and a sinister smile fills his face. After a second or two, he slides backward through the door, leaving his eyes on me until he reaches the locker area. He flips open his and pulls out his phone, typing quickly, then tossing it onto the metal shelf and jumping a few times in place before jogging back to the ring, climbing in and moving as if someone is in there with him.

He shadowboxes, his eyes as focused as they were before, but this time all he has to work with is the enemy he can imagine. He's fearsome, and he's flawless. And when Leo and Fake Omar walk back into the gym, Memphis isn't even out of breath, despite having fought a shadow for several minutes while my uncle sucked up his pride and came back before he was ready to.

I don't move to the bench like I did before, but I do watch. Memphis points his gloved hand toward me, and my uncle looks my direction, slowly flipping the toothpick in his mouth before slipping into a grin. He loves conflict, and he thinks breaking a man down will only make him stronger. He may be right about that. Only Memphis has already built himself back up from nothing. He's built himself into a champion. And for the next hour, he soaks up every weapon my uncle and Fake Omar try to throw at him, and he turns it into domination.

The way he moves brings me to my feet, and I'm unable to stay in my self-imposed cage any longer. I need to see him do it. My soul aches to watch him overcome every little thing my uncle can throw at him—the mind games, the speed—it's meaningless in his path.

There's just something about the way he moves...like a ghost.

Like a fighter.

# CHAPTER FOURTEEN

Memphis

There's a sixteen-year-old girl a few racks to the left of me, and she looks miserable. It must be homecoming. That's the only thing I can think of happening this time of year that drives mothers and daughters into a mess like this. The girls in my group home were always worked up over school dances, and one of my foster siblings practically pushed our foster parent into a nervous breakdown over it.

Homecoming, and dinners with potential sponsors with thousands of dollars on the line that I'm not entirely sure I want...or *need*. Two good reasons to be stressed.

The girl has tried on about a dozen dresses, some short and too tight—as in I would never be okay with my daughter wearing that—and some that belong on a wedding cake...from the nineteen eighties.

I'm waiting on a dress I ordered online. The store put it on hold, but now no one can seem to find it. I used the few pieces of clothing Liv left at my place to pick out what I hope like hell is her size. I went plain and comfortable. The dress is gray, and all that I really cared about was it had those thin straps on the shoulders. If I get lost at all during this dinner tonight, I plan on finding home right there on Liv's skin. I think the trail of freckles on her left shoulder might be my favorite constellation.

"Every dress is too small, Mom. Even the big ones. And I don't have a date, I'm going with Hannah and Taylor. I feel really stupid because everyone is going to know I just got dumped. Let's just forget it." It's impossible not to hear her monologue.

She's sixteen, heartbroken, and as a result, insecure. I've been there. Only I never had a parent to take me somewhere nice to pick out clothes. I had Sister Monica, and the St. Vincent de Paul Thrift Store on the corner, where—for as long as I can remember—I got new slacks and a decent white-collared shirt at the start of every year.

"This one looks amazing on you, Sam. Please...at least get the dress so you're ready, if you decide to go..." Her mom stops abruptly, reaching into her purse for her phone. She holds up a finger and moves to the front of the store to hear better.

Somewhere in that time, the girl's gaze has found me. When I turn back to keep spying, I'm hit with a crinkled brow and a slight death stare. My crooked smile sets her a little at ease, so I glance back at her mom, then move a little closer so I don't have to shout.

"Your date is going to be knocked on his ass when he sees you in that," I say, and she looks down, dragging her hands along the skirt that sways out ending just above her knees.

"He uh...we broke up," she says, her gaze still down at the skirt of the dress.

I exist in a world where I get an edge by tearing the other guy down. It might be nice to lift someone up.

"Well then, you should *definitely* get that dress. Dude's gonna feel sorry as hell watching you have a good time without him."

And just like that, her eyes flit up and her mouth curves.

"I found it, Mr. Delaney. I'm so sorry for the wait," the clerk says as she weaves through a line of formal dresses back to me.

"No problem at all. My girl is going to love this dress, but if you couldn't find it, I was gonna see if you had that one in her size," I say, nodding over my shoulder to my teenaged friend.

Not in on my plan, the clerk awkwardly nods and smiles. It's enough, though. I don't look back until I'm nearly out the door, but her mom's returned, and they're both smiling.

I bank the good karma all the way home, stopping at the coffee shop to pick up Miles's favorite donuts. I drop them off with him at the park, and give him a peek at the dress I chose, maybe just needing one other person's approval since Liv has no idea it's coming—let alone what it looks like. His reaction is a little more than I expected, though; I think maybe he's been drinking today. His whistles are loud, so I take off before his pervy side comes out.

Leo's waiting in the gym when I walk in, so I check the clock on the wall. I'm not really late; I'm right on time. And technically, buying a dress is business, so just as his mouth starts to fly off the handle with my lack of dedication, I cut him off completely, walking straight into Liv's office and closing the door behind me.

"Shit," she startles. "Umm, you still get to knock, okay?"

My lips tighten for a smile. I'm actually excited to give this to her. Fuck me if she hates it.

"Cinderella? Meet your gown," I say, resting the box on the less-messy side of her desk.

She stares at me suspiciously for a few seconds while her hands work at removing the lid, and I can tell when she starts to piece together what's happening. We haven't talked about the dinner once since the big blowout with Angela. There wasn't a need, really, until there was a date. Angela gave it to me yesterday, again insisting she come along. I dismissed the idea and ordered this dress, which Liv is now lifting slowly in front of her, holding it by the two thin straps that I've already imagined over her shoulders.

"A woman helped you with this, didn't she? Come on; you can tell me," she says, and I exhale.

"This is all me. Well...it's really all *you*, but it just looked like it belonged on you I guess. I knew it when I saw it," I say.

Her thumbs and fingers rub the fabric, which is soft and well worn, just as I knew she would like it. She lowers it back into the box carefully, recovering the lid with a soft smile painted on her lips.

She likes it.

"I guess this means I have to go to a dinner party, huh?" Her mouth quirks up on one side, and I'm not looking forward to the part I have to say next.

"Good news, though," I say.

She cocks her head.

"It'll be over soon." My voice rises at the end, and I wait for her to get it.

"Tonight?" She doesn't quite shout, but there's a hint of surprise... maybe frustration in her tone.

"I know, I know. I'm sorry, I just got the date yesterday," I say, scooping up her hand and playing with her fingers, trying to distract.

I fail. She takes her hand away.

"So that was before I fell asleep at your place—after we sat up until two in the morning talking. So much talking, Memphis. Somewhere in there, maybe an 'Oh, and that dinner you're dreading is *tomorrow*.'" She rolls her eyes and falls into her seat at her desk, scooting back a few feet.

"To be fair, you never fall asleep at my place." That one wasn't nice, and I feel sick for saying it the instant the words hit the air. Her eyes droop, and the fact that I made them look that way stabs at my side.

"I didn't mean—" I start to apologize, but she cuts me off.

"What time should I be ready?" she asks, sliding her chair back into its place at her desk then turning her focus on the computer in front of her. She's mad.

"Liv," I say, about to step toward her. She stops me again.

"Time, Memphis?" she says.

I pinch the bridge of my nose and think about waking up every morning. Just once, I'd love to wake up and have her still be there.

"Seven. We need to leave at seven," I say.

"You need to rent a car," she answers, leaning back and tapping a pen on a notepad in front of her a few times before glancing at me one last time. "I'm not wearing that beautiful dress on your...*Commando*."

My mouth ticks up on the right, and even though she doesn't smile back, I see the playfulness dust her eyes. As satisfying as that is, though, it's not crystal clear. I'm never going to be vague with this girl.

"I'll get a car," I say, pausing at her doorway, pulling the handle closed with me, but stopping to say one last thing before I leave to let her uncle rip me a new asshole for four straight hours.

"Hey Liv?"

She looks at me sideways, her hair twisted at the base of her neck and held in place by a pencil. When I get the attention of her pale, blue eyes, I hold onto it for a few seconds because sometimes, it's good to feel lucky.

"When I wake up, and you're already gone..." I say, noting the way her eyes fall just a little, a hint of a dent above each brow. "I just really wish you were there is all. That's why I said that."

Her skin evens out, and sad eyes look a little frightened, but there's also something in them that looks excited, too. I nod lightly and close her door the rest of the way. I don't let her or dinner enter my head again until my body has been fully spent and every move Omar Morales knows how to make is imprinted in my brain.

---

THE ONLY THING really fueling my exhausted body for this dinner is seeing Liv in that dress. That and the New York strip I intend to put away with a second helping of...another New York strip. I get how vampires feel now. This level of hungry is something I've never experienced. I've never worked this hard for a fight. The stage is so big, though, that I want to make a statement.

I need to make a statement.

Vegas comes with odds. Not that the local fights don't, but the odds are almost more important than the glory when it comes to fighting in Vegas. Right now? I'm the underdog. It's actually right where I want to be, too, because whether he realizes he does or not, Omar Morales has started to think of me as the underdog too.

He's training right now. He's putting his body through the same regimen it's experienced a dozen times. I'm the new kid; he's the king whose crown I intend to take. But he's the favorite, which means his hunger...it's not as rabid as mine.

It gets harder to stay hungry when you're on top. That's why I don't believe in a ceiling. When I defeat Omar, there's a bigger title in my sights. And when I conquer that one, I want the world. When the world comes, defending titles are next, and I will defend until my death.

For now, though, I am helpless. No one has ever shown me how to tie a tie. I can usually get away with it, but this place—El Carbon—is strictly jackets and ties. I feel like I'm choking every time I put my head in this noose.

"Gah!" I give up on my last attempt and leave the ends undone on either side of my neck. I grab the jacket I bought along with Liv's dress, and slip my arms in the snug fit. Everything I'm wearing is gray —the suit dark, the shirt light, and the tie somewhere in-between. Miles actually taught me that. "A big man can't go wrong in gray," he said. I think he suggested it sometime after I dripped ketchup on my shirt from a burger we shared in the park.

I run my palms under water in my bathroom sink and comb my fingers through my hair a final time.

"This is as good as I get," I mutter to myself, lowering my eyes and meeting myself in the mirror. With my head turned slightly to one side, I draw my lip up and smirk at myself—in a gray suit. I think maybe Robert Delaney would be proud of his boy right now.

I feel fucking dapper until I step out my trailer door to see a goddess waiting for me. Everything about her is so simple, and that's what makes it perfect. Her hair somehow seems longer like that, over her bare shoulder. She's golden, even more so thanks to the setting sunset reflecting all around. Her bare neck and the hint of her breasts is going to draw every man's eyes one direction, and I can't even be pissed off about it because holy damn, this woman.

"Wow," I say.

I roll my shoulders back and let my free hand sink into my pants pocket while my other holds the jacket over my shoulder. My head shakes slowly as my grin spreads, and all I can do is lean into my doorframe, cross my ankles and appreciate her.

"Stop gawking. It's uncomfortable," she says, chewing at the inside of her cheek.

"I can't, Liv. Goddamn."

Her eyelashes bat nervously, and her gaze flits to me briefly before falling down to the skirt of the flowing, silky dress that she gathers in her fists and squeezes.

"Thank you," she whispers.

I jump from the step of my place, pulling the door closed behind me, and Liv starts to sway her skirt from side to side as I get closer. My hand gravitates to her chin, and I coax her head up just enough to look right into her eyes as we stand toe to toe.

I don't have cheesy words to say. I'm not going to kiss her. I'm only going to look at her this close to me with nobody around to interrupt us, and I'm going to appreciate every breath I get to have her—right like this. Her hands climb up my chest until each is gripping an end of my tie, and she tugs lightly while letting her head fall and her lip tick up.

"You need a little help, champ?" she teases.

I nod with a light chuckle and helplessly let my hands fall to my sides.

"It may as well be a bandana the way I tie it," I say, noticing how wrinkled it's become from my pathetic attempts.

"Let me show you the trick," she says, pulling the tie from my neck and wrapping it around her own. "Watch carefully. This one is long, and it travels here...then here."

I'm not paying a damn bit of attention to her hands and the tie; I'm too far gone looking at her lips move. She bites the bottom one when she concentrates. I've seen her do it in the office when she doesn't have a pencil to chew. Her eyelashes flicker, like a humming-bird's wings, while her eyes dash from one movement of her somehow perfect fingers to the next. Her skin looks so soft, and she smells so good, like the beach and summer.

"You get all that?" she asks, looking up into my eyes as she slips the finished tie from over her head then loops it over mine, her hands working at my collar to put it in place.

"Absolutely not," I chuckle lightly, giving her a guilty, crooked smile.

Her lips draw into a tight, closed-lip smile, she folds my collar over the tie and straightens it in the center of my neck. It's still a little constricting, but I don't dare adjust it. As far as I'm concerned, it's perfect.

"You got a car, right?" Her eyebrows raise just before she glances to my bike, then down to her skirt. It's the first time I notice her feet, and the silver toe ring that shimmers from a diamond stud through the woven straps of her shoes. I like the way they crisscross and lace up her leg.

"I was thinking you could drive it again to get us there?" I wait for the brief second it takes for her to realize I'm kidding, and then I manage to catch her fist in my palm before it nails my arm.

"Yes, Liv. I got a car. It's parked out front," I say, holding my arm out like a proper escort.

She glowers at me for teasing her, but slips her arm through mine, and I press her palm down flat against my bicep. We're running a few minutes late, but I don't give a shit. There is nothing I plan on hurrying right now, even walking a beautiful girl through a dirt alley in ninety-four degrees.

When we get to the sedan I rented for the night, I open her door and help her gather the skirt of her dress, noticing the small bag clutched around her wrist almost like a bracelet. It looks old, the outside covered with pearl-colored beads, some of them a little yellowed from time. She follows the trail of my eyes to it and turns it in her hand, pulling the strap from her wrist.

"I don't have a lot of purses, so I stole this one from my mom. She used to let me hold it when I was little," she says, shrugging and looking at the bag as she runs her thumb over the beads. "It made me feel grown-up back then."

I smile and wait for her to look up at me.

"It suits you," I say, somehow knowing that the small purse is one of those good things she's holding onto. A sad smile hits her cheeks, and she mouths *thanks*.

I round the car and lay my jacket in the back seat, then climb in next to her. This is the second time I've had something big like this happen. The first was when Omar's people requested a sit-down to set something up. I let Angela and Leo do the talking for me, which was probably wise. But this—someone like Fuel wanting to tie themselves to me, to consider my brand worthy of theirs—this is big, and it's something I have to take the reins on.

I'm nervous.

My hand pauses on the gearshift, my elbow on the center console, and I glance up to catch my reflection in the rearview mirror as I exhale methodically, like I do before a fight. Liv's hand is soft; it glides over my own, and I open my palm so she can hold my hand completely, squeezing it while I breathe just one more time.

"You've got this," she says. I lay my head sideways on the seat back to look her in the eyes. They steady me somehow, and my heart slows with the rise of my chest. The rise of hers.

"Can't we just stay here," I breathe out. I almost mean it.

Her blink is slow, and she shakes her head in tiny movements.

I look down and exhale one more time before moving my eyes back to the roadway, a little less nervous than before. I turn on the car and drive us to the most expensive dinner I will ever have.

The valet takes the car as soon as we pull up, and all too quickly Liv and I are inside and being led to a table by the windows, overlooking the city's sports district. Angela requested this table, I'm sure of it. She once told me that part of selling yourself is selling where you're from. I'm not really from anywhere, but I guess I'm from Phoenix now. The glitz of the billboards, rush of people, and thump of bars and restaurants lining the arena and stadium make *this* look bigtime. And *this* makes *me* look bigtime.

"Let me guess...you must be Memphis?" Paul Wolseley is short, but he's made up for height with muscle. His jacket and shirt are both rolled up at his elbows, and his arms are red from the loss of circulation. He's just as uncomfortable in a suit as I am. Maybe that's the reason he's led off with such a flat joke that I can tell Liv is having a hard time faking laughter for.

"Nah, man. I just handle the books. This here is Memphis," I say, pointing with my thumb to Liv at my side. This time her laugh is genuine. She knows I'm only making fun of him.

Paul pauses for a second and draws in his brow, but then it fades away as he laughs with us.

"Ahhhh I get it. Funny guy," he says.

I think maybe Paul Wolseley is a douchebag, but I'm going to hold out judgment...at least through dinner.

"I'm Cadence," says the woman to his left, reaching across the table to take Liv's hand. Cadence looks to be about Liv's age. Paul, on the other hand, is fifty-four. I know he is, for a fact, because before this dinner, I researched him.

"Nice to meet you," Liv says, shaking Cadence's hand a lot harder than the woman probably anticipated.

We all take our seats and Paul ushers over a waiter who lists off a bunch of different things, none of them steak, and before I can open my mouth, the Fuel CEO places all of our orders. I'm almost dizzy by the speed at which it all happens. What's worse—I'm pretty sure he ordered fish. I fucking hate fish.

"It's the tilapia with jalapeño glaze...it's to die for, I swear. Best thing on the menu," Paul says, leaning in as if he's telling us all a secret.

Before I can open my mouth, I feel Liv's leg brush against mine.

"Memphis is actually on a pretty strict training program, and his diet needs to include red meat tonight..." Liv smiles with gritted teeth and hunches up her shoulders in a gesture of apology for stepping all over Paul's order.

"Oh...uh...sure. Duh, I mean," Paul says, laughing loudly and getting the attention from the dozen or so tables around us. "I'll get the guy. Hey..."

He waves his hand catching our waiter across the room, and before Paul can talk to pick out something else, Liv steps in for me and orders the strip steak, and one for her, too. Paul looks a little offended when she changes her order.

"She always gets the same thing when we go out so I can have half. It's a sacrifice she makes," I say, winking at her.

It seems to satisfy Paul, and it earns another obnoxiously loud laugh from him that might haunt me in my sleep.

There's a brief awkward silence after the waiter leaves, So far, this dinner has me leaning toward a hard *no* for linking myself in any way with this man. His company's name is on the center of every ring I've ever fought in, though, so I owe it to myself to see what I can stomach.

"So Liv..." he begins, leaning on the table with his elbows, twisting the gold watch around his wrist to let his hands breathe. Everything this man wears is so tight.

"Mmm," Liv reacts, her tiny purse in her lap and her thumbs obsessively running over the beads.

"Archie Valentine's daughter...that must have been some life, huh?"

Everyone is looking at Liv, and that's the only reason Cadence and Paul don't notice the sharp breath I take through my nose and the heavy fall of my eyelids as he starts things off by entering into really messy territory. I want to rescue her from this.

"I tell you what, it's something, training there...at that gym. Leo's pretty intense." I try to steer the conversation, but Paul has tunnel vision. Part of it is her beauty, and I know it is. Paul is the kind of guy who wants the greener grass on the other side. He has a date—a *young, beautiful* date. But I brought Archie Valentine's daughter, and she's the most beautiful thing in the room. And he wants her. Her attention, at the very least.

Her *undivided* attention.

"Did you get to see a lot of his fights? I mean, I'm not sure how young they let you go in. I heard the Atlantic City years were bloody, but your dad was this godlike fighter and he just wouldn't go down." Paul pauses, waiting for a reaction from Liv, and I notice her leg starting to bounce under the table.

"I didn't really see the fights. I was busy going to school, and I never traveled with them when they would go." She keeps her answer simple, leaving out the gruesome things I'm pretty sure she did see there in the gym.

"Huh, too bad. That was history, you know," Paul says, glancing to me and gesturing to Liv. "That's some girl right there— boxing royalty. Ha, I bet the kids at school never fought you, did they?"

He laughs a little less loudly this time, and Liv plays along.

"No, I was pretty much left alone," she says. Paul is hearing what he wants to hear from her, but I hear the undertone in what she's saying. She's not really lying—she was pretty much left alone. And I know her well enough to see the sadness cast in her eyes in that response.

"Memphis, check this out...I remember this one radio interview he did, when he was talking about how he had a daughter, and he made this threat to any guy who ever dated her that they'd have to go through him. Imagine now, huh? Did you have to fight him to bring her as your date?" Paul's question lingers for a few awkward seconds while Liv's attention is turned to the waiter pouring a glass of water. She begins the drink the moment he's done.

"I would never fight Archie Valentine," I answer, not knowing any other way to respond to this line. First of all, the man can barely leave the bed, let alone the house. And second, I'm not so sure defending his daughter's honor is a priority.

"I bet it was awesome growing up with him, huh? I bet you got just about anything you wanted, and then you had this dad you could show off at school who looked like frickin' superman, haha." Paul's obnoxious laugh is like a punctuation for everything out of his mouth.

Liv swallows her water so hard I hear the gulp. She lifts the napkin from her place setting and covers her mouth to cough, then pulls her lips in tight and raises her eyebrows.

"He was an amazing dad. You pretty much nailed it," she says, and I slip my hand to her shaking thigh to settle her.

"You must have some great stories. Go on...give me one time where it was cool having Archie as your dad," Paul requests.

His enthusiasm is ridiculous, as is his obsession with Liv's dad. But there are a lot of people like him out there. Archie was the last of his kind in many ways—this huge personality in the ring and on the air before fights. His face was so recognizable with the hard-cut jaw and muted blue eyes; his build was thick and impossible to knock down. He was heavyweight in every sense of the word.

"Paul, I was curious about how you got your start with Fuel?" I try one more time to redirect this, but Liv's already given in to sacrifice. Before Paul has a chance to take my side trail, she begins to dazzle him with exactly what he wants to hear.

"I remember once when he was coming back from a fight on the East Coast, and I was at school. We had a nanny, and she was taking care of me while they were gone. Anyhow, I was sitting on the steps waiting for the nanny to show up with my lunch, because I'd forgotten it that day, and there were these mean boys who were teasing me about not having lunch and all of those dumb things kids do to make other kids feel bad and whatnot. Anyhow, I blinked, and all of a sudden my dad pulls up in this huge truck that he just bought after winning the fight in Atlantic City. He rushes to me, picking me up and swinging me at the steps, telling me he's taking me out of school for the rest of the day and we're going out for pizza..."

Paul is riveted. I feel sick. Liv is lying.

"You know those boys totally wanted to go, but I whispered in his ear that they had been mean to me," she says.

"Oh my god, what did he do?" Cadence pipes in, now invested too.

Liv smiles with tight lips and leans back in her chair, her leg no longer bobbing. She's either given over to the lie, or she's so pissed she's actually crossed over to calm.

"Nothing," she says.

"Nothing?" Paul can't believe it. None of it is true anyhow, so she may as well make this story go the way she wants.

"Exactly," she says. "He picked me up and carried me into the office, signed me out, and then drove me away in his big-ass truck."

Both Paul and Cadence are mesmerized, eyes wide in wonder and slight smiles pasted on their lips.

"'Some people just aren't worth fighting,' my dad said." Liv finishes her tale just as a basket of bread is delivered, and she reaches in and takes the largest piece, breaking off a bite and putting it in her mouth because she is done talking now.

"Amazing," Paul says. "Just...isn't that amazing?" He brushes his date's arm with the back of his hand to make sure she's as amazed as he is. She seems to be.

We spend the rest of dinner hearing about Paul and his rise to the top of the sporting-goods empire, but every now and then, he slips in more questions about Liv's dad. She keeps the answers vague for the most part, and by the end of dinner, I can tell that the lies have drained her. I want her to give them all back, to never have told them. I want to reverse even more and say *no* to this dinner. And I want to make that lie she told true—because I think deep down that's what she always wished for—and I hate like hell that it never happened for her.

It never happened for me either, but at least I never had the world's imagined reality to live up to. Not having a dad in my life means nobody is ever going to ask for glory days stories about my blissful childhood.

After nearly two hours of bullshit, Paul is drunk and tired, and he's also ready to offer me a deal that I don't deserve. I manage to get him and Cadence into a cab without any more business talk, though, and I beg the valet to rush our car out so I can get Liv out of here.

"I'm so sorry," I murmur as she stands at the curb waiting with me, her hands fists, one clutched around her tiny bag, both of them at her sides, arms stiff like a soldier.

Liv's eyes are lost to some other dimension, her face void of emotion. She's staring into nothingness in that way that makes colors and lights blur together, and she doesn't snap out of it until the car rolls up right in front of us.

I open her door and shut it for her after she gets in, tipping the valet and rushing to my side because I just don't want to leave her alone. I begin speaking the moment I close the door.

"Liv, really...I'm so sorry. I should have left when he..."

"It's fine," she cuts in.

That word—*fine*. It is never fine. It's always anything *but* fine.

"No, it isn't. That guy was obnoxious," I say.

"He was." Her response is clipped.

"I don't need to take this deal. I was already uneasy with it anyhow, and there is going to be something better for me down the road, and..."

"Memphis," she says, her eyes still ahead...lost. "You have no idea how many times I've had to pretend that life in the Valentine house is amazing for people. I've done it for fans. I've done it for the media. I had to do it for my mom when I was little because I thought if she was happy, then I would be happy. When I say it's fine, I swear I mean it. It's fine."

I let her words sit there for the few minutes it takes to drive; the quiet in the car hangs thick as we wait through two stoplights on our way back home. I can't just let this be it though—I can't let her do that for me ever again. I promised her I am not her family, that I'm nothing like Archie, Leo or her mom, and if I go on with this story she's put out there—that her life was amazing and that she is fine—then I'm breaking that promise, because it's exactly the thing they would do.

I pull the car into Leo's small driveway, and I kill the lights and engine so all that's left is dark and silence.

"No, Liv. I mean it," I say.

She sighs.

"You aren't fine. That...was not fine. And I don't need a sponsor-ship deal from that obsessed fan man. He'll want to have dinner again someday, and next time he'll want you to tell him more stories, and you'll feel like you have to because of money, and frankly Liv, I've been fine with very little so far."

Her head rolls to the side and her eyes meet mine. A gaze that begins as blank fills as her brow pinches, making that sad wrinkle on her forehead.

"Next time," she whispers.

I shake my head and shrug, not sure what her argument is. She swallows and slowly licks her lips as her mouth parts and a tiny breath escapes.

"You said *next* time, as if I would be there with you, as if there is an *us* that goes into tomorrow, next week, next—"

"Liv," I stop her rambling. We sit like this, my head turned to face hers, inches of actual space between us, but somehow it feels like a mile because there's no way for me to easily pull her into my arms in this goddamned car.

"I said next time because that's the only way I see things for you and me. I don't know what you are, what *we* are—I don't think we're supposed to put a word on whatever this is. But it is something. I close my eyes at night when you're there and I don't think. I just sleep, like the calmest fucking sleep of my life, and when I wake up and you're gone, I feel..."

I draw my lips in tight and shake my head, the feeling scratching at the inside of my chest—just like it has the last few mornings.

"Liv, I feel so goddamned alone when you aren't there, and it's weird because I have never felt alone once in my entire life. I was born that way—*alone*. And then I met you, and..." I breathe out a laugh and roll my head back against the seat, looking up at the car's ceiling before closing my eyes to remember.

"You walked into your uncle's kitchen, all pissed and surprised and funny, and it was like...yeah...I know this girl. Something inside me knows her, like her world gets my world, and we're the only two that get any of this crazy shit. I can tell you my worst, and you don't even blink. And you tell me yours, and all I want to do is make it better. I don't think anyone else will fit you like I do, Liv. And I don't care how punch-drunk that makes me sound, it's the truth. I know it because I don't think anyone else will fit me either."

My eyes fall open after my last word and I roll my head to the side again. I don't think Liv's eyes have moved from me once, and she looks terrified. I don't know what I'm supposed to do here. She looks so scared, but she looks so broken at the same time. I've never wanted a girl so badly in my entire life. I want Liv—I want her heart, I want her body, and I want her goddamn crazy shit, too.

"I just wanna quit waking up so sad in the morning, Liv. I don't think I can do that anymore. Part of you isn't enough. It...it isn't even close." I breathe in slowly and hold my chest full as my mouth rests in a tired smile. We stare at each other for what feels like minutes until Liv rolls her head back to face the front, pausing for a few seconds before turning toward her door, pulling the handle, pushing it open, and exiting the car.

When it closes behind her, I feel like I've been given a shot of morphine—shivers run down my spine, my heart throttles, and my head feels light. The panic lasts only a few seconds though, because Liv doesn't leave. She stands there, just outside the car, arms folded, purse clutched, shoulders hitched high, and the warm night breeze wrapping her dress around her legs.

I exit on my side and watch her over the roof of the car. When I shut my door, she turns to face me, and our eyes lock. My steps are slow and cautious, and I work to unravel my tie as I slowly round the front of the car; Liv's body turns with my movement so she's always facing me. Once my tie is undone, I undo the top button on my shirt so I can breathe, unsnapping the cuffs next before I push the sleeves up my arms.

This is where I should stop—here, four steps away...maybe three. I should make sure that she doesn't really want to run, but what if she does? If she ran now it would leave a scar. I'm in deep, and Liv has the power to sink me mentally, but I know none of that matters right now. I meant what I said to her in the gym the other day. I am no champion if she isn't there to see it. If I don't have her, then what is it all for?

I close the gap between us to three steps, then two, reaching for her face with my hands as feet become inches and when my fingers touch her skin, I know there is no going back now. My mouth takes hers and my hands fall deep into her hair as her fingers claw at my shirt, pulling my body closer to her as she stumbles back on her feet. I catch her, sweeping one hand behind her neck, my lips not leaving hers once as I reach my other hand under her legs and scoop her into my arms.

I carry her to my modest home, holding her to me, kissing her just outside the door, my feet on the bottom step, and the only thing between us and my bed is a damned door I could easily kick down right now.

My grip loosens enough for her to slide from my arms to her own feet, and I lift her to the top step, pressing her back against the door, my forehead against hers, leaving only enough room for me to be able to look down at the few inches between us.

We're both breathing hard, but it's not exhaustion. My hand sinks into my pants pocket, desperate for the key to my house, and I fumble it, nearly dropping it to the ground as my mouth finds hers again. My knees bent to lower myself to her level, I kiss her raw as she tilts her chin up. I stand tall, and I blindly find the lock and open the door, spinning my way inside with Liv's taste on my tongue the entire time.

We both kick away our shoes, and as she sinks her hands inside my button-down shirt, pulling free the buttons and tugging up on where my undershirt is tucked, I slip my thumbs under the thin straps I've become obsessed with on her shoulders.

The weight of her dress tumbles to her hips, sliding from her wrists as soon as I move the straps over the curve of her arms, and Liv wriggles the rest to her feet.

I lift her under her arms as her cold palms touch my cheeks, her mouth panting and her lips brushing against mine with stuttered breaths. Our kiss breaks as I raise her as high as I can up onto the loft bed and lift myself right after her. She's caged beneath me, between my arms as I move over her and she slides back, arching until her breasts brush against my chest, causing her to moan.

I've held her like this for nights, and I've always obeyed the line I let her draw, but I obliterate it now with her permission, my mouth sucking at the tender spot under her chin, leaving a trail of kisses on her writhing body until my tongue feels the hard peak of one of her breasts.

Her voice breaks with a sweet moan, cut short by the way she moves her hand to her mouth so her teeth can latch on to her fist, her body arching into my touch in search of more pressure. I give it to her, first a gentle bite and pass of my tongue against her nipple, then I suck hard, circling the tip with my tongue in my mouth until I'm sure I've left it raw.

Liv's hands fall to my hair, and she grips tightly, urging my mouth to make her other breast just as sore. I let my bottom lip linger on it, lifting my chin and dragging it against her until the rough stubble of my chin scrapes against the sensitive peak.

"Ah," she breathes out, tucking her chin and lifting her head enough to meet my gaze.

Her eyes are hazed, and she's drunk with lust. The tip of her tongue is pinched between her front teeth, and she's letting out short pants in anticipation, which I draw out until I feel her lower body begin to squirm underneath me.

She needs to be touched.

My lip draws up on one side and I breathe out a light laugh, myself drunk on this power she's letting me have over her body. I lick her nipple and blow, chilling it until it's so hard that I can bite it with a little more force, and the feel of my teeth makes Liv buck her hips up and pound her fists down at her sides, grabbing fists full of the blanket beneath us.

I nestle into her side and suck on her breast until she moans out loud, so loud that I hope someone can hear it outside of these metal walls. I want to pound my chest in pride for making her feel like this —for making her feel something. She feels something for me —*with* me.

My fingertips drag from the center of her chest to her trembling, bare stomach until I feel the lace of the top of her panties. I brush my knuckles along the band then dip my thumb inside, moving it slowly across the width of her body from hip to hip. This is one of those lines that I've held as a hard no with her, and it has been torture. I both want to make this last and be certain it's allowed, so I slowly add more fingertips just inside the soft cotton and lace under her belly button until I have enough to tug into my palm.

Liv cries out softly, her voice vibrating with the word.

"Please," she begs, and I move my hand just a little more, my palm flat against her bare skin and the soft tickle of her teasing against my fingertips.

I glance to her face, and her eyes are closed tightly while her tongue takes a slow pass over her bottom lip, her imagination already there. The only thing left is the reality.

My eyes fall closed, and my mouth finds its way to her raw skin, to her now warm and wet breast that rises and falls with each breath she takes, and I kiss it while my fingers flex against her lower body. I hold her here, on this cliff, for nearly a minute until I'm satisfied that her body is telling me she wants more. Her hand wraps around my forearm, and she coaxes me lower as I suck her nipple hard one final time, my fingers falling deep inside her while she grabs my arm with both hands and holds it against her tightly.

"Oh my god, Memphis..." My name falls from her lips over and over again, her hips moving for more as I shift my weight and eventually pull my hand away from where she wants me to touch her most.

I position myself between her knees and hook my thumbs on either side of her panties, tugging them over her ass and hips quickly, letting her lift one knee to slip her leg free. Her eyes open on mine, but I drift my gaze down her body and take in every bare inch of her, from her hair splayed in messy, golden waves around my bed to her hands flat at her sides, fingers curling and scratching at the blanket beneath her.

I rest my hands on her hips, my thumbs stretching toward her middle, grazing the light trail of hair that leads to soft pink skin. I tease her, letting my thumb take gentle strokes against her hot, wet center. I touch her like this until the pressure in my cock becomes unbearable, and I breathe out raggedly, my eyes connect with hers, reading them.

My stare bonded to hers, I sit back so I'm on my knees, and my hands drag along the insides of each of her thighs until I reach her knees. I push them wider, and her legs fall open willingly as her body rolls in slow waves.

"So fucking sexy," I say, moving my hands to the button on my pants, unclasping it and pulling my zipper down enough to free my cock. I hold it in my hand, stroking slowly, taking pleasure from her waiting body laid out in front of me to take. I can smell her sex, and it makes me want to be rough, but I restrain myself because that feels just as good.

"Are you on something?" My eyes dim with my question, and she nods quickly.

"I've been on birth control for a year. I'm fine," she says, her words coming out breathless.

I groan with the knowledge that I'm inches away from sinking inside her, and I position myself so I'm towering over her, holding my weight up with one arm, my other hand still stroking my cock. I let the tip slide against her wet center, taking slow drags up and down until I'm slick with her.

My chin tucked to my chest, I taste her belly button and lick my way up her body until my lips are on her neck and my cock is just at her entrance. With one thrust, I slide inside her and feel my entire chest crush like I'm drowning in an ocean. I move slow at first, our bodies finding their fit together until everything is perfectly matched, and when my lungs fill again, I begin to pump into her harder.

Liv's legs wrap around my waist, and my right hand finds her thigh, holding it high against me as I pummel into her, rocking until her body has slid to the deepest corner of my bed. Her hands reach up to brace her head against the wall and she arches her chest, begging me to suckle her skin while my cock fills her over and over.

I let the weight of my body ease onto her and tuck my head enough for my tongue to reach her hard tits, flicking her nipple with short passes until she begins to moan. Her hands hold my head against her, pressing me harder into her flesh while my hips rock and I groan, chasing this building explosion that always seems to just be out of reach.

"Fuck me, Memphis. Fuck me so hard that I will feel you for days. Fuck me so you can fight, and it's the last fuck you get until you kill that man in the ring. Fuck me because I'm yours. This body—my pussy—is yours. I give it to you."

Her dirty mouth drives me over the edge and I growl as I push into her, wrecking our bodies with pleasure, my eyes wide with desperation and my cock swollen with power.

"You are mine," I grunt out with one final thrust, her body quivering and convulsing as her hips rock hungrily, wanting her orgasm to last.

I come in her and she squeals from the slick heat as I keep pushing into her, my hand now touching her center, my thumb pressed into her swollen, pink skin. I rub in circles, and she begins to shake with every pulse until her back arches enough to lift her shoulder blades completely from the bed, and she starts to vibrate out a hum.

"Ohhhhhhhhhhh, Memphis."

Fuck me, the way she says my name like this, with that voice. I've never felt more alpha than I do right now, and I don't let her stop, pushing into her, touching her, holding her orgasm hostage until her nails dig into my back and she begs me to stop.

I ease up finally and stare at her, my hips still moving in slow drags, and I move my hand to grip myself again, guiding my cock in and out, torturing her until her eyes open on mine and she bites her lip, ready for me again.

"You sleep here tonight," I say.

She exhales slowly, a blissful smile stretching her mouth wide as she nods.

"You sleep here every night," I say.

Her eyes pause on mine at this, and her focus moves from one eye to the other. I'm not sure if the hesitation is because of me, or because of her, but it's there, and I don't want it to ruin any of this.

"Or just tonight. We'll start with tonight, and then we'll see what happens tomorrow," I say, falling into her, cradling her back against my chest, our bodies still connected where I pulse inside of her, still hard and unable to use reason because of it.

"I'll stay," she finally says, her voice hoarse and frail, but nothing sad about it. She sounds high on the sensations still numbing her body, and my muscles are so jacked with adrenaline I feel like I could go rounds with the best right now.

I rock my hips into her slowly, filling her again, and my lips rest on the center of her back. Her skin is so silky and warm, and the beads of moisture that dampen it is salty and sweet to the taste. I consume her while I have her, and I never let my mind go to what happens tomorrow.

Tonight—here—I am her champion, and that's all that matters.

# CHAPTER FIFTEEN

Liv

I didn't sleep. I think Memphis knows because I felt his eyes on me most of the night. I pretended—a little for him and a little for me. My eyes remained closed even though my body was restless. I'm not afraid, but the fact that I'm not makes me suspicious somehow. There isn't an easy way to put it into words, not that I have to. Memphis seems to understand the things that make me how I am.

Maybe he just accepts my imperfections.

He's a fighter. I wasn't supposed to fall for him.

But I am.

The morning sun is warming this small space, and my skin is damp from our body heat and the heavy quilt sheltering us. I've never been so comfortable lying naked in a man's arms. Enoch was always cold after sex—both literally and emotionally. He didn't like to talk, and he rarely liked to touch.

He'd compliment me, and shower me with sexy words, but only long enough to get me to let him sleep—or leave for the office. I wonder now if that's where he really went.

So many lies.

Memphis's lips press into my hair, and his hand shifts beneath me enough to reach the strands that have fallen across my face. I smile as he tucks them behind my ear.

"Good morning." His voice is a gravelly whisper, and I feel it vibrate in his chest.

"Good morning," I hum, snuggling in, heat be damned.

"You didn't sleep at all," he says through a chuckle.

I knew he noticed. I shrug one shoulder.

"I'm okay. I have this ability to operate on very little." It's Sunday, which means I really don't have anything to do. I may crawl into my bed upstairs and crash for a while, but not until I know Memphis is busy with something else. I don't want him to think I can't sleep here. I can hardly sleep anywhere unless I'm alone. I think there's something built into my fabric that's always on alert that whomever I'm with is going to disappointment me.

But Memphis isn't. Somehow, I just know it.

"You have to run," I say, preparing my body to be let go. He doesn't move, instead wrapping his arms around me tighter.

"It's Sunday. How about today is a day of rest?" I feel his lip raise against my cheek.

"Uh uh," I say, shaking my head and wiggling loose, finally sitting up to look down at him.

My hand feels along the side and top of my head, and I realize that my hair is probably tangled and teased from our night's activities. I blush a little and close my eyes, drawing his quilt to my chest. Memphis tugs at it, though, and when I open my lids to look at him, he smirks, pulling one more time until my breasts are bared.

"Goddamn, you're beautiful."

My chin tucks and my cheeks round from the heat of his attention. His eyes roam down my face to my arms and breasts until he reaches forward with the back of one hand and traces my profile with a feather-light touch.

He's quiet, and the longer he showers me with his seductive affection the more his brow draws in. Something is weighing on him, and I assume he's worried about me.

"I like staying here," I say, wanting to set him at ease. His eyes perk up a little and his slight frown shifts to a smile as his gaze comes back to mine.

"Yeah?" His voice is quiet.

"Yeah," I say. I take his right hand in both of mine and I begin to massage each finger. Even these small parts of him are exhausted yet strong. His eyes grow heavy from my touch.

"I could put you to sleep like this," I say.

His chuckle is soft, but deep.

"I'm completely on board with this." His laugh is raspy, the morning kind.

I work his hand until the tension in it is gone, then I hold my palms out for him to give me his other one. He smiles faintly and rolls to his side, resting it on my legs, and I begin to massage again. His eyes are focused on my hands while I study him. There's this flicker that happens in his eyes when he's thinking. I've seen him do it when Leo talks to him about fighting defensively, as if he's soaking information in and dissecting it at lightning speed and applying it to every possible outcome. His eyes...they're doing that now, their focus rapidly scanning from knuckle to knuckle. The movements are miniscule, yet they're there. I can't ignore them because they mean he's thinking hard about something.

"Hey, lost boy?" I finally say, shaking his hand against my lap. His eyes widen and he breathes out a smile, coming back from wherever he was when his gaze meets mine.

"Sorry, I was..."

"Thinking?" I finish for him.

His lip ticks up and his eyes settle on mine for a few long seconds.

"You can tell me anything, you know?" I actually mean it; I'm not even afraid.

Memphis moves closer to me and rolls onto his stomach, holding his chest up with his elbows, his hands both cupping one of mine. His face softens as he gazes at our fingers touching, his enormous hands swallow mine completely, and I love that they do. Somehow, nearly a minute passes, and the quiet in here grows even thicker.

"I never want to lie to you," he says, his eyes lifting to meet mine, his hands stopping to hold me still. There's a gentle squeeze, and I wonder if that's what keeps me calm or if it's simply Memphis, who has somehow become this rare exception to everything I've ever known of this world.

"Okay," I say, breathing in slowly through my nose as my mouth curves, my lips closed.

Memphis reflects my expression, and lets the moment be while his eyes flit between both of mine with their focus. He's being thoughtful with his words. I'm sure of it. My stomach tightens in anticipation, but somehow, I know it's still going to be okay. Everything...Memphis and me...we're going to be okay.

"The other night, when I was looking for you, I saw...something... in Leo's house." His lips hang open and his head tilts slightly while my eyes narrow, pushing a wrinkle onto the bridge of my nose.

"Something." I repeat his vague choice of words and smirk a little.

His eyes roll as he chuckles, but he holds on to my hands, eventually coming back to our quiet.

"I saw them...*more* than kissing." His lips fall shut and he waits for me to catch up. The strangest sensation washes right through me —it's similar to amusement, but it's tinged with a little disgust too.

"You...you knew, didn't you?" Memphis asks.

I breathe in deeply, and hold my breath while I think about it. Perhaps I did. I'm certainly not surprised.

"I'm not sure. It..." I pause to think, and my eyes move from my lap to his face as I breathe out a small laugh. "It feels like nothing, so maybe I did. If that makes sense."

He holds my stare for a beat then begins to nod slowly.

"It does," he says, his eyes settled on mine. "I meant to tell you days ago, and I would have...or I didn't mean to keep that from you. I just needed to find the right time or way, and I had to make sure it didn't hurt you to hear it."

"Thank you," I say before he begins to worry any more than I think maybe he already has.

I pull my hands free only long enough to crawl closer to him and lean forward and press my lips to his briefly. I hold his gaze for a full breath while I'm only a few inches away, and I let the feeling settle in my chest. There's a balance inside of me, and as gross as my family's behavior is, it isn't surprising to me anymore. I don't think it has been for quite some time, since I was a little girl forced to grow up fast and see people for their ugly sides.

"You, mister, need to get some miles in." I smirk as I back away and let my right foot feel for the stepladder out of his loft bed. "Those lungs of yours have a handful of days left to grow as big and strong as they can be. So hit the pavement, champ, before it's so hot that it feels like hell outside."

"It always feels like hell outside," he grumbles, rolling to his stomach and wrapping himself in his blanket. Once my feet are both on the floor, I pull the edge of the quilt with a hard tug, leaving him without any cover at all. God his naked body is something to behold.

"Fine, but when I'm done, you and I are going to do a bunch of lame couple things," he says, climbing from his bed without the use of the ladder. He turns to face me and presses my cheeks between his palms, forcing my lips to pout just before he kisses them. "I mean I want to do the most cliché, dumbest couple shit you can think of."

"Like sharing a soda with two straws?" I shoot him a wry smile because that sounds awful. I like my own soda, and usually nobody likes the same flavors as I do.

"Exactly!" His smile grows, and I instantly regret suggesting that.

"Goody," I mutter, pulling one of his large shirts over my head and searching for a pair of sweats to borrow. He hands me one, but doesn't let go until I roll my eyes and laugh.

"Fine, I'll be a good sport," I say, and he leans in for one more kiss, then lets me have his sweatpants. I snap them at him as he walks away.

"Careful," he taunts.

Our eyes lock one last time before he pulls the slender door closed on his bathroom. I slip into his pants and loosely tie my sandals to my feet before gathering my clothes from the night before in my arms. I slam the door closed loudly enough behind me to alert him that I've left.

It's already warm outside, but Memphis will run far anyhow. He'll push himself to dangerous levels. I've watched him do it for days now, and I know that he's been pushing himself like that since the day he found his father's gloves.

He doesn't know any other way.

I take my time making my way back to Leo's, already missing the small camper behind me that feels so much more like home than anywhere I've ever slept. Maybe one day, I'll be able to sleep there... in Memphis's arms. I feel like I'm close. The act of closing my eyes and giving in to the pull of slumber under someone else's watch is one of those things for me—it's a wall I have a hard time scaling. Even with Enoch, before the world came crumbling down, I didn't sleep soundly. It's like I always had one eye open, or I kept dreams at bay in case I needed to jolt awake.

There has never been trust.

I trust Memphis.

I start to smile at the thought, the way trusting him sits in my chest and makes it feel warm and right. I easily push open an already-unlatched door to Leo's house.

"Olivia Valentine?" A man in a dull blue suit stands at the side of Leo's kitchen table the moment I step through the door. There's a coffee mug resting on the table behind him, and it's still steaming, which means it's fresh. He hasn't been here long.

My mom and uncle are sitting with him, and there's an eerie vibration in the air—they've been talking about me.

"What's going on?" My steps have turned into slides, my feet like magnets on a metal floor. Something isn't right in my gut, I just can't tell what.

"Are you Olivia Valentine?" The man repeats his question, walking directly to me, his jacket over his arm, sweat stains on his dress shirt.

"That's me," I say, sliding a foot or two back as he approaches.

In a smooth motion, he unburies an envelope from beneath his coat and hands it to me.

"You've been served."

My eyes flutter and I get dizzy, instantly feeling my mother's eyes drilling holes through me with her judgment. The process server leaves and my uncle leans back in his chair and takes a long sip from his coffee. He smiles at me over the mug, somehow satisfied by this. No matter how many things I've been through, there is always something new to drag me down.

"Why did you let him in?" I shake my head and squeeze the envelope in my palm. My stomach clenches with a brief wave of nausea, and my head grows hot. The sick feeling shifts into anger quickly.

"My job is not to worry about *your* problems," my mom says, standing and turning her back to me as she whisks her half-filled coffee mug off to the sink to pour it out and rinse. She's here for the show. She lives for this tension, and I don't want to give it to her. I hate how I get sucked in—what our push and pull turns me into.

"Right, my bad. You're only my mother; why would my problems concern you at all," I say, moving quickly to the stairs.

My foot lands on the first step when I'm suddenly yanked backward by my hair. The painful tug surprises me at first, and I scream from the sting.

"What's wrong with you?" I shout.

My mom slaps the envelope and my clothes from my hands then grips the center of the shirt I'm wearing, pulling the material closer to her seething eyes.

"What is this? Are you whoring yourself out to our fighter now? You walk in here, into this house that we were kind enough to let you stay in, wearing *his* shirt and...and...you're wearing his pants? Where did you get this?"

My mother kicks my beautiful new dress, and I hear some of the stitches tear.

"Stop!" I yell through gritted teeth, bending down to pick it up, my hand never reaching it because her knee comes up to kick me.

"Oh!" I cry out and cover my eye, my cheek burning and a bruised sensation beginning to throb at my brow.

With half of my face covered, I stare at her. Her eyes are red. I've seen her like this before. This is how she reacted when Charles left our gym, and it's the way I imagine her face looked when she found out Enoch had stolen her money. It's a mixture of shame and hatred for me and everything I've made hard in her life.

"None of this is my fault," I say in a low tone.

Her brow draws in, forcing a deep line between her eyes. Her lips look as if she's tasted something sour. Something...*bitter*.

I lunge at her, causing her to flinch, and then I reach down to pick up my damaged dress and the envelope. When I stand back up, I make myself tall, only inches between us. I've never been afraid of her. She hates that, too, because she's powerless.

"You had me on purpose, and it just kills you that none of it worked out like you thought it would." I smirk, then take a step up, forcing her to lift her chin to keep her eyes on me. "Dad never really loved you. Leo uses you, because he's just as empty as you are. And Memphis is never going to stay here and make money for you like you think he will. He's going to win, and he's going to move on to some-thing bigger—to better people."

"I suppose you're going to make sure he does?" Her eyes dim, heavy makeup weighing down wrinkled lids. She works so hard on the façade. I see right through it—*everyone* sees right through it.

"I won't have to. It's just how your life is going to go," I say, turning and leaving her there to be pissed and throw a tantrum at the bottom of her brother-in-law's stairs. I don't turn around until I get to the top, and when I do, her eyes are like lasers waiting to burn a hole through me. The effect is nothing.

I don't need her. I don't need my uncle.

I never did.

# CHAPTER SIXTEEN

Memphis

I don't think she sees me. I've been watching Liv through her window for the last ten minutes, ever since I got back from my run. I'm supposed to be drowning myself in water to stay hydrated, but I think I may be drowning in her instead. It's a good way to die.

She's on her phone, and I think maybe she's pissed about something. She likes to use her hands when she talks, and she's dropped her phone twice so far because her movements aren't subtle. She keeps pointing downward, and I feel pity for the poor soul on the other line who is getting an earful to match her gestures.

I tip my water bottle back and let the last few drops fall on my tongue before tossing it inside my place and pulling myself up to stand. My legs are teeming with the blood pumping in my veins, my muscles primed from fast miles that didn't make me breathless in the least. Omar is in for a rude awakening—my biggest weakness in my last fight was endurance. I've erased that for him. Nothing tires me—not even the body of that angel born in hell one story above.

It's going to be hard to stay away from her for two weeks, though.

Superstition or not, I think I'm going to need every weapon at my disposal, and pent-up sexual frustration does wonders for a right hook.

I step back into my doorway, my hands holding the top of the frame, giving my bent arms a place to stretch. When she sees me, I'll head in to shower, but I don't want to go just yet. She walks by the window, pacing, a few more times, and I stare intently trying to draw her gaze to mine. I start to laugh silently, because she's come close to looking at me a few times but our eyes always just miss each other. Then she pulls her hair back and tucks it behind her ear; my mood shifts in an instant.

There's a fucking bruise forming on her cheek and her lip is a deep red, most likely busted. I don't remember leaving my place. I have no idea how I got inside Leo's house. But my hands are on his throat now, his back jammed into his refrigerator. Spilled coffee and a busted mug mark the trail I took him on when I lifted him from his now-broken chair and shoved him several feet backward. I know Angela is here, and I recognize her screeching voice, but I'm so wired with fury that I can't stop to decipher what she's saying.

"You are a fucking coward, you hear me? You want to teach me a lesson, you use my face! You don't touch her, you sick motherfucker! You...don't...touch her!" My face is throbbing with heat and my teeth are clenched as I growl at this man I could so easily kill with my bare hands right now. I can feel how fragile his windpipe is under my hands.

He kicks me in my stomach with his knee, and it knocks the wind from me a little, but I don't let up my grip. My head is swimming with what I just saw, Liv's voice echoing in my ears. She's come down stairs, and her mother and she are both pulling at me.

"No! He doesn't get to touch you. These people..." I'm shouting so loudly that my words echo throughout Leo's home. I push into Leo again, and his face begins to glow pink, a sick sound gurgling from his lips as I push air from his body with a thrust.

Liv's hands are furiously gripping at my arms, and that's the only thing that stops me from slamming into him again. I hear her words.

"Stop!"

She's pulling one of my hands free, and I begin to breathe hard now. I'm not winded. I'm manic. I'm...not here. Rage blanketed everything else, and all I could see was her pain, and I had to fix it. My fingers begin to unfurl, and Leo pushes me away as I stumble a few steps. He slides to the side and begins coughing as Liv grasps the front of my shirt and coaxes me to the other side of the kitchen.

"Stop it, Memphis! It isn't what you think. It...it wasn't him!"

Her eyes are pleading with me, her stare close as my focus moves from one eye to the other. Leo continues to cough behind her, and I can make out shadows of action behind her, but Liv is the only thing I can see clearly. Her eye swollen, her cheek purple, her lip divided with a line of blood—dried.

My breathing slows and her hands press flat against my chest, but my fists are still tight at my sides, my biceps primed so much I can't relax my arms. My nostrils flare.

Liv centers herself in front of me, her chin tilted up and her eyes never letting go of mine.

"It wasn't him," she says faintly.

There's a resolve to her expression, and like a tsunami, everything falls together in one wave that crashes over me and my eyes move from this special woman in front of me to the terrible one with her back against the wall ten feet behind her.

"What is wrong with you?" My voice shakes as my body comes down from the high and a sadness takes over my chest. I'm so sad for Liv—and I'm sad for Angela, too. What must have happened to make her the way she is?

"Memphis, this is what she does..."

Angela's words come out desperate, and I actually interrupt them with laughter.

"You are a terrible person. You...you're actually rotten to your soul, and...and evil. You're just evil." My lips bend in sickness and my hands relax, automatically moving to Liv's elbows, and holding her to me.

Angela shakes her head slowly, and her eyes move from me to her daughter, dimming in disgust. I don't know how Liv survived this, how she's able to have so much compassion inside of her despite never having anyone to learn it from. Somehow, she was born with good and nobody destroyed it.

"Get out," Angela says, her eyes now on Leo, but her hand waving at both Liv and me. "You've done enough here. Your fight is soon, and you're not thinking clearly."

I turn to Leo and his heavy eyes look drunk, his lip turned up on one side as if I'm the one who got a lesson here today. Perhaps I did.

My arm shifts. I pull Liv in close to me, and I begin to guide her out the door with me.

"I need to take care of something; hold on," she says, her hand dragging along my chest as she leaves my hold and rushes up the stairs. I sway where I stand, somehow surprised by these people, though I shouldn't be at all. I've watched the disguise deteriorate for a year now.

"I'm not signing the deal, Angela." I decided I wasn't taking the sponsorship during my run, probably before that, if I'm honest with myself.

"Don't be a fool," Angela seethes.

I smirk.

"You just want the twenty percent." I shrug.

She rolls her shoulders and Leo spits in the sink before turning around to defend her.

"You don't know what you're doing," he says, a messy stagger in his footsteps as he tries to fold his arms and look tough. He has a tell; it's the way his hands tremor when he's unsure. Leo's a tough bastard, but I think he's also gotten his ass kicked plenty of times. I've thrown him off.

"I know exactly what I'm doing. I'm holding out for more because I'm worth more. And that's why that deal is coming now; because

Paul and his company want me cheap." I shake my head with tight lips. "Speaks volumes about him if you ask me...that he plays the game cheap."

"That's business, son. You best get to understanding it, too, or else you're gonna find yourself living in that shithole on wheels for the rest of your life."

"Ha," I chuckle, shuffling my feet and looking off to the side. He just doesn't get it. I don't care about any of those things. I care about my legacy, and starting something that might make the man up in heaven who gave me life feel like he left one behind for his son. I care about leaving one for my son one day. And I care about the way Liv looks at me like I've made her proud.

I care about Miles, and about where I'm going to be a year from now as a human being. I won't be here. There was a time when I thought I would be, but no—they don't deserve me, and I sure as shit don't deserve their judgment.

"That's not how I do business," I say as Liv takes the final few steps until she's next to me again. She glances at me and I smile faintly on the side closest to her. Taking her hand, I lead her through the kitchen door down the side alley back to my home. My "shithole on wheels" that I wouldn't trade for the world.

She follows me inside and pulls the door closed behind her as I move to my freezer and pull out a frozen slab of beef wrapped in plastic. Liv sits on the small bench for the eat-in kitchen, and I shove aside the cups and wrappers from days of protein drinks and bars so I can kneel down and rest my forearms on the table across from her.

"Hold this to your face. I swear it will help," I say, putting the meat in her hand and covering it with my own to guide her to the right spot.

"Ah, it's cold," she says, flinching a little with her hand.

I reach up and pull my shirt up over my head, wrapping the frozen beef in it once to take away the sting of the cold.

"Here," I say, helping her put it back in place.

Her eyes settle on mine, and I look right back into her, holding the makeshift cold pack against her skin for almost a full minute in silence. I reach up a few times and tuck loose ends of her hair behind her ear.

"I don't know how you kept yourself from hitting her back," I say, followed by a smirk and chuckle that fades quickly.

Liv's shoulders lift with a short and quiet burst of a laugh.

"I can show incredible restraint; what can I say?" She shrugs and her lips fall into a wry smile.

I pull back the cold compress to check her skin.

"I don't think it's going to be as bad as I thought after first looking at it," I say, lightly running my thumb over the reddest part. Liv's eyes squint from the brief sting.

"Good. Then I don't want to look at it. I'll be better off pretending it isn't there," she says.

She takes the cold meat from me and holds it to herself, slipping back to find a more comfortable position on the bench. I hold the edge of the table and sit back slowly until I'm completely on the floor, with my back against the small set of kitchen cabinets that hide most of my mess. My knees pull up and I rest my elbows on top, folding my fingers together in front of me.

"You want to tell me about it?" I let my head fall slightly to the side as a gentle urge for her to share. I know I can't fix her broken family; I just want her to feel comfortable enough to talk to me.

Liv briefly lifts one shoulder in sync with the side of her mouth.

"I just pushed her buttons I guess," she says, her brow pinching and her gaze falling to the tabletop. "She does not like that you and I..."

She doesn't finish that sentence, but she doesn't really have to.

"I'm sorry." It's the only calm thing I can think of saying.

"Don't be," she says, pulling the meat away again and resting it on the table.

She lifts up an envelope with her other hand and slides it toward me. I lean forward and take it in my hands before sitting back on the floor. I lift my eyebrows and glance at her while turning the thick, opened letter over and over in my hand.

"I've been served," she says through a dry laugh. "I ran all the way here to this place to get away from the nightmare—that I ran away from this place for—and still...Enoch's fucking legal troubles chase me down."

She sighs. I slip the letter out, sliding loose multiple pages, mostly language I don't understand.

"It's a civil suit for damages. He didn't get the punishment he probably really deserved on the criminal end, but the civil case... that's going to decimate him financially. Of course, he really doesn't have much to take at all. That's the entire problem. He sold dreams and turned his profit to dust. Just...*poof*."

"This says next Friday." My eyes are down at the letter balanced on my legs. My fight is Saturday.

"I know," she says quietly. My gaze flits up to hers, and her eyes are bathed in guilt. That's the last thing she needs right now. "I guess they sent a letter that was forwarded here, and then called to notify me that I would have to testify, of course...I'm not the one who answered that call. Leo doesn't believe in writing shit down, or they just didn't care since me being held in contempt of court is like... whatever to them."

I'm quiet. My heart and head battling over how my road got so misguided. This fight means so much to me. The name—Delaney— having that stand for something is all I've ever wanted, at least as long as I've known the name was mine. And now all I can think about is how if Liv isn't there, I won't have a chance. And maybe it isn't as important as finding her. Maybe that's what all of this cosmic bullshit that led me to this place was for—for finding her and giving a damn.

"I'm charging the flights on my credit card. My name is still on an LLC for a small business Enoch set up for me. I was going to help with estates, for low-income seniors. I got to help one woman—*one*. She still calls me with questions. I haven't called her back, but I'm all over her paperwork, and the LLC is still there, which means in a way,

*I'm* still in Washington. They gave me a stipend to cover the travel, which..." She pauses to laugh, and it comes out nervously and desperate.

"I can't even afford the red eye, but I have to go. I'm staying in a hotel that...well let's just say the place is decorated with crime-scene tape. And I'll be taking public transit, which is probably how the murderers who left the dead bodies at the hotel got there and back. And I'm going to have to pack granola bars and drink tap water, because forget food costs. I can't eat in the city. Everything there is expensive and..."

She's rambling, and her face is growing pink from her lack of taking a breath. She's adding to her own stress, so I stop her, sliding up on my knees and running my hands forward on the table, palms down until I'm near her. I twist them open for her to take my hands, and she does, shaking a little with the sensation of defeat that slips out in her long exhale.

"I'm going to miss your fight." Her eyes look so damned sorry. I have to lie to her and say it's okay. I hate it though, because she's the only person who I really feel is in my corner.

"It's okay." I can tell I didn't sell it well. I mean it even though I don't. How did I get so selfish? Is it this place? I crawl around the table to her lap and slide my hands up her thighs, kissing her stomach through her shirt and looking up at her like a begging man. I would beg, too, if it would somehow make a difference. I know it won't.

"It isn't okay, and I'm so sorry," she says, a tear getting through. She runs her arm along her eyes then squeezes me to her in a tight hug, kissing the top of my head. My hands slide around her waist to hold her back. We remain still, like this, for almost an hour. I trail my hand up and down her thigh while she stokes my hair as I rest my head in her lap.

"You're not going to believe this but...Memphis?" I lift my head at her question and look into tired, sad eyes. She forces a slight smile on one half of her mouth, so I lift myself up higher and kiss it, taking my time and brushing my lips over hers slowly until I feel the muscles in her mouth stretch more, the curve growing stronger and more genuine.

"What is it? Anything...tell me, or ask me. I'll do anything." I lean my forehead into hers and she lightly chuckles.

"I actually really want to go somewhere and share a fucking soda."

My lips pucker, trying not to laugh at her request, but when she breaks, so do I. I lift her to stand, brushing her hair behind both ears and cradling her face in my hands, kissing her gently as I grin against her lips.

"My baby wants a soda with two straws. Done and done," I say, stepping back and taking her fingertips in mine, pulling them forward until her feet follow.

"And...I'm regretting it," she says, words drizzled in her brand of sarcasm. She's feeling better, which makes me feel better. I have thirteen days until the fight of my life, and somehow, for the first time in the seven months since we booked it, I feel like Omar Morales has the advantage.

# CHAPTER SEVENTEEN

Liv

Yesterday was the first time my mother kicked me. She's hit me before—a few slaps, really. She and I have gone rounds with shouting matches, and I've said some things that have triggered her. I know where all of her buttons are, and I'm guilty of pushing them in the past.

It's how I was raised.

The abuse, though—that's on her. She's the one who reacts like a monster.

My dad always pretended nothing was wrong. He would whisk in from somewhere else and call me princess for a day then ruin it all in the next twenty-four hours. When he was happy and here, my mom played the part of doting mother. When the luster faded, so did her fake kindness—every single time. Pretty soon, I started to call her out on it. That's when she grew violent.

Now I've threatened her livelihood, though—her business. I know things, and she hates that. She doesn't want me close to Memphis, because she believes I'll poison him, but she's doing such a great job on her own, all I have to do is watch. He deserves better than her and my uncle. He can mooch off their clout and then he needs to get out of here.

I need to get out of here.

Memphis had a hard time motivating himself this morning, and I don't feel right about that. There's a part of him—the respectable part —that doesn't want to associate himself with Leo after yesterday. But he needs him for now. If anything, to get through next Saturday's fight. My uncle may be a shit of a person, but he's one hell of a corner man. He sees things, sometimes before they happen in the ring. He'll know when the heavy rounds are coming. He'll be able to tell Memphis when to hold back. More than any of that, though, my uncle is invested. There's money in this for him, and I'm sure he has a buddy splitting money on the line somewhere too. He never bets against his man. Leo is Memphis's best shot, and after a lot of persuasion, I convinced him of it, too.

My morning is a lot less predictable. I'm pretty sure I still have a job. As essential as Leo is to Memphis's success, I'm kinda key to my mom's taxes. At least for this year. The books aren't done, and I still haven't been able to bring the balance to black from the deep, bloody red it's in. I'm not sure I'll actually be able to, but my mom knows that her best shot at getting some of her questionable moves through an audit is by letting me turn them into legitimate business expenses. Anyone else would flag half of that office.

I take my time after Memphis leaves, showering in the small space that smells of him. I use his shampoo, lathering the musky scent in my hands and smoothing it over my entire body. My clothes are still on the other side of the alley, in a house I'm not ready to walk into again yet, so once I'm dry, I look around for more sweats and T-shirts I can thieve. The one he slept in is slung over the driver's seat of his RV, so I pull it over my body and hold the front up over my nose, breathing in him. Pants seem a little trickier, and I eventually find a smaller pair of sweats tucked under the dining bench, a storage area hidden under its cushion.

I slip into the dark blue pants and begin to close the lid on the bench when something catches my eye. A shoebox marked with Memphis's name bears familiar handwriting, an address scribbled on the corner of the lid.

It isn't mine and I know I shouldn't, but something nudges me to keep reaching for it until I've grasped it in my hands and held it close. I know before I admit it, and I use that as the excuse to sit down with the box in my lap and remove the lid. The things inside are exactly as he said they were. I'm careful with the old boxing wrap rolled neatly and bound by a band, the rubber brittle and ready to break. There are unsent birthday cards, and meaningless notes and receipts, a few from restaurants, mostly just junk. There's a golden ring that I can tell isn't real, and a green stone is embedded in the side. A birthstone for a pinky ring, I'm guessing. I find a stack of old photos at the bottom, pictures of people wearing styles from years ago—men in shorts that creep up high and Hawaiian shirts hanging open. The visual makes me smile briefly until I see his face and the earth drops.

The box falls to the floor, spilling everything and leaving me with nothing but this one photo in my hands. He's on the bike, Memphis's bike. I don't know how I didn't recognize it as the one Leo used to ride, and my young mind never considered that Leo could have borrowed it or that it was someone else's. But it was. It was *his*.

My dad rode that bike, too. He rode it once—on a road trip from here to New Orleans with some guy who had been working out at the gym. Some wannabe fighter who was just getting started. Some guy who my dad took an interest in right after Charles left. He was one of dozens that they tried to groom, but nobody was Charles. Especially not in my dad's eyes—or heart.

I remember answering the phone and getting my father's drunken slurs when he called from the road. I handed the phone over to Leo, but I sat at the kitchen table and listened to his end of the conversation. He called my father careless. He told him he was weak. And then he hung up and forbid me from picking the phone up again when it rang. It did ring. It rang all night, and eventually Leo ripped the phone cord out of the wall.

Dad didn't come home until days later. The bike was gone. He said he needed to sell it. I never thought about the fact that it wasn't his to sell. I thought it was Leo's, and my dad selling something that belonged to my uncle for cash wasn't strange at all. It was exactly the dick-move they'd always done to each other. My father came home angry, and he started to box sloppy. Booze, women, men, drugs—inconvenient distractions. This was the beginning of the end—a golden career marred by ugliness. Though, I guess my dad was just finally showing everyone else how ugly he was while I knew all along.

I was fourteen then, which means Memphis was fourteen, too. There are some gaps in this puzzle, but my gut is filling them in, and I'm pretty certain that I'm right.

With numb and quivering hands, I scoop up the things that spilled from the box and put it back in its place under the bench lid, but I keep the photo. I stuff my feet into my tennis shoes and lock Memphis's door from the inside so it's secure when I close it behind me. It's early still, which means my mother will be in her room. She'll hear me, but not before I can ask my questions.

I grab the keys from the hook inside Leo's house and unlock my parents' front door, opening and closing the door as quietly as possible. I pause at the creaking sound and hold my breath, my heart hammering in my chest and my inner voice begging my mother not to hear me come in. I wait a full minute, at least, then lock the door behind me and take soft steps up to my dad's room.

His bed is lifted when I walk in. He's sitting up enough to look out the window at the traffic congestion below. His room is hot, and I wonder if he likes it this way or if my mom just forgets to check on him sometimes. The door clicks behind me, and my dad's attention comes to me with the slow swivel of his head.

I didn't want to come back in here, to see him or talk to him again. But this is too important. His eyes are heavy with sleep, his mouth drooping on one side where it's been numb for years now. I move to the space next to his bed, standing between the chair and his mattress, near his head, and I waste no time getting to my point.

"You knew this man," I say, holding up the photo of Memphis's father, standing in front of the bike.

My father's eyes stay on mine, the whites scarred with red veins, and deep wrinkles underneath, just above his high cheekbones. I hold his stare and leave the picture where it is, knowing he won't bother to look at it. He doesn't need to see it. He knows who it is, who Memphis is.

"Does Mom know?"

His eyelids close in a slow blink, so heavily I wonder if they'll open again. His expression is unchanged when they do, not that he can express much anymore. I could always read his eyes, though. And the lack of anything in them means I'm right so far.

"The man in this photo is Robert Delaney, isn't he? He was here —he was your friend after Charles left. You took him to New Orleans. I remember, Dad. I remember enough, and I think I can guess the rest," I say, swallowing the surge of bile creeping up my throat.

I lift my father's dry, frail hand in my own and curl his fingers around the photo, squeezing while my mouth bunches in frustration and anger. My father's nails are long, in need of a trim, so they scratch and puncture the photograph as I force his fist to hold it on his own.

The entire time he leaves his gaze on mine, but the subtle changes I've been waiting for happen in his face. The right side of his mouth frowns, and he swallows hard, a short burst of breath coming out his nose and forcing his lips to part to help him get more air.

His eyes close again and this time open on the image that he's balanced in his fist against his chest. He blinks several times, and the longer he looks at the photo the more his mouth curves downward until he looks sick.

"You were different when you came back," I say while he

continues to stare at the picture, holding it close and forcing his eyes to scan and take it all in.

"What'd you sell the bike for?" I wait, knowing he won't answer. His speech is pretty much nonexistent; the sounds he is able to make consist of moans and grunts. He's lost the ability to form words. "Did you have to pay someone off? Was it a trade to make a problem go away? Did you kill him in the ring? Or did you beat him up again after the fight, while you were drunk or high?"

My father's lip ticks, and he struggles to keep his mouth from quivering, a slobbery breath shaking loose.

"It was in the ring."

My mom has been standing behind me for a while. I heard the door click open, but I'm not afraid of anyone in this house, and I wasn't going to stop asking questions just because she could hear them. They're questions for her, too.

My dad's hand falls flat against his chest with the photo underneath. I will take it back before I leave, but for now, he can suffer from the touch of it. I've grown so cold toward my parents, and I used to regret it and let it make me sad. Now it just is what it is. There are better people in my life, people worth my heart and effort. People whose lives have been forever changed by my parents just like mine have, unfortunately.

"How did you know where to send the box?" This question is for my mom. It's her handwriting on the box. The Tennessee address I assume is the hotel where Memphis found the items when he was fourteen.

"Seemed as good a place as any," she says.

My eyes fall closed, and I hurt for Memphis. He's built a life around a lie my mom orchestrated on a whim.

"You just picked a random hotel and shipped away his things. Why didn't you just send them right to his son? You knew he had one...*clearly*! How did you send the post card from Memphis? Why would you spend so much time on this?"

My mom remains silent, and my head swirls in frustration. I want answers, and Memphis deserves to know. I'm not sure when, but he deserves to know.

"You've known this entire time...that he is who he is. Did you know, Dad? Did she tell you?" I pull the photo away from him, and his eyes are swollen and redder than before. His forehead creases as he struggles to shake his head.

"Your dad didn't need something like this out in the public. We were struggling to keep this place together, and his name was the only advertising we had. That name needed to stay whole, and that fight in New Orleans was just unsanctioned amateur shit. He was making that poor sap's dream come true by stepping in a ring with him."

The way my mom always tries to justify things is twisted. She applies logic to situations that call for compassion, and I wonder how I can feel so much when I come from a woman who never seems to feel anything.

"So why not leave it alone, just throw away his belongings and move on? Why did you have to torture a fourteen-year-old boy?" I twist to look her in the eyes as I ask this question, and her expression is calm and almost superior.

She folds her arms and leans into the doorway to glare at me. Her mouth forms a smug line, pulled tight at the corners. She isn't wearing makeup yet, and everything she does to fool the world that she's still young and relevant is still in a drawer. Her pajamas are old, and her hair looks thin, twisted in a bun on top of her head.

I don't think she's going to tell me, so the best I can do is guess and try to read her reactions. I think of plausible scenarios, and I begin to laugh at how outlandish they seem. My parents orchestrated it all to steal money from the man. They were trying to take bets on the fight and it went wrong. My dad is secretly a murderer. I begin to utter the craziest of my ideas out loud, until something I say suddenly strikes near the truth.

"Dad knew Robert a lot longer than anyone thought. He was a real friend."

My mother's eyes widen and her mouth pulls tighter. I'm close; I can tell by her discomfort. I stand, clutching the photograph, and begin to move toward her. She squirms a little but doesn't move from her spot blocking the door.

"You didn't like Robert," I say, my head tilting a little with this sense of being right. I begin to smirk just as my mom begins to frown, her eyes dimming with angry shadows.

"You were glad he was dead. In fact…Dad didn't kill him at all, did he?" I push my theory over the line on a gamble, and my mom takes the bait.

"Stop it, Olivia. Your dad killed that man accidentally. He knocked him out. Robert died of a brain hemorrhage. And your dad wanted Robert's son to have his things…"

She slips, and I catch it.

"He knew he had a son," I confirm.

Realizing we're in this deep—and that I'm only going to make up worse stories—my mom sighs heavily then licks her bottom lip before rolling her eyes.

"Yes, Olivia. We knew he had a son. We knew his son was in Philadelphia. We're the reason he sent him there when that woman showed up at my apartment, right from the hospital demanding money or a ring. She was just some junkie boxing-groupie looking to hitch herself to a fighter, and your dad and Robert were good friends. Robert was actually going to marry her. Can you believe that?" My mom scoffs, and my stomach begins to churn with a boiling sensation. "Your dad and I weren't even married yet. Robert was being stupid, getting taken by her con. I threatened to call the cops because I just knew she was tweaking, and surprise, surprise…she took off."

My mom's eyes finally settle on mine, and she stops talking abruptly, as if she's surprised she's said so much. I knew she wouldn't be able to help herself once she began spinning her version of the past. It's probably mostly right, only the perspective is warped, per usual.

"You got knocked up on purpose, and dad was married to someone else. *You* were the groupie, Mom. Robert was just a dad. Or he could have been, until you had to ruin it. You wanted everyone miserable, though."

I glare into her and search for the nugget of truth. It's in there, and I've pretty much gotten it all. Just a few details remain.

"Who wrote the note in Philadelphia?" I match her slow breathing to prove I can wait just as long as she can in silence.

"Leo," she finally says with a shrug.

"And the postcard, from the hotel..." I lead her.

"Leo," she confirms.

I chew at the inside of my lip and nod, glancing down at the place where her fingernails are digging into her own arms.

I look up into her eyes when it hits me, and my lips part as my eyebrows lift and I suck in a quick breath.

"You left just enough of a trail for Memphis to find his way to you when he was ready," I say, her eyes widening again. It's all I need to know I'm right. "You were making an investment in your future. Dad was mourning an old friend. Just like you always do, you manipulated the situation. I'm not sure if it was just because Robert was a better fighter than you let on and you were betting on his son having the same talent, or you liked the idea of his presence reminding Dad and torturing him just a little. I think maybe it's both."

My mom almost looks proud hearing my retelling of the past. I've always known my mom was a psychopath. Her ability to remain calm and feel absolutely zero emotions while destroying others for her gain is pretty much the clinical definition. I didn't have a name for it until I took psychology in college, but as soon as I read it, I knew. I just never thought the effects from her manipulation would reach beyond our family, would hurt others.

"If you tell him, you'll fuck his head up and he'll never have a chance against Morales," my mom says. I don't argue with her, because she's right. But my stomach does sink with the sensation of free falling from a high-rise. My body rushes with tingles from a flash of panic. I didn't know it would go this way until it was too late. I didn't know this is what he'd hear. If I'd known, I would have told my mom Memphis has been standing behind her the entire time. Maybe he was looking for me, or maybe he came to talk to my father on his own. Whatever the reason, a fucked up coincidence aligned our paths and brought him upstairs seconds after me and put him steps away from hearing the awful truth.

I should have stopped this, but I was being proven right—my mom was being proven evil. I'm not much better than they are it seems, because Memphis has heard every word, and I let him take the bullet while I watched. I've ruined him and all of his hard work, because it was more important to me to hear her admit to her atrocities.

And now I have to live with the broken heart and devastation staring at me from just over her shoulder. I did that. Me...and me alone.

# CHAPTER EIGHTEEN

Memphis

It's nothing like the movies. When I'm prepping for a fight and I literally have days left, I start to panic that I'm resting too much, and at the same time that I'm resting too little. Workouts phase down, running amps up and I'm hungry as fucking hell.

Weigh-ins are in exactly six days. I get in the ring with Morales in seven. I have ten pounds of flexibility. I have eleven pounds to lose then gain back overnight. It sounds impossible, I know, but I've done it before. I'll do it again.

The problem is I can't stand to step foot in the place I'm supposed to train. I can't stomach food, so I'm losing weight too quickly. And I'm a ticking time bomb.

I'm a ticking bomb because of the very people I thought would make me a champion. Maybe that was their plan all along. It was only a matter of time before Angela broke the news, and I'm sure when I turned down the Fuel contract, it eliminated any reason she had not to stir my emotions.

Liv hasn't left my side. She packed the few things she had in her suitcase and dragged it into my RV minutes after I punched the wall in the hallway across from where Angela stood and spilled her guts like one of those moms who purposely make their children sick just so they can take care of them. I've been trying to remember the name of it all day. It's this obsession I can't let go, because if I'm not thinking about it, I'm thinking about all of the lost time with my dad, about all of the things I could have known, and about these awful people.

"Munchausen by proxy syndrome," Liv says, finally looking it up on her phone, and I breathe in deeply, relieved by solving one fucking problem. Too bad it isn't the bigger problem.

"I'm pulling out."

Liv gives no response. I've said those words at least a hundred times since everything came crashing down last week. It's the only solution I have. I can't fight for Leo. I can't be their prized horse. I'd rather start over than serve them in any way at all. Liv, though...she sees the big picture, and maybe that's because she's been their victim before.

The only thing I can stomach is running. The first night, I was gone for three hours, and Liv was worried I'd done something. Hungry...angry...she understands how those two compounds can be explosive. Boxers can be irrational—it's the result of pushing the human body to extremes. Now I run the same mile over and over. Liv sits on my steps and pretends to read, but her eyes are up every time I pass by, scanning the sidewalk in anticipation. She waits for me, counting the seconds, knowing my pace by heart. Sometimes I think about not passing by just to test her—to see if she'd worry again, like a gut-check to make sure her concern is real. This place has torn apart my ability to trust and to see good in people. It has to end.

"I'm really pulling out," I say again, standing from the blanket we've laid on the ground next to Miles. His life out here doesn't seem so bad now. There's a freedom to it, no attachments or promises to lose.

"Sit down, you damn fool," Miles says, pulling the hat away from his face. I thought he'd fallen asleep an hour ago. "It's late, and when you stand and make noise in the park people think you're open for business. Potheads will come looking to buy and the angry fuckers over there will try to pick a fight. You ain't quitting shit. Now sit down and fix your head. You've got some adversity to overcome in a week."

I do as he says only because I don't want to make him miserable too. Liv hasn't moved once. She doesn't even dare look at me.

Liv feels responsible. She won't come out and say it. At least, not directly. She's constantly trying to prove to me that she's on my side—leaving Leo's to stay with me instead, quitting and refusing to handle the quarterly tax reports for the gym, and pouring over the contracts I *do* have in search of ways I can get all of the money I'm owed without having Angela involved.

I should tell her she's not the one who did those awful things. She isn't. She's just the one who let me hear them. We made eye contact in that house, just outside of Archie's room, and I stayed quiet, ready to back her up in what I thought was an argument with her mom. I was blindsided by what was said. There's a part of me...a part that I'm not proud of...that's a little angry at Liv for it. It's not fair, but that feeling is there, in the pit of my stomach. It's why I'm not talking; because if I talk, I'll say something I regret.

"When I was in the Middle East, we had a lot of...let's just say *covert* operations that went on. It wasn't a clear-cut war. They used words like *conflict* and *scandal*. It wasn't so different from life on the streets. I think it's why I can survive out here so well. This life feels more like home, because it's literally just like the world I'd left."

Miles doesn't talk about his military days much. The mention of his service paralyzes me, forcing me to think about something—*someone*—else rather than my problems. I'm not sure if he's just trying to distract me or if there's a lesson to be learned, but I hold my breath and roll to my side, my eyes grazing over Liv's profile as she looks up at the stars. She's lost in them, and worry lines weigh down her mouth, dimpling her chin.

"Sometimes, it's hard to see who your enemy is. Sometimes, it changes." I glance to Miles's profile again, his hand holding the top of the old ball cap his wife gave him years ago. It's the only possession he never lets out of his sight; even when it isn't on his head, it's on his body somewhere. He draws the brim back down over his eyes, and I wonder if he's done sharing and ready to fall back to sleep.

"Over there, we had no idea who the enemy was. Seemed like a lot of really nice people just trying to survive—go to work, take their kids to school, buy groceries. It got to the point where we were getting orders that just didn't seem to add up with the world in front of our faces, so this one day...we just refused to fight. A whole church full of people wasn't blown up. Was a bad guy in there? I don't know. But I saw the kids come out, and I can live with my choice. I'm good with it."

My eyes move from Miles to Liv again during the silence after he speaks. I know what he's saying...but boxing doesn't work like war. Hell, *war* doesn't work like war most of the time. If I give this up now, it might not ever come back.

"He's right, you know?"

Somewhere in the midst of my thoughts, Liv rolled to her side and her eyes found mine. She tucks her palms under her cheek to rest on them and shifts her eyes a hint so they almost beg me to consider what Miles is suggesting.

I breathe in slowly and imagine the scenario, and it makes me sick. The worst flavor is resentment—I would resent them all for losing out on this. I'm afraid I would resent her, and I just don't want to do that. I think I love her. There's no room for love in a resentful mind.

"It takes years to get boxing to take you seriously, Liv. You know that," I say. It comes out condescending, so I reach forward to her arm, brushing the ends of my fingers on her elbow. She doesn't give me her hand, and I know it's because she's hurt.

"I know it's a lot of money," she says.

"I could give two shits about the money," I cut in. My eyes stick to hers, and my words sink in for a few quiet breaths. "But the shot at being considered worthy of a major bout? Liv...that's not gonna happen again if I back out. You know it. I know it. That's just how this world works—*one shot.*"

Her eyes slip lower, to the blanket between us. I reach forward again and this time her hand tentatively slides toward mine. I lie flat on my other hand, my arm folded under my head, while my fingers dance with hers. What a cruel joke life has played on me—to give me dreams but wrap them up in nightmares.

"You really don't care about the money?" Her hand continues to move with mine, and when I look at her face, her eyes are distant again, like they were at the stars, but this time at our touch. She chews at her lip.

"I really don't. I mean I would never turn it down. I'm not stupid. But if I'm talking priorities? Money ranks pretty fucking low, Liv."

I think it's hard for her to understand that kind of response. She comes from a family where money is at the heart of everything that's wrong, yet it's all they fight for anyhow. At that very thought, her eyes flit up and meet mine.

"I know someone..." Her words come out in a slow whisper. Our hands have stopped moving. "Either he gets your contract, sits in your corner and earns fifty percent of their take..."

"Or they get nothing," I finish for her.

Her eyes blink slowly as she nods.

"You really think that will work? That they'll give up owning me just to get a little now?" I doubt it as I say it; Angela and Leo are just so vengeful.

"I really do," Liv says.

I sit up, a shot of adrenaline rushing to my heart with hope, kicking my nerves in and pushing me to move. I'm ready. I'm ready for this now if Liv really thinks it will work.

"Why are you so sure?" I need one more convincing argument—something more than my gut instinct and hers.

"Because the man you're going to ask? He's the one man they can't refuse. They owe him too much," she says, still lying on her side, her hand stretched out to where mine left it, her gaze fixed on a nothingness. I glance to her fingers, and they remain there lifeless. Something about this makes her nervous.

"I'll call him in the morning," she says, moving slowly to her knees and then her feet. I stand with her, uncertain because of how distant she seems.

She senses it. After reaching down and gathering my favorite quilt in her arms, she pushes her hair back over one shoulder, and tucks the rest behind her ear. Our eyes meet in the filtered light of the moon that paints us both in spots because of the thin blanket of leaves on Miles's tree.

"And yes, Memphis. I am incredibly sure that this will work. And this is right," she says, swallowing back emotions. Her voice cracks. "This...it's the most-right thing that's come along in a while."

I know there is still fear buried under her brave face. I see it in the way her eyes slant with worry, the way they won't focus on me for long, because they're too busy searching for a way to jump to the future...or the past—to fly to any time but this one right now.

I take a few small steps until I can reach for her, my hand sliding under her trembling arm to the warm curve of her back. Her eyes fall closed and I draw her in, pressing my lips to the top of her head as she nestles into my chest, my blanket rolled and tucked under one arm while her free hand grasps at the front of my shirt, holding it close to her face.

"I'll talk to him...or them. Whoever it is. I'll say you sent me, and I'll explain. I mean, other than me, who turns away free money, right?" I smile against her hair, but just as the air begins to feel light, Liv adds more weight.

"It's a him. This needs to be me. And he's not interested in the money, either. He'll do it because he loved my dad, and my dad loved him back. And that's enough."

That's enough.

I echo her final words over and over in my mind as I wrap my other arm around her and keep her close. This here...it's enough, too.

# CHAPTER NINETEEN

Liv

I looked up Charles Francisco de la Rosa on my eighteenth birthday. There wasn't a cake or presents. My mom had just fired the part-time caregiver who was helping her with my dad after the stroke. She convinced Leo that the nurse was stealing from them, but I know the truth—insurance only covered a fraction of the cost, and my mom had other things she'd rather spend money on.

She also loved the pity party. How could she throw a birthday party when she needed to bathe my dad? How could I think about presents when she needed to lift and stretch my father's legs to keep him from getting atrophy? Why would I need a car? Or to borrow the car? Or money to ride the bus? It's not like I had many friends.

Of course I didn't. My younger years were spent being pulled out of school early for fights I didn't really get to see, but could only listen to. I never wanted to invite people over, because I'd have to explain why my dad only came to visit my mom in the bedroom then left before dinner. As I got older, and after they married, the drinking began. So did the drugs. If I had friends, they'd see through my carefully constructed lies. It was easier having people think I was mysterious, and that my dad was just strict. He fit the part of overprotective if people didn't really know him, and I could get away without talking about my mom at all.

And so I turned eighteen all alone, and for the first time ever, I let it get to me. It hurt. All I wanted was to find someone else who would understand that pain.

Charles was easy to find. He came up, as he still does, with a few clicks on an internet search. He lives in Chicago, and he trains teens who fight on the streets to use those emotions for something better. He turns broken kids into fighters, and then he finds them someone else to turn them into champions. He's never in it for the money, and when he's given credit, he brushes off the fame.

I wanted to call him so badly. I didn't even know him that well, but I just had this feeling that he would understand. I could never bring myself to finish dialing the numbers, though, and even now as I sit here on Memphis's steps with the phone pressed against my ear, I fight the instinct to hang up and pray he doesn't call my number back.

"It's ringing," I whisper, glancing up at Memphis where he stands in front of me. His hands weight down the pockets of his jean, and his arms are stiff. He's afraid to give this idea too much hope.

"Sisco here. How can I help you?"

I close my eyes at the sound of his voice. It's the same as it was the day I listened to him leave. It's been more than a decade, but he sounds as if he hasn't aged a day.

"Charles..." I let his name linger, offering a clue. Only a handful of people called him that. *We* called him that. Everything else he did was as Francisco—his middle name. His fights. His gym in Chicago. He was Charles to only a few.

"Who is this?" The suspicion in his voice is obvious, and warranted.

I swallow hard and look down to the metal step between my knees and the dirt ground beneath that.

"It's Olivia...Archie's...ummm, I'm Archie's daughter?" I was so sure this was going to be the hard part, but the tightness in my chest has only gotten worse. Even more, I can hear it choking him on the other end of the line.

"Liv," he says softly. "Your dad...is he okay?"

I breathe in quickly and let the tingles roll down my spine. I never even thought he would assume I'd be calling because of dad, but of course.

"He's fine. He's...well he had a stroke a few years ago, but other than that." I lick at my lips and close my mouth tightly, avoiding saying too much. It's quiet on the other end for a few seconds.

"Oh," he finally breathes out. I can hear people in the background, the sounds of speed bags and coaches shouting. It's two hours later there; he's probably been open for a while.

"Listen, Olivia. I'm not sure why you're calling, but I have a family. I have a wife now, and kids...what I mean is I moved on. Your dad and I were close during a really crazy time, and I think maybe he needed me more than I needed him. I cared about him, don't get me wrong. I truly did. But I am not looking for reunions. What he maybe thought was love for me was...I don't know...finding myself, maybe? Forgiveness for what he did came with time, but I don't really think he needs to hear me say he's forgiven. Is he even in a state where...shit..."

Even as Charles talks, as he says the things I fully expected to hear, I still know he'll help. I know he will, because of the reason my father admired him so much. He'll help because he does what's right, but he also believes in karmic justice.

"I've met someone, Charles. He's important to me, and my mom...she's going to destroy him," I say. His initial response is more silence, so I wait.

"He's a fighter?" He knows he is. It's the only reason this call would need to take place.

"He's going to be the middleweight world champion," I say, an automatic smile taking over my mouth. Memphis reflects the same expression and kneels down, running his hands over my knees and leaning forward to kiss the top of my thigh. He holds me here as I continue to listen.

"He's under Leo." It isn't a question. He knows he is.

"He's gotten him ready," I say.

I can hear his breath rustle against the phone, and the sounds behind him begin to fade then cut off completely. He's moved to an office or outside.

"Liv, Jesus. I know why you're calling. They've got him, though. You need to tell him to do his time and when it's done, he'll have a name and I'll help you find the right people. There just isn't anything I can do, Liv. I don't even manage fighters." Even as Charles gives his reasons, I can hear the yearning in his tone. He wants to help. All he needs is that little push.

I'm good at little pushes. Charles left my family because they stole from him, but that's not what kept him away. *I* kept him away. I hated my mother so much that I wanted to hurt her the only way I knew how. I told her that my dad didn't love her the way he loved Charles. I needled her with the idea—with the truth—even when she wrote it off as lies and me just being a hormonal teenager. I planted the seed and nurtured it until she felt discarded. It's the only way I knew Charles would be free, and the only way I could think to make her suffer.

If only I'd let it play out on its own. Maybe they'd all be different people.

"His dad was Robert Delaney. Dad ever mention him?" He must have. I'm sure he did to Charles.

There's light laughter on the end of the line.

"Sure I did. He wasn't a very good fighter, but damn did that boy have spirit. He'd come and go, odd jobs and all. Never really could stay settled in the same place for long. We'd always go out drinking when he was in town, and damn did he get your dad shitfaced. He was training there, at the gym, when I left. I didn't know he had a son, though."

This won't shock Charles. It will be that little push, though.

"That's because my mom had him sent away. He never got to meet him," I say, waiting for him to process.

"Shit," he finally mutters.

"Dad killed him with a blow to the head. It was in the ring, but I'm pretty sure dad was drunk and it wasn't a sanctioned fight." I stop and chew at my lip, realizing Memphis is hearing every word of this for a second time. His thumbs run over my kneecaps, but his head hangs low. He's fighting through feeling, and it's not healthy. He just doesn't have the mental space to handle this right now, though. If he lets it all in, he'll become toxic to himself.

"When's his fight?" Charles asks. It isn't a promise, but I feel it coming. I just need to clear this hurdle now.

"Saturday," I say. Memphis lifts his head and our eyes meet, both of our lips ticking up at the absurdity of this enormous favor we're asking of a man that's by most stretches a stranger to us both.

"Aww hell. Liv...Saturday?" He laughs on the other end, the rumble filling my ears. It's such an impossible challenge, he's considering taking it for the mere level of difficulty.

"I know, but he's really ready, Charles. I meant it—Leo's gotten him ready. And awful as he is, you know there's nobody better."

Charles is quiet again, a breath of laughter vibrating against the phone and in my ear.

"Nobody better, huh?" My smile begins to curve more. You can take a boxer out of the ring, but you can't take the ego out of a boxer.

"You know how much this means. You know you're the only guy for the job. And you know they'll have to let you take over because if they don't, Charles, my guy...he's gonna walk," I say.

"Who's he fighting?" I've been waiting for this.

"Omar Morales." There's another chuckle on his end of the line.

"Morales. Saturday." I've got him. He's there; he's invested. The next step is to get him in so deep he won't want to give Memphis up.

"Saturday," I repeat.

My eyes remain wide open, my stare locked on Memphis's, both of our breaths held. He's hearing bits and pieces, whenever Charles speaks loud enough, but mostly he's reading my expression and filling in the gaps with what he hopes is being said.

"Put your man on the phone." I smile at his request, and hand my phone over.

"Yes, sir," Memphis says, showing respect from the very start. It's a well-honed move, and I'm sure it did wonders on Leo, but Charles won't care about that. He'll care about what's in Memphis's heart. I know he'll see it when he meets him, but I just hope he can sense his passion for this sport over the phone.

"Memphis, sir. I mean Charles. Sorry." His eyes flit to me briefly, and I laugh. He's already being coached.

"I'm going to ask that you get fifty percent," Memphis says, standing and pacing a few steps away from me.

"I'll make weight...no, never....not in the least." I wait through the pauses and glean what I can from his short answers. Charles wants him clean. While my dad was great, sometimes his fights came with questions. The gambling on the side never helped, but there were so many knockouts that felt impossible yet came easily, even as he aged. I think my dad's only true vice was himself—booze, drugs, careless sex—it was all about short-term happiness and a high. He was nothing unless he could make himself happy, and he didn't care how fleeting that sensation was. But I don't think he ever cheated. He liked to win outright, so he had something to hold over someone else.

For Memphis, it's about something else. It's about a name.

It's about a ghost.

About a man.

"Yes, sir...Charles," Memphis stumbles into a laugh. "I will. Thank you. I'll make you proud."

He hands the phone to me, and I hold it to my ear, not sure if he's still on the line or if he's gone.

"Liv." Nerves run with electricity when he says my name. I'm not sure what else I have to say—what else he has to ask.

"Yeah," I respond.

"No money. They can keep it all. You tell them they get their full cut, and I get their fighter. And you make sure Angela knows where he's coming," he says.

"Okay." My answer is fast, and just as quickly he's off the line.

My eyes blink a few times at how quickly that happened. There are some things that will need to be worked out—a commercial later this month, a few local endorsement deals. He never signed Fuel, and that's good. He'll find more in Chicago.

He's going to need to go to Chicago.

"It's done." I decide to tell him that Charles is giving up the money later tonight. I want him to enjoy this without the little revenge string that's attached. He should get to. And when I explain more, he'll understand what's in it for Charles. And eventually, they'll form a real bond, Charles becoming the coach he's meant to be, and Memphis getting the attention he deserves.

And he'll need to go to Chicago. I'll be here. Unless I leave...and follow some guy across country, just like I did before.

I leave my doubts in my head, too. Those are other things that Memphis doesn't need to hear. These are all things that can be worked out after Saturday. After his hand is held in the air by a referee, and Morales's title is his.

I'm going to miss it all. Because of the first boy I followed somewhere.

Fucking hell.

# CHAPTER TWENTY

Memphis

They must know it's coming. They can't live the way they do—pushing people to breaking points—and not expect the blowback. I think it's pretty clear that they're due some blowback from me. There's a fucking hole in the hallway of their house as evidence of my anger. Angela's lucky I didn't tear down her whole damn house.

Leo's ready to fight. I know the second I open my mouth he's going to put on a show. I just don't know what. I'm the one starving to make weight yet he's the one who's like a bomb waiting to explode. For the first time in days, I'm calm. I'm more than calm—I'm ready. That edge Omar Morales gained, the minute my carefully assembled fantasy about my dad and his death came crashing down, grew narrower when Liv found me a lifeline.

She told me about Charles—about the things she knew of his time here. As much as Archie was the dark, it seems like Charles was the light. Maybe that's what Archie was attracted to. Maybe he admired his focus and simplicity. Archie was like a rock star, and this sport is meant for discipline. The two lifestyles don't mix, and maybe Charles brought him a sense of balance.

I wait for Liv to lay out my plan on the table. We spent two hours at the office supply store this morning figuring out how to print something she had to write on her phone. It's fairly basic—a list of bullet points and dollar amounts. The only thing that should really matter to Angela and Leo is that bottom line.

"You still owe me the quarterly taxes you know?" Angela lifts her reading glasses from the chain they dangle on around her neck, pushing them up the bridge of her nose, but stopping to stare at her daughter over the rims. I can barely stomach looking at her now that I know what she did.

"You're not paying me to finish them, so I wouldn't hold your breath," Liv says.

I reach my hand out to the side and brush it against her thigh to get her attention. She glances at me and I wince. She's going to fire them up too early if she isn't careful. I know it's hard to hold back, but I need her to now. Just this once.

"I believe that's the job I *was* paying you for. You never finished, so maybe you owe me some of that salary back," Angela mutters as she slides my plan toward her on the table. Liv titters, but covers it with a cough.

"What is this horseshit?" Leo reaches over Angela's shoulder and takes the paper in his hand, his neck slung forward and his head hung low as he reads. I can tell when he's reached the end, because he crinkles the paper in a fist and throws it back on the table.

"I want out." I keep it simple. If I say more right now, it's going to be threatening. Nobody in this room is surprised by this move, but Angela begins to pretend. Before she can play the "I don't understand" line to its full effect, though, Leo ruins it.

"Fine. You're out. Good luck winning that fight with nobody in your corner," he spits out, folding his arms and leaning against the brick wall behind Liv's mom. His frayed toothpick is fat with saliva, and he bends it in half with his tongue before spitting it on the ground and kicking it into a corner.

"You get paid either way," Liv says, and both Leo and her mom scoff.

"Yeah, like a few thousand if he loses versus fifty if he wins," Leo says.

"Seventy," Angela corrects.

She always knew the number. She's added the details of every contract to the penny. If prompted right now, I bet she could calculate the cents. It's thirty-four; Liv calculated it last night.

"You can't do this alone. Get over yourself, kid. You're being childish, and you're going to lose a lot of money," Leo pipes in.

I sit back in the chair and stretch out my legs while I fold my hands together and rest them on the table. Angela peers at me over her glasses while Leo paces, hovering like a lion.

"I won't be alone. I'm with Charles de la Rosa now." I stare Leo in the eyes while he reads me trying to tell if I'm being serious. Eventually he cracks a hard laugh and looks away, but his eyes come back again and his laughter stops.

"I'm not kidding. He's taking over this fight. I am done here." I let my gaze linger on Leo's for a few seconds before I move to Angela. She refuses to look me in the eyes, instead scanning the row of numbers we've laid out on the page she's trying to flatten again on the table.

"Charles is just doing this to hurt us. You don't know the history there, Memphis. He's using you. I can't let you get taken like this," Angela says.

I glance to my side and meet Liv's pursed lips and stare just as her head shakes. Every second so far, almost down to the word, is exactly as she predicted.

"I know who Charles is, Angela. And he's not interested in the money. In fact, you get to keep it all—every single penny you're due if I win," I say, sitting up and leaning into the table, weight on my elbows.

Angela and I stare each other down, her lips bent in this sinister angle that puts me on edge and ratchets up my already easy-to-set-off pulse.

"No," she says, that slight curve in her mouth stretching into something a little more smug. She doesn't even see it coming.

"Then I'll walk out. I walk, nobody gets a dime. Not me...not you." I match her stare and wait her out, knowing she can't hold her expression longer than a few seconds. She's bluffing. I'm not.

"You'll be ruined," she says, her eyes lowering.

"He's being stupid. Memphis, you're being an idiot. Just finish what we started, yeah?" Leo adds.

I don't move my eyes from Angela's, though, and the longer I hold her hostage, the more her expression begins to shift into something that isn't so sure. The confidence drains her eyes first. Her mouth falls next, and eventually, she pulls the glasses from her face and leans back in her chair—defeated.

If there were a referee here now, he'd rule her down by contact.

"You won't get paid, and you can't afford not to get paid. Your back taxes are..." I lean my ear closer to Liv and wait for her to fill the number in.

"Just under fifty-two," she says, clearing her throat as she sets one more paper on the table for Angela to consider.

Her mom lets her eyes drift down long enough to get the gist of what's on that page. Most of it was from memory, but the scary numbers are what they are. She's been nose-deep in those books for weeks. This bill was coming due whether she or I were here or not.

"He wouldn't do that. Ange, he's testing us. He needs us; don't even fall for this shit," Leo says, stopping his wild pacing just long enough to point at me a few times and attempt to convince himself that he still has a card to play.

"I don't need you, Leo," I say, looking him in the eyes just long enough to let him see just how serious I am. "You taught me what I need to know. I'm grateful for the knowledge. And that is all. I can't even stomach the sight of you."

My eyes move back to Angela because that last part wasn't a lie. They both deceived me, and I detest them for the part they played. But of the two, I spent hours every day with one of them. I gave him a piece of me—I gave Leo trust. I won't make that mistake ever again.

The room grows smaller somehow, everything in the gym looming with shadows. The doors are locked and the sign is out for a temporary closure. Angela didn't want interruptions. She didn't want an audience here. That means somewhere deep down, she knew this wasn't going to end the way she wanted. The twist, though, is she still gets paid. She expected a fight over that, but there won't be one. It's the price paid for my freedom.

"Done," she says, and a beat after Leo punches a metal plaque hung on the wall, his knuckles instantly busted open and red with his own blood.

"Sign...right..." Liv leans forward and draws a line along the page of terms, "here."

She hands her mother the pen, and Angela scribbles out her name, then passes the pen and page to the left for Leo.

"I'm not fucking putting my name on that. I don't care. He's not getting you. I worked *too* hard. I made you. No, I'm not signing." Leo leans into the wall again and holds his wrist, his injured hand likely throbbing now with pain.

I glance to Liv, and she shifts her eyes to mine and nods once. We both stand, leaving the paper and pen on the table for Angela to force on Leo. He'll sign it. He has no choice. If he doesn't agree, then this place will be forced into bankruptcy, and that's not something they can survive.

We leave the two of them alone, and the second the gym door shuts behind us, the shouting begins. Liv doesn't utter a word, she just slips her hand in mine and pivots her body in front of mine, lifting herself up on her toes to place her lips on mine. Her other hand rests on my cheek, and when she falls away, I hold my hand over it, keeping her close.

"It's done," she says, and I breathe in deeply. I believe she's right.

There's a nagging thing I need to deal with before I can close the door here mentally, though.

"I have to talk to him one more time," I say, looking toward the porch just behind her.

Her hands are warm, and they wrap around mine and squeeze tightly until I lower my gaze back to her. She shakes my palms a few times, brow pinched and lips somber as she stares at me. She's asking me if I'm sure I need to do this. She's asking without words, and probably because she's been in my shoes too—not for the same reason, but for the same man.

Her chest sinks as her shoulders lower, and her eyes flit to my chest then to our hands. She nods while looking at our feet.

"Okay." Her hands offer one more squeeze and she slips around me, heading toward the trailer where she'll wait for her mother to reluctantly deliver a signed paper that probably wouldn't hold up in court. Thing is, Liv owns Angela and Leo. She knows what they owe the government, and sometimes that's more powerful than knowing where bodies are buried.

I've only been in Angela's side of the duplex a few times, and it always strikes me how homey it is when I enter. If I didn't know the neighborhood that was outside, and the people living here, I would think I stumbled into a loving grandmother's house, cookies in the oven and yarn in a basket by the sofa. The illusion is masterful and it makes me laugh to myself seeing it now in broad daylight.

The reality becomes more apparent with each step up toward Archie's room, where canes and walkers to assist him are propped against the hallway wall just below the hole I made with my fist. When I first came here, I thought it was strange that a man like him— a god, really, of his sport—was kept in a dark room up a set of stairs he probably wouldn't be able to get down quickly if there was a fire. I get it now, though. Angela was just hoping this place would burn down one day.

He's exactly where he was the last time I saw him. I push open the door completely, and his neck shifts enough for him to catch a view of me sideways. His body slumps into his bed, the top half bent up during the daytime. I wonder if anyone bothers to lower it at night.

His eyes struggle to look at me from the side as I enter, so I close the door behind me and move to the chair next to his bed. He looked excited the last time I visited with him, though it has been nearly two months. This man—his expression—is far different this time. He isn't afraid. I don't think Archibald Valentine knows fear. I think if this house were to catch on fire, he'd take on the flames, even in his condition.

A fighter to the bitter end.

"I don't even know what I am right now," I begin, leaning forward in the chair to rest my elbows on my knees. I rub my hands together as I think, and Archie's eyes follow the movement.

"I have so many questions, and the hardest part...the thing I think I'm angriest about...is you can't fucking answer them." I choke up a little, my words hanging in my suddenly dry throat. I cough the feeling away, pushing it deep, but it still burns.

I shift my gaze from my hands to his eyes, and he's still not looking at me directly. He can't—not while I'm talking about something so raw. This is his defensive move, and I can wear him down as much as I'd like and he'd still outlast me. He's had years of practice holding things in.

"Was he a good man?"

The room is quiet, and I swear I can hear my own voice asking this question over and over, somehow echoing off the piles of junk and dusty articles framed on the walls. Archie's eyes dart in short movements, and I'd think he were truly heartless if they weren't glassy. I'm patient, and eventually he nods shakily.

My father was a good man, or at least so says a rotten one.

"Did he ever want me?" My tongue pushes at the back of my teeth and I mash my lips together tightly fighting the shaking sensation in my chest. I am not impenetrable, and these wounds are fresh and old at the same time.

Archie's eyes pass mine on their search around the room, pausing for just a breath. They're so fucking sad. He nods again, the movement bigger than before.

I nod in sync with him as I gaze down at the floor, short carpet stained with ink and medicine. Angela brings her puzzle books in here sometimes to waste time while she visits. I wonder if she's broken pens in anger and frustration, or maybe Archie has in a fit, trying to pull it from her hand and force her to look at him.

I wonder...can Archie write?

I glance to the left to the side table for the bed. It's covered with medications, filled Sudoku books and a plate with half-eaten eggs and a cold piece of toast. I take one of the puzzle books in my hand and flip through the pages in search of something blank, finally settling on the inside cover. I crease it and fold it inside out before pulling open the small drawer and fishing through dozens of shortened pencils and broken eraser pieces. The first pen I find doesn't work, but deep in a corner, I feel a marker. It's fat, and black, and permanent—not ideal for a man who likely lacks hand control, but I take it in my hand along with one of the sharpest pencils.

There isn't much room on Archie's bed, so I drag the chair close and sit on the armrest, holding the folded book in my palm like an easel. Archie's eyes widen slowly, every movement he makes delayed in response. I'm already forming his fist around the pencil when he looks down to where our hands touch.

"Tell me something. Here, on this paper. Tell me the most important thing. I know you can't give me what I want, but just give me something—one goddamned piece of him. Something I can take with me anywhere. Just...ahhhhhh...just..."

I grit my teeth as I grow frustrated. Archie's hand isn't able to hold the pencil well, and the sharp end snaps off leaving splinters of wood on the paper.

I let my hands fall away and hold the folded booklet against my leg while I breathe—first in...then out. My heart is racing with rage, and I have to calm it. I'm dizzy and sick.

"I just want something," I whisper, feeling the soft edge of the book's pages with my thumb. I rub it fanatically until it bends so much it's rounded.

"Pe....ennnnn." The sound creeps from deep in his chest, rough from his dry throat and awkward out of his mouth that only works on one side.

With wide eyes, I shift my focus to his chin that he's fighting to tuck to his chest so he can better see the marker I left in his lap. His hand crawls slowly along his blanket, over the crisp gray sweatshirt that practically swallows his frail body whole. Quickly, I move my palm over the top of his hand as he struggles to curl his fingers around the marker resting on one of the sweatshirt folds. Once it's caught in both of our grasp, I pull the cap away and throw it to the foot of the bed, holding the book back where it was before, just beneath the tip of the felt from the marker.

The ink smells strong, and our hold together is uncomfortable. The black draws lines along the sides of both of our fingers, but Archie doesn't stop. His tongue is pinched between his teeth and lips on the right side of his mouth. He nods with each mark he makes on the page. It takes minutes for one word—HIS—and I start to worry we'll run out of room. I'll rip away more book pages, tear down old articles from this wall if I need to for him to finish with this message. Everything feels desperate, and I grow restless the longer it takes, afraid that someone will come into this room and put a stop to it, destroying the little he's been able to write.

His fingers shake, but he nudges me away, my hand falling just under his wrist for support as the black ink drizzles as if it's coming off a feather. More minutes pass, and another word comes into view, and after almost half an hour, his message is complete. The marker falls into the bed, staining the sheets, so I pick it up and toss it opened into the drawer.

HIS BIGGEST REGRET

It's nothing earth shattering, yet it is so deeply what I needed to read. My father wrote those same words in his diary, but when the truth came out, I began to doubt he meant any of it. I started to think Angela and Leo made it all up—his words, the bike, the birthday cards. I knew deep in my heart that it was real, but their selfishness made me doubt it all the same.

Archie's hand slides toward the edge of the bed, brushing into my leg, and I look away from the words he wrote to his hand. I stare at it for long seconds because that hand is many things. It's pitiful, for certain. It's also capable of killing a man, even if it was in a ring where that man went willingly. And that hand is repentant. It's strong enough, even in its weakest state, to communicate to the little boy in my soul, who is more hungry and desperate than the fighter standing in this room.

I take his hand in mine briefly, squeezing.

"Thank you," I say, moving it up to his chest and leaving it there. It's all I can give him, and I'm still not sure if he deserves more or less. But that is something.

# CHAPTER TWENTY-ONE

Liv

Being grilled by both sides of a legal battle makes a person start to question which side is right and which one is wrong. It messes with my head; makes me feel abused. Enoch's defense team is strategic, and their questions come out in such a way that it's almost impossible to counter or poke a hole.

"Yes, I did take those documents to this building, and no Enoch... I mean Mr. Rostram...was not present when I did that."

"No, he did not request that of me directly, but his secretary reports..."

"Oh, you didn't ask that."

"No, he did not request that of me directly."

"Yes, I took those to the agency alone."

"No, I do not have any copies from him."

The jury must know, though. They can strike things from records and ask people only to consider so much when they're making a decision, but is that really how they act? Could those people really see me struggling for ways to say what I really knew

—that Enoch was at the helm of every decision that ultimately robbed those people of millions—and then ignore it completely when trying to assign some sort of number that these victims are owed?

I don't think they can.

I've been in Washington for a little less than two days, and already I'm afraid that my mom and Leo have somehow managed to wiggle their way into Memphis's life and turn him against me. Paranoia's greatest ally is experience.

My fears are irrational, though. I know they are. I've talked to Charles twice. Memphis is working out of a different gym, one on the east side of town, in a space borrowed by an old friend of Charles's who also happened to be screwed over by my mom and dad and uncle.

I spent the entire night trying to find a way to be there—a way to get to Vegas today. There weren't even seats on a bus, and by car, I'd never make it on time. I was close to trying, but Memphis told me not to. An eighteen-hour drive in the dark on my own with very little rest would not keep him calm, he said. He has plenty of extra noise in his head thanks to my family. This isn't how a fighter walks into a challenge.

Instead, I had to settle for the hotel business office, where for the last hour, an older gentleman named Gary has been trying to fax vacuum cleaner orders he got during his trade show to the main office in Kansas. I've become Gary's IT administrator, and in return, Gary promised to listen to the fight as I stream it on my phone and somehow try to talk to Miles at the same time.

My space has been set up for a while now. I got here early to make sure nobody else had ideas of taking the only chair in here or sucking up the Wi-Fi connection for their stupid multiplayer phone games.

"It's up!" I align my chair with my screen, my phone resting against a hardwired one I doubt anyone has used in a year.

"Your friend call yet?" Gary hovers over my shoulder, and I'm so nervous that I don't even mind the smell of day-old coffee on his breath.

"I need to call him. I'm just so nervous," I say, giggling through the words.

I sit on one hand and press my fingertip from my other hand on my phone screen, minimizing the video to get to my contacts. Memphis insisted that Miles be there. I think in his mind, he's as close to a dad as he'll ever have. I think Miles is okay with it, too. A healthy codependency. Something shifted in Miles's perspective when he learned the truth about Memphis's dad. His heart broke a little along with us all, and maybe he's more willing to leave behind that tree and the life that goes with it.

Maybe he's ready to heal.

I press to call Miles, and it rings a few times, ratcheting up my nerves because without Miles on the phone with me, I'm going to feel helpless when I see Memphis take a punch. No offense to Gary, but he's already said a few things to indicate to me he has no idea what he's about to see.

"Hello, hello...Olivia? You there?" I can almost imagine Miles cupping the phone to his ear.

"Yes, I'm here! Miles...can you hear me?" I left him a pair of earbuds, and I hope he brought them, because as loud as that arena is now, it's about to quadruple in decibels.

There's some sliding noises and a little static as the phone moves around, so I wait and check my screen to make sure I still have the video feed up. It buffers every few minutes, but only for a second or two. I hope it doesn't cut out when...no...I won't think that way. It won't cut out, and there won't be anything scary to see.

"Liv, you there?" Miles comes in clearer this time, but the noise of the crowd is still thick behind him.

"I'm here. Can you hear me?" I'm shouting, and it echoes in this tiny room, drawing the attention of people walking by in bathing suits on their way to the pool.

"I sure can. Damn, lady...these headphones you gave me are nice!"

I laugh and run my palms over my face, my lips numb and my teeth pulsating with this uncontained energy I can't seem to dodge.

"How does he look?" I move both hands under my thighs and I rock forward in the seat, trying to make out everyone on the screen. They haven't announced his entrance yet. This was always my dad's favorite part. He liked the pomp and circumstance of hearing someone call him The Heavy, and the cheers from the crowd. He loved the fight, but that jolt of testosterone that came from having a crowd root for him to knock someone else down was the real drug.

"He looks like a champ, Liv. Just like a champ. You don't worry, okay? This next part is all just formality so he can brag about it. I've seen this one already, and let me tell you how it turns out—*Memphis wins!*"

Miles laughs so hard he starts to cough, and my knees begin to bob nervously under the table, causing my phone to slide flat onto the desk.

"Shoot," I say, sliding it back up.

Gary rips a piece of tape from the dispenser on the guest desk and rolls it into a ball then lifts my phone a little to squish the tape underneath and stick my phone in place.

"There you go. Now you can thump your leg all you want," he says, chuckling at his wit. I laugh lightly, then immediately begin to wiggle my leg again.

"All right, lights are out." Miles gives me the play-by-play about five seconds before I see it on my screen. The delay might kill me if he says the wrong thing and I can't see it to confirm whether or not Memphis is okay.

I close my eyes and listen to the noise piping through the phone speaker, and I imagine waiting through this entire fight under layers of concrete in a sub-basement of the arena. These sounds are more than my mom got during those early years, when she wasn't supposed to be seen with him and I was just some baby this woman brought in a carrier. If I try really hard, I wonder if I can remember those early sounds I heard, too.

My eyes remain shut while I hear them announce Omar Morales. There are boos and chants reverberating through my phone, so I open wide and lean forward to see if I can tune in the sound for the fight. It comes in decently, and from what I can sense most of the professional world is handing this to Omar without a lot of faith in what Memphis can bring to the table.

"Showtime," Miles says. I tune down the sound from the video again and open my eyes waiting through the delay. I don't need to hear what other people have to say about him. I know in my heart what he's made of, and I know what he has that Omar doesn't—heart. So much heart.

I can hear the doubters through the phone, though. They're loud and loyal to the favorite. It's easy to root for the favorite. I wish there was a way I could find out who the haters were so when Memphis becomes World Champion, they wouldn't be allowed to be in his court. They'd regret it, because once they see him—when they *know* him—they will love him.

I've fallen in love with him. I've known for a while, and with every new obstacle thrust at us, trying to tear us down, I've held on hoping there would still somehow be a *we* at the end of it. I don't know what happens from here—when I come home and he's ready to make home somewhere else. That place—it isn't my home either.

"He's in the zone, Liv. Can you see it? It's incredible!" I can barely make out Miles's words over the buzz of the crowd nearly drowning him out, but I get his prompt and lean in close waiting for the camera to zero in on the greatest fighter I've ever seen.

In a blink, he fills the frame. Gary says something behind me, and I nod, not even knowing for sure what he said. I don't have time to listen to anything but the bells and Miles's reassurance.

His stare is lethal. He's been trained by the best intimidator I know. Leo Valentine knew how to make an opponent feel threatened, and with the polish from Charles in a few days, Memphis paces around his corner with a stone-cold confidence in his eyes.

I smirk when he jogs, bouncing as Charles pulls his robe from his shoulders and tosses it over the ropes. I'm pretty sure I see Miles in the background, seated directly on the floor right behind our man.

"Nice gray suit," I say through a grin. My phone sounds with his raspy chuckle.

"Why, thank you. First one I've ever had. Got married in uniform. Champ said I needed to show up classy, so he took me out shopping. That little shit was cranky as hell, though," he says.

"He was hungry," I laugh out.

"No reason to be an asshole about things. He said I was indecisive or some shit. I think we were in the store for seven minutes," Miles says.

Gary's found a spare chair from somewhere outside and he's pulled it up next to me. He slides a soda in front of me on the table and pulls back the tab.

"Vending machine out there. You looked like you could use a snack." I hear him open one for himself a second later, so I turn and smile.

"Thanks," I say, pulling the can in my trembling hand. I can barely take a sip, but I force myself to because that was really sweet of him.

I listen in live from Miles, watching Memphis's face for clues about how he's going to handle this moment. They've rattled off stats and weights, and both men have come to the middle to be schooled by the referee. These are my favorite pictures my mother has of my father. If I were to lay one on top of this moment right now, every detail would match up perfectly. Two alpha men, bodies damp with sweat already, muscles primed to punish, jaws rigid and mouth guards being chewed away by rabid teeth. It's so primal, boxing. So violent, yes—two men beating the shit out of one another for the right to say they're king.

But Memphis *is* king. I can see it already in the way he swaggers back to his corner but never takes his eyes off the target. They are both the same height, yet somehow Memphis seems to tower over him, even as he moves away. He nods to Charles, weight shifting from one foot to the other while his eyes sear into the man staring back at him. He's waged war, and my chest burns with excitement and fear.

His father died in a ring just like this.

"There's the bell," Miles says, briefly bringing me out of my trance. I go right back in, watching it happen on the delay.

Memphis is quick to the center, wasting no time showing Omar he isn't afraid. Where Omar is thick, Memphis is lean and fast—his muscles rounded by discipline and passion. It's the defensive strategy Leo deployed, but there's an edge to it, and that's strictly Charles. He's not playing it safe, and that terrifies me.

The first swing comes, but I'm already okay, because Miles hasn't told me to worry yet. I'll have time to prepare myself...that's the only benefit to being here instead of there. If I die inside, I'll have a warning.

There's reaction from the crowd on the phone and I start to ask Miles, but instinctively he knows and tells me everything's fine.

I see it play out, hard right hook that Memphis dodges. He's poetic on his feet, and it's beautiful to watch.

Somehow shutting everything out, I focus on him—on the way his legs remain steadfast, his balance perfection and his movements unpredictable. There is no pattern to discern. He moves by heart, where instincts tell him to go, always just out of reach but close enough to tempt.

There are some taps—first Memphis at the side, then the face. Omar returns them. They're testing each other—teasing, mostly. Nobody wants to go out in the first. That isn't good for anyone, so when the clock starts to close in on zero, I exhale knowing things are fine.

"Jesus Christ!"

Miles jolts me back from calm, and for a brief moment, my heart stops beating.

Memphis dodges, his body weaving low, then right, then center, and in that same breath his left hand fires away, two jabs to the right side of Omar's face. It wasn't part of the old plan, but this new plan doesn't follow rules. It plays to strengths. Memphis's strengths.

He's faster. And he isn't afraid.

The bell sounds on my screen and they both back into their corners, only Omar's dominant side is going to have a hard time seeing things coming at it now. His eye is swelling. Memphis is swaying in his seat, his feet itching to go in for more.

"He was not ready for that," Gary says.

"Neither was I," I say.

The break is never long enough, and I've barely caught my breath when it rings and both fighters come in for more.

"Ohhhh wow!" Miles is emphatic, and it plays out for me a second later.

Memphis isn't wasting time. He's making a statement, going in hard and early, taking Omar off balance. He throws him a combination that sends him to the ropes and brings his stumbling body back toward Memphis, where he holds on just to get a break.

Once separated, they both gain some distance again, each taking half of the ring, circling in their dance. Omar lunges, and Memphis doesn't flinch. He's fighting like Leo here—balance above all else. That bastard was right about one thing.

Omar lunges a few times, all idle threats, until the round is almost over and he comes in hard, landing a punch to Memphis's side. He blocks some of it, but it isn't enough. That one hurt.

It's impossible to be in this sport and not get hurt. At this level, there are so many wins by decision. That means ten rounds of trading fists and flesh, leaving bruises and breaking open skin. For two rounds, Memphis is doing okay. At least he can see.

"He's all right. I can hear him," Miles says. I watch him go to his corner on the delay, and his mouth is moving a lot.

"That one hurt," I say.

"Yeah, it did. It hurt," he yells. "But he's all right. Champ is talking trash, just like I taught him to."

"Oh, you taught him that, did you?" I laugh, and Miles adds in a "Mmmm hmmmm."

I'm starting to sweat, so I pull my sweater over my head and toss it on the desk and catch a glimpse behind me. It's no longer just Gary. This small crowd has grown to five—the three reception desk employees now invested in a boxing match being shown on a three-by-five phone screen.

"We're rooting for that guy," I say, touching my finger to his body on the screen.

"Hell yes, we are," the woman says. I give Gary a sideways glance, and he laughs.

Round three kicks in and is over without much action. I can handle this if more rounds pan out like this. I know it isn't likely, and I know the crowd doesn't like defensive fights, but when your heart is invested, you wish every round were this boring.

"I think the secret is out," Gary says, leaning into me. I glance over my shoulder again, and a few guys from the bar have stumbled into the tight office now, one of them sitting on the printer table so he can see.

"Hey, I got money on Morales. Think you can hold that up a little higher, sweetheart?" My eyes linger on his for about half a second before I turn around, glancing at Gary again along the way.

"Awe, don't be like that. Come on," he says, just as the fourth round is getting under way. My skin is tingling with nervous energy, and assholes have a tendency to make me do rash things, so I fight to keep myself calm.

"I don't know what Charles said to him, but it looks like this is the round where things are gonna happen. Time to hold on, sister."

I see what Miles is talking about just as he finishes his warning. Charles and Memphis are nose to nose, heads both nodding, Charles shouting to make sure Memphis can hear. This scene is familiar, too. I watched it on TV a lot, Leo shouting at my dad. He used his hands a lot when he talked, but he told me once that he was always careful to make sure his gestures never gave anything away. Charles's hands are perfectly still.

Memphis doesn't look fatigued, but neither does Omar. I can't read the scores they're throwing on the bottom of the screen, but the hater behind me must be getting them from some app he's on.

"They've got them tied, right now," he says. "Bullshit."

I grit my teeth as the bell rings and Memphis moves in.

"Bullshit because Delaney's up three rounds to one," I say, no longer able to keep it in. Gary moves in his chair. I didn't look, but I think maybe he scooted a few inches away from me.

"Fuck that. This wannabe is getting his ass knocked out in seven. You wait," he says.

I keep my head forward, and I remind myself that this man isn't Angela—I don't engage. I also know that he's going to lose that bet he made, and I'll take satisfaction when it happens. I hope it was for a shitload of money.

This round is different. Miles was right; there's a strategy happening. I can almost see it, but I don't know Charles enough. My guess is that they expected Omar to be prepared for a slow start. They were working to let him take it easy, too. They'd both save, then fight it out in the late rounds. I guess the outcome is the same— they're both still fresh enough to go the distance.

"He's down!" Miles yells, and I stand with wide eyes, fists at my side and my stare fixed on the screen waiting for it to happen.

"What the fuck? Who's down? Is that dude there?" I want to punch the hater myself, but I can't because Memphis has lost his footing. He isn't down completely. He's stumbled, and he relied a lot on the ropes after Morales laid into him with his entire body.

I hover on my feet and wait for Memphis to find his center and right himself, and it feels like it takes forever. There's always blood, and it's there now. His beautiful face is red on the right side, his cheek bleeding where the thin skin barely covers the bone. Omar hammered it to nothing. Charles will need to fix it.

I slowly sit as Memphis begins to move more steadily. His hands are up. He's defensive, and I don't like it. He needs to have his gloves up, but he needs to swing first. He needs to hit him harder. He needs to win and get out of that ring.

He needs to come home.

Home. Where is home?

I have to close my eyes. Thoughts spin out of control and start to make me crazy.

"Ooooooh," the room swells behind me. The crowd has grown again, and I can't bring myself to look. Gary reaches over and squeezes my forearm, and I stutter out a breath.

"He's out of that one. Thank God, because that was rough. He got another shot in right before the buzzer," he says.

"Bell," I correct, letting out a weak and pathetic laugh.

"Just make it to seven, baby. I've got you in seven, Omar!"

I sway in my seat, and the taunting behind me begins to blur together, like I've been drugged or like I'm the one getting punch drunk. My chest feels tight, and the eyes staring out on my phone screen are lost. That fire is dim, and I wonder if it's because of everything that's happened. He's lost it because of me—because of my family. Leo's woven himself in so deep that Memphis doesn't believe he can do it without him now. He's succumbing to doubt and intimidation. He's falling victim to the game.

There isn't enough time to fix him. There's never enough time. Charles can't say enough to force the will back into his fists and legs. The bell rings and Memphis lumbers toward Morales. He dodges, but some light jabs land. More points—more rounds in his favor. He started so well, but this fight, it was too much.

I'm becoming her. I'm praying—a girl who has never set foot in a church is praying for a violent end, and for my man to stand victorious. It's twisted, and it scares me. More than anything, though, I'm terrified that this fight will change him—that Memphis will never be the same. And I can't lose him, all of him, because I love every piece. I love every bit of the man he is mentally. I love him inside. And his eyes, his face, his body—his good soul.

Robert Delaney made a beautiful man, and I fell in love with him...tragically. I can't lose this. *He* can't lose this. It's his namesake, his promise—it's everything to him, and it will be the foundation for us. I believe in him because he isn't like Archie Valentine at all. He's everything Archie isn't, and that's why this fight—it's about to be over.

The bell rings, and another round goes to Omar. I don't care. It doesn't matter. None of this matters. It will all be forgotten because Memphis is going to make them forget. They'll only remember him tonight.

The hater behind me is rooting for seven, and he's so confident he's starting to count his money. This bitch goes down in six.

"You have to tell him I love him, Miles. I need him to know. Tell him...say it loud." There's a short pause, and eventually Miles chuckles along with his trademark cough.

"Olivia, he knows," he says.

"He doesn't. Not really. Nobody knows until they hear it. You have to tell him." I bite at my nails and watch the clock count down, seconds left, water washing away the blood on his face, jelly closing wounds and slowing down the gush. His chest is heaving. His brain is fooling him that he's tired. He isn't. He has so much left inside; I know it.

"All right," Miles says, and I wait, pulling my phone to my ear and pressing hard, ignoring the boos and hisses from the room full of people who weren't invited to my party. This was just supposed to be me and Gary. They can all go to fucking hell.

"Olivia! The girl loves you! Come on, man. You do this for her! Olivia loves you!" I smile against my knuckles and blush even though nobody can hear this on my phone now. Miles yells my confession out to the world until I hear the bell.

"Did he hear you?" I ask, heart pounding at a sprint.

"Oh, he heard me. Him, that Omar fellow, his trainer, the woman on the other side of the ring. This makes us family now, you know. I don't do this for just any woman," he says.

"Best family ever," I say, meaning it. My only family, really. I don't want the real ones. I'm completely open to replacing them all —trading up.

I set my phone back down and take a deep breath as both men pace toward each other, then away. Memphis's legs are stronger now, and that look is coming back. He's been damaged, but he can work with this. He was trained to work with this, and his heart is pounding harder now. I know it is, because I know he loves me too. This shitty world put us both in the same place for a reason. We were meant to be—and maybe it was for this moment right now.

A calmness rushes through my body. I twist in my chair, pointing a finger at the drunk heckler who is about to lose his bet.

"Your man is going down in six," I say, boldly. It induces laughter at first, then a shade of detest. The man's heavy eyes sink lower and he nods for me to turn around, but I give it one more second just to show him that I'm serious.

I know things.

I have faith.

"Oh damn!" Miles announces the first blow before it comes. Memphis keeps his weight back and dodges Omar, coming up swinging on his own, catching him on the chin.

He does it again, and Miles warns us once more.

It's like a broken record, Omar repeating the same failed attempt, and Memphis waiting calmly for the bait, punishing him four times in a row before Omar switches, dipping and working the other side.

It fails, and Memphis cuts in again, this time harder. With every step Omar falls backward, Memphis closes in, until Omar is clinging with limp, gloved hands to the ropes, steadying himself for the blow that's about to come.

The hater predicts it before it happens, and my heart explodes the moment his fist connects. It happens fast on the screen, but my eyes somehow slow everything down. I see Omar's eyes close, his chin jerk, and his cheek indent. Sweat drops fly from his body and drip from Memphis's arm. His skin twists and his legs give. His first step fails and his body falls. Memphis circles, then moves to his corner, like a predator waiting for his pack to finish what he started so he can go in and feast.

Omar grasps at the bottom rope, and his hand slips. He crawls, and the referee crouches down low to read his eyes. He counts.

We all count.

Eight.

Nine.

Ten.

# CHAPTER TWENTY-TWO

Memphis

"It's sappy, huh? Don't lie." They've been showing my post-fight interview on the news all damn day, and Miles can't get enough of it. He's commandeered my phone so he can play the video over and over.

"It's not sappy, brother...it's love," he says, shaking his head slowly like he's listening to some sweet jazz or something. He's mocking me. I slap at his left arm, which is covered in one of my sweatshirts.

He hits play again. It quit being embarrassing, and to be honest, I like hearing it. I'm truly happy, and I can hear it in my own voice.

> *Reporter: Correct me if I'm wrong, Memphis Delaney,*
> *but did I hear that gentleman sitting over there in*
> *your corner shouting that he loved you? Are you*
> *telling the boxing world that all you need is love?*
> *Memphis: I don't know, man. It's not magic or*
> *anything, I swear. And he was talking about a*

*girl. God, baby...I did it! I'm crying, baby. Do you*
*see this? I'm crying. Big, fat happy tears, I love you*
*so much.*

*Reporter: You looked like you were down there in the*
*fourth and the fifth. You were gassed. You think*
*you came out too early?*

*Memphis: I don't know. It wasn't really the plan. We*
*thought maybe it would work to surprise him, but*
*then he was just so strong.*

*Reporter: But you saved something, didn't*
*you? Haha.*

*Memphis: Heart, dude. Right here, in this chest. That*
*fight, Omar...he's amazing. To be in this ring with*
*him. It was all heart that did that, and it was her.*
*It was you, baby. You've gotta come home. Come*
*home now, baby, because this ain't real. It ain't*
*real until you're here. You know that. This...all of*
*it. I'm no champion yet.*

*Reporter: Who's baby?*

*Memphis: Come home, baby. I love you so much.*
*Come home to me. Come home, come home,*
*come home...*

This is always the part where Miles is laughing so hard, no sound is coming out of him. It's still a little embarrassing I guess.

"You look like a...what do they call that? A meme! You're a meme!" A rush of air hums from his chest, and I yank my phone back from him.

"You don't even know what a meme is, old man," I say, checking the time on my phone and comparing it to the flight tracker on the screen in front of us. It hasn't changed. She's probably touching down on the runway right now.

"Oh I know what a meme is. It's when grown men act like they're in a boy band on national TV; that's what a meme is," he says, only breaking long enough to get the words out before he busts into laughter again.

"It wasn't on national TV," I mutter.

"Oh yeah? You don't think this video's been viewed in Arkansas?" he fires back.

I glower at him then roll my eyes.

He starts to brag about being right, but I don't hear him. All I can focus on is the shift in the airport screen that says FLIGHT 4109 IS AT GATE C1. I can see it in front of me. Cosmic luck put the security gates right in line with the family area and this one particular gate—the gate her jet was pulling into.

It's late as hell, and my body is exhausted, my fight barely twenty-four hours old. I never really slept. I spent the entire night with my head pressed against my phone in the hotel room just listening to her breathe.

Somehow, out of all of this—out of the pain and wrecked histories and coulda-beens—I got her. I got the good Valentine.

"You should have made her a sign," Miles teases. Let him tease, I don't care.

Her bright eyes begin scanning the moment her body clears the gate door. She's the last flight in, no more flights out, and this place is practically a ghost town.

"Come home, baby!" I shout so loudly it alerts the TSA workers who are just counting down the minutes until their shift is over, nobody left in line.

"I love you, baby!"

Miles laughs loudly behind me, but he's clapping, too. He's proud, and he's pushing me out there, making me give my heart away to this woman who took a chance and leapt. She fell for me—a fighter. The kind of man she swore she'd never be with. I idolized her father when I came to this place, but I idolize her now. I bow to her.

Fearless. She lost everything and went right into the fire. She led me out. She came home.

She clears the security point so I run at her full force, and she drops her bag along the way to me. She leaps at me and I catch her in the air, her arms and legs wrapping themselves where they belong, her soft voice humming under her teary eyes. Hair wild and heart thumping so hard I can feel it in her bones when I hold her close.

"I did it, Liv. I did it, and you're the only reason. I love you so goddamned much, and you gave me this..."

My mouth stops talking long enough to taste her lips. It's been days, and I'm starving for her. My hands push back her hair, fingers threading the tangled strands, her eyes tired from the late travel and the abuse of testifying. Both of our nightmares are over. She never has to see those lawyers again. We never have to see V's again. We're home; she came home. I meant it when I said it. Her home—it's with me.

"You were a god, Memphis. A fighter—from somewhere else, some other time. I am so proud of you...you...inspire me. You amaze me. And I don't know how I'm going to survive another fight, but there are going to be so many. You are the one they all want to defeat now. You're the name being spoken out there, the guy they're all looking to take down."

I kiss her again and replay her words in my head, my chest warm from hearing her be so proud of me. I've fought for so long for a name that I never really knew, for a ghost and a man who wasn't strong enough to fight to keep me in his life. I'll never fight for them again. I'll fight for this woman—I'll fight for us.

My arms hold on for a few steps, her body finally sliding down my legs, but remaining under my arm as we walk in stride with one another. I pause to run back to grab her bag, then start our trip toward Miles together again. She rushes him with a hug that surprises him, and I can tell it scratches at something inside—a feeling he lost a while ago.

"Thank you," she says to him, stepping back and kissing his cheek before looking in his eyes. "I couldn't be there, and it killed me. You made it okay, and nobody else could have done that—nobody else would have."

"That's 'cause pretty boy over here doesn't have any other friends," he says, and I laugh hard and loud. Even now, when I know her words have touched him deeply, he takes a shot at me.

It's how I know we're family. The three of us. Lost souls find each other sometimes.

I take her hand in mine and I squeeze tight, not wanting her to let go for even a second. A few guys waiting near the exit to the parking lot reach out to shake my hand, and I give them my left because my right one belongs to her. They congratulate me—they recognize me. Fucking wild.

We make our way to the center of the empty lot, the only cars around those that are spending the night and waiting for their owners to return, and one, newly-running RV. Turns out Miles was a mechanic in the military. He knows a thing or two about engines, and making things work for cheap. Not that money will be a problem for at least a year.

Leo and Angela, and I suppose Archie, got the money they were due, and not a penny more. Charles brought me a few new options to the table, and they come with the Chicago market. Sportswear, pizza, and a Chevy dealership—as well as a Corvette of my choice—are all in negotiations. The only thing I didn't look over the details on was Charles. I didn't need to. He said he likes to keep it simple.

One handshake and a promise was all he asked of me, and it's all he offered in return. It feels right, and it feels like everything that I went through led me to this.

"I can't believe you drove that around the airport," Liv says, biting her knuckle as she surveys the beat-up exterior of our home.

"Not gonna lie, we were tailed on the way in," I say, and she looks to Miles who nods in agreement.

"Motorcycle cops can be real pricks," he adds.

I roll my eyes, because I don't want them tailing me on the way out, but he's right. Sometimes they can. So can fighters, though, I guess.

Liv steps inside, most things just as she left them, only a few modifications made to make sure Miles has a place to sit and sleep on our way to Chicago. Liv turns in a slow circle and raises one side of her mouth when she sees the open passenger seat.

"Where...ever will you do your laundry?" She chuckles, then drops her bag in the floor space between the two cab seats and nestles in, pulling on her buckle.

"I boxed a few things up and took them to UPS. We'll get them from the gym in Chicago, then we can look for a place," I say, stopping when I feel her eyes frozen on me.

"We," she repeats.

I simply laugh and lean toward her before I sit in the driver's seat.

"There is no Champion without you, and I kinda like being one, so I'm afraid you're stuck," I say, dropping a kiss on her lips then falling back into my seat. "You weren't planning on going back to Leo's, were you?"

She smacks my chest, and it actually hurts.

"I didn't think so," I grunt out, exaggerating, but only a little. I rub the spot where I have a broken rib, then adjust myself to get ready to drive.

"This beats the tree, huh?" she says over her shoulder. Behind her, Miles has slid into the bench seat that's cushioned by blankets held on by tape. It isn't ideal, but it's warm and it's with friends.

"Ya know, it would be all right if this dumbass driver would get his shit together and get on the road," he says. I lift myself enough to glance at him in the mirror. He's already laid back though and pulled his hat over his eyes. He looks good in my clothes. They swallow him, but I think maybe that's just a matter of time.

Liv stares at me until I stare back, and we sit silently for a few seconds while I crank the motor and feel the rumble of the makeshift engine.

"You okay with this?" I whisper, lifting my brow and tilting my head toward the man behind us.

Her lips stretch into the surest smile I've ever seen.

"I can't imagine life in Chicago without him," she says.

I hold her gaze just a little longer, and before I guide everything the three of us own onto the highway for a new beginning, I let the moment matter. I feel it and I memorize it—the musty air from the vents, the dust on my windshield, the gurgling sound under the hood, the scent of lemon from the tiny freshener dangling from my rearview mirror. I soak it all in, and I save her for last.

For the rest of forever, I promise to put her first.

# EPILOGUE

Two Years Later

Miles

Ghosts are funny things. I know they aren't real—at least, not tangible. But they're real in our minds. We can't hold them, but that's what makes them so important. We *want* to hold them. I lost my wife and my baby girl—the lights of my life—and I thought that if I laid there under the stars long enough, eventually they'd see me from heaven and know I came home for them. I wanted them to know I'd never be the same without them.

They can't hear me, and I never hear them talk. But I feel them. They're in my heart and their lessons have made me the man I am now.

I used to spend so much time worrying about the wrong people. I gave pieces of myself to people who weren't worth the dirt on the bottoms of my shoes, and I had too many sleepless nights spent worrying about their opinions. I should have been spending that time with Anna and Felicity. Perhaps, if I knew how short our time was, I would have. But I didn't know what I know now, and a person can't look back.

People can learn.

People can grow.

We move forward.

When I found my new place, I held on.

Memphis reminds me a lot of myself, and I think if I had a son, our relationship would have been a lot like this. When I met him, there was something inside me that told me this one...*this chance meeting*...it's meant for something more.

I think back to that day in the ER three years ago, and I truly think something bigger was giving us both what we were missing. But we weren't whole. We weren't even close until Olivia showed up.

Their electricity was serious right from the start. She razzed him just as much as I did, and a person only does that when they're comfortable with someone—when two people are meant for each other.

To watch that woman pick herself up from the bottom, brush off having her name dragged through the mud and become one of toughest contract negotiators in the sporting world—yeah, I'm proud like a father.

No one else was meant to manage Memphis. And he wasn't meant to fight for anyone else.

They live a few blocks away from me. They're on the seventeenth floor and every room in their apartment looks out over that beautiful Lake Michigan water. My place is simple—one bedroom and a nice fire escape that I slip out on from time to time to indulge in a cigar and look up at those stars in search of Anna and our baby girl.

There was never really a question of whether or not those two would get married. It was always just a question of when. Seven fights later, and one World Championship belt, now seems just about perfect. And in less than one hour, I'll be walking a beautiful girl down the aisle of this church to meet her future, to hand her over to her now and to forget about her past. Nothing has ever felt so right. And nothing has ever been more worth fighting for.

## THE END

# ACKNOWLEDGMENTS

Thank you all so much for spending time in the ring with my battered and bruised, with my strong and weak, my damned and beautiful, and precious darlings Memphis and Olivia. If you've read me before, you probably know I have quite the love affair with baseball. I find some sports to be hopelessly romantic, and I could probably teach a college course on all of my reasons why with some great examples—*Bull Durham*, anyone?

Boxing hits that same spot for me, like an arrow through the heart. I have a few reasons, actually, the most prominent being 1976. That's the year I was born, and the year one of the greatest films ever made and scripts written won the Oscar. *Rocky* is more than a story about boxing. It runs deeper than good guy versus bad guy. It's a love story, it's a family drama, it's a tragedy, and sometimes it's funny. That's the kind of boxing book I wanted to write. I wanted to twist things inside, I wanted to turn conventions upside down, and I wanted you to have someone to root for.

*I also wanted it to be a little bit sexy. It kinda was, wasn't it? ;-)*

I'm enormously proud of this story, and I have a lengthy list of people to thank for helping me get from that first chapter to these acknowledgements at the end. I think the first mention should be for that truly sexy man on the cover there. (I know a lot of you agree—you've been heard LOL.) That's Trevor McCumby. He's 23-0, with 18 KOs as of right this minute. That number is going to go up, and he is going to be something special. He's the real deal, the kid who had the dream and fought his way up. I admire the hell out of his discipline and dedication. Trevor, go get it, sir! #Alpha, as you all say ;-)

With Trevor comes some of my peeps from way back when—the people behind the man, making him strong, booking his fights, telling his story to the world. Emily Pandelakis, you are the woman in so many ways! Thank you for kicking off this journey and connecting me to this world. Kiona and Daniel Arellanes, thank you both! Kiona for the wrangling and help at the shoot, and Danny for making Trevor such a bad-ass! And my sweet, amazingly talented friend Frank Rodriguez of DLRfoto—you take it up a notch every single time! This cover is going to be hard to top, my friend. Thank you for making the shiz in my head look so damn good.

There's a lot of my home city and the stomping grounds my family grew up around in this book. Central Boxing in downtown Phoenix was my muse, and manager Tom Garcia is the warmest and kindest. Thank you, Tom, for letting my crew come in and create in your ring. As much as Trevor is the star of the cover, Central Boxing is the co-star. There is magic in that building, and I hope I captured a little bit of it in this book.

To my beta readers—Shelley, Ashley, Bianca, Jenn and TeriLyn—I don't know if I could have gone 10 rounds without you guys! (See what I did there?) Tina Scott and BilliJoy Carson of Editing Addict, I definitely needed you in my corner. I guess that makes you my ring girl, Autumn...or maybe you're my manager. I think maybe you and Wordsmith Publicity are my Michael Buffer. Thank you for helping me get this baby seen, and for being just as excited as I am to see it fly.

Kerie Shea Trindle Byrne, you are my ambassador of legal eagleness. Thank you for playing out my scenarios and answering my random messages as deadline loomed. I love you, friend.

I saved my boys for last, but not because they played a small part. I always have a hard time putting into words what they do for me, and it requires thought and a paragraph that stands out. I wouldn't be doing any of this "living my dream" stuff if it weren't for you, Tim. And Carter, you make the little things possible. You are forever my joy and the fuel in my engine.

Engine...

Hmmmm...

I think maybe a racing book is in my future...

# ABOUT THE AUTHOR

Ginger Scott is an Amazon-bestselling and Goodreads Choice Award-nominated author from Peoria, Arizona. She is the author of several young and new adult romances, including recent bestsellers The Hard Count, A Boy Like You, This Is Falling and Wild Reckless.

A sucker for a good romance, Ginger's other passion is sports, and she often blends the two in her stories. When she's not writing, the odds are high that she's somewhere near a baseball diamond, either watching her son field pop flies like Bryce Harper or cheering on her favorite baseball team, the Arizona Diamondbacks. Ginger lives in Arizona and is married to her college sweetheart whom she met at ASU (fork 'em, Devils).

 facebook.com/GingerScottAuthor

 twitter.com/thegingerscott

instagram.com/authorgingerscott

## ALSO BY GINGER SCOTT

www.ingramcontent.com/pod-product-compliance
Lightning Source LLC
Chambersburg PA
CBHW060905250626
47159CB00008B/2871